AGED FOR VENGEANCE

(A Tuscan Vineyard Cozy Mystery—Book Five)

FIONA GRACE

Fiona Grace

Fiona Grace is author of the LACEY DOYLE COZY MYSTERY series, comprising nine books (and counting); of the TUSCAN VINEYARD COZY MYSTERY series, comprising six books (and counting); of the DUBIOUS WITCH COZY MYSTERY series, comprising three books (and counting); of the BEACHFRONT BAKERY COZY MYSTERY series, comprising six books (and counting); and of the CATS AND DOGS COZY MYSTERY series, comprising three books (and counting).

Fiona would love to hear from you, so please visit www.fionagraceauthor.com to receive free ebooks, hear the latest news, and stay in touch.

ISBN: 978-1-0943-7361-4

BOOKS BY FIONA GRACE

LACEY DOYLE COZY MYSTERY
MURDER IN THE MANOR (Book#1)
DEATH AND A DOG (Book #2)
CRIME IN THE CAFE (Book #3)
VEXED ON A VISIT (Book #4)
KILLED WITH A KISS (Book #5)
PERISHED BY A PAINTING (Book #6)
SILENCED BY A SPELL (Book #7)
FRAMED BY A FORGERY (Book #8)
CATASTROPHE IN A CLOISTER (Book #9)

TUSCAN VINEYARD COZY MYSTERY
AGED FOR MURDER (Book #1)
AGED FOR DEATH (Book #2)
AGED FOR MAYHEM (Book #3)
AGED FOR SEDUCTION (Book #4)
AGED FOR VENGEANCE (Book #5)
AGED FOR ACRIMONY (Book #6)

DUBIOUS WITCH COZY MYSTERY
SKEPTIC IN SALEM: AN EPISODE OF MURDER (Book #1)
SKEPTIC IN SALEM: AN EPISODE OF CRIME (Book #2)
SKEPTIC IN SALEM: AN EPISODE OF DEATH (Book #3)

BEACHFRONT BAKERY COZY MYSTERY
BEACHFRONT BAKERY: A KILLER CUPCAKE (Book #1)
BEACHFRONT BAKERY: A MURDEROUS MACARON (Book #2)
BEACHFRONT BAKERY: A PERILOUS CAKE POP (Book #3)
BEACHFRONT BAKERY: A DEADLY DANISH (Book #4)
BEACHFRONT BAKERY: A TREACHEROUS TART (Book #5)
BEACHFRONT BAKERY: A CALAMITOUS COOKIE (Book #6)

CATS AND DOGS COZY MYSTERY
A VILLA IN SICILY: OLIVE OIL AND MURDER (Book #1)
A VILLA IN SICILY: FIGS AND A CADAVER (Book #2)
A VILLA IN SICILY: VINO AND DEATH (Book #3)

CHAPTER ONE

Arriving for work on a breezy winter morning, Olivia Glass was surprised to see a woman in a chic gray business suit pacing impatiently outside La Leggenda's tasting room door.

Olivia was puzzled, because the winery's opening times were well advertised online, and also displayed on the shiny brass sign at the gate. She had arrived an hour early to get the place ready, and didn't expect to find anyone there.

She hurried along the paved driveway while she tugged her scarf into place and patted down her shoulder-length blond hair.

Enthused by the change in pace, Olivia's adopted goat, Erba, capered ahead, her shaggy, orange-and-white winter coat rippling in the wind. The young goat detoured mischievously to one of the ornate stone planters in the parking lot—where, Olivia noted, a brand new silver Range Rover was parked. Erba jumped nimbly into the planter. There, she tugged at the geranium bush, swathed in a bed of straw to protect it from frost.

"Erba! Out!" Olivia reprimanded her goat. Clearly, she was taking advantage of the situation to show off to this early visitor.

"*Buon giorno!*" Olivia greeted the strange woman. She guessed from her dark hair and stylish outfit that she was probably a local. "*Posso aiurtala?*"

Although her pronunciation was still clumsy, Olivia felt proud to be asking "can I help you?" in the local language. She was making enormous progress. A month ago, she'd never have been able to do this.

Disappointingly, the other woman didn't seem impressed with her efforts.

"You don't sound Italian," she said in a crisp British accent after glancing disapprovingly in Erba's direction. "You're not one of the Vescovis who own this place, are you?"

Busted, Olivia shook her head ruefully.

"I'm not part of the Vescovi family," she admitted. "I work here. I'm the head sommelier."

She took a breath to ask who the woman was, but before she could speak, the woman continued hurriedly, as if she didn't have time for any chitchat or explanation. "I'd like to take a look around, if I may."

"We don't open for an hour, so we can't offer you a wine tasting. Would you like a tour of the facilities, or are you looking for some other reason?" Olivia asked. She hoped this strange woman would agree to come back later, once they were properly open. Or, at least, explain why she was here.

She did neither. Instead, she folded her arms, tilted her head back, and stared down her perfectly straight nose at Olivia.

Olivia had a nasty feeling that asking anything further might offend her. And what harm could it do to let her have a quick look?

"Please come in," she invited, taking out her keys and unlocking the imposing wooden door. The diamante cat token on her key chain, a gift from her new boyfriend Danilo, glittered in the low morning sun. Looking at the cat always made Olivia feel happy.

Smiling, she stood back as the charcoal-suited stranger powered into the lobby, her heels clip-clopping on the granite tiles.

What was she doing here? Olivia wondered. This was very mysterious! Although the woman knew about the Vescovi family, she didn't seem to know them personally. None of the three Vescovis—Marcello, Antonio, or Nadia—had mentioned anything about this yesterday.

Olivia hoped this stranger didn't think it was too chilly inside. Lighting the fires in the lobby and tasting room was one of her first daily tasks, and the main reason she came in early on these sharp mornings. The spacious, high-ceilinged rooms were freezing cold at the start of the day.

"It's much warmer with the fires burning," she said helpfully, knowing that she was stating the obvious, but wanting to make *some* conversation. Even though this woman was in a rush, there was no reason why she shouldn't be put at ease.

To Olivia's alarm, the woman rummaged in her large leather purse and took out a black clipboard. She began jotting notes on it.

Was she a health and safety inspector? Olivia wondered. She'd only been working at La Leggenda a few months and had no idea if in-person visits might be made from time to time. Although she would have expected such an individual to be Italian, and to drive a more ordinary car than that bright silver statement vehicle outside.

2

"Are you inspecting?" she asked, hoping to get a handle on the situation.

"Open up for me, please," the woman said, indicating the wide, arched doors that led through to the tasting room.

Doubtfully, Olivia pushed them open. The customer was always right, but this encounter felt very untoward. Was she going to explain why she was here?

No, she was simply going to march into the large, neat and tidy tasting room without so much as a thank-you! Olivia wondered if she felt a thrill of excitement at seeing this majestic space, with framed posters and information on the walls, chairs and tables placed throughout the room. And, of course, the centerpiece—the long, wooden tasting counter, with its dramatic backdrop of wooden barrels, and the La Leggenda logo in gold above.

The woman paced around the room with Olivia following a few steps behind.

"Where are your bathrooms?" she asked suddenly.

"They're down—" Olivia began, but she was interrupted.

"It's all right. I see the signage now. Not prominently displayed," the woman said disapprovingly.

She headed purposefully down the corridor and, to Olivia's consternation, marched straight into the men's restroom!

"That's the wrong one!" Olivia called out, but there was no response from inside.

She *must* be inspecting, Olivia decided. She couldn't have made such a basic mistake. The signage wasn't that un-prominent! At least, at this early hour and with no other visitors, there would be no chance of embarrassing incidents.

Olivia waited at the end of the corridor, fidgeting uneasily.

A minute later, she was out, and into the ladies' room.

Then the door swung open and the woman stomped back to the tasting room, scribbling notes as she walked. What notes? Olivia wondered, wishing she wasn't frowning as she jotted her impressions down. It made Olivia worry that they were negative.

She gazed across the tasting room to the doors at the far end.

"You have a restaurant on site?"

"Yes. It's quite famous," Olivia supplied, hoping to improve on her track record of not impressing this woman by anything she'd said so far.

3

"Let's see." Clearly still unimpressed, the other woman addressed the comment to herself, but even so, Olivia followed in her wake as she strode purposefully through the double doors.

"Why are you looking around?" Olivia tried, hoping her words struck a note that was closer to "conversational question" than "I'm becoming suspicious of your behavior."

She didn't get a reply, and sensed that the woman thought her questioning to be nothing more than irrelevant background babble.

After a swift glance around the restaurant, with its polished tables and furniture sparkling clean and ready for the day ahead, the woman went into the kitchen.

"Wait!" Olivia squeaked. The woman ignored her, of course.

Olivia felt her stomach twist. This was the domain of her rival, Gabriella. The tawny-haired restaurateur was Marcello's ex-girlfriend, who had kept her job after the relationship had ended. Ever since Olivia had arrived at the winery, Gabriella had regarded her as a threat, and the relationship between them had been nothing but stormy.

If Gabriella were to walk in now and find a stranger nosing around her kitchen, she would be furious—not with the dark-haired woman, but with Olivia, for allowing it.

At that moment, Olivia heard an impatient scrunch of wheels in the parking lot. The sound of Gabriella's sporty Fiat was unmistakable. At the worst possible moment, she was arriving!

Olivia swiveled around to stare anxiously at the parking lot, and then turned back to the kitchen, where the woman was still busy.

"Are you finished in there?" she called, but the only sound was receding footsteps as the woman prowled even further into Gabriella's territory.

From outside, a car door slammed. Olivia felt like waving her arms in consternation. It didn't seem possible for her to remove this officious stranger without grabbing her arm and physically hustling her out. But if she didn't act fast, World War Three might erupt at any moment. In fact, Olivia revised her ideas as she heard the hurried click of Gabriella's heels on the paving outside. There was no "might" about it. They were moments away from an explosion, unless Olivia could come up with an emergency plan to avoid it.

4

CHAPTER TWO

There was only one strategy Olivia could think of on the fly. She needed to buy time by delaying Gabriella at the door. Since the strange woman seemed to be in a hurry, she probably wouldn't spend much longer looking around. If Olivia could stall the restaurateur, trouble might be avoided completely.

Olivia rushed to the restaurant's side entrance, arriving at the same time as Gabriella. With her tortoiseshell hair pinned in a perfect chignon, and her makeup flawless, though heavy on the mascara, Gabriella looked as picture-perfect as always.

The moment she saw Olivia, her mood soured, and she glared combatively at her.

"What do you want?" she demanded.

"I wanted to ask you something," Olivia said innocently.

Gabriella looked immediately suspicious. "What?"

That was a very good question! Olivia felt her synapses smoldering as she racked her brains for a topic.

Luckily, inspiration struck.

"That pond there," she said, pointing to the scenic water feature in the distance, beyond the restaurant gardens. "One of the customers asked me yesterday if there were fish in it. I had no idea, so I thought I'd ask you."

Gabriella gave her an incredulous look, as if Olivia had started babbling in Ancient Greek.

"There are no fish in the pond. It is ornamental only. Why are you asking me this, anyway? I am too busy for stupid questions about pond life! Next time, ask Marcello. Or go and look for yourself." Her glare was so intense, Olivia felt as if she were getting an X-ray. "You should be doing your work. I see the fires aren't yet lit!"

Olivia bristled at the unsolicited career advice. Did Gabriella think she was Olivia's boss? What was she doing, ordering her to light the fires, when for the past two weeks, Olivia had lit them before Gabriella had even arrived?

5

That was the problem, Olivia decided. Gabriella did think that she was her boss, and that was partly why she didn't have any respect for her.

Gabriella wasn't finished yet. Warming to her topic, she continued.

"Your job is to sell wine to the guests. Not to encourage them to roam the grounds in search of fish!"

As Olivia bit back a defensive comment, she heard footsteps behind her. Hopefully, that meant that the gray-suited woman had finished her lightning inspection.

"Thank you for the information," Olivia said coolly, turning away. She'd gotten an answer, even if one heavily cloaked in rudeness. More importantly, she'd managed to avoid the explosion of Gabriella finding a stranger in her kitchen!

Gabriella stomped inside, still muttering in angry tones, "Fish! Fish?"

Olivia hurried back to the tasting room, wondering if the woman needed any more help, and hoping she'd finally explain who she was and why she was here.

But she was too late. The woman was already marching out of the lobby. By the time Olivia rushed outside, the Range Rover was accelerating down the driveway, its engine growling.

She had left without even saying goodbye, or providing a reason for her mysterious appearance, and Olivia couldn't help worrying that this odd visit would end up landing her, or La Leggenda, in trouble.

Trying to put the incident out of her mind, Olivia hurried back into the lobby to start the job she would have done even without Gabriella bossing her so rudely. As she arranged the wood in the fireplace, Olivia seethed over the restaurateur's disrespectful attitude.

Olivia was all out of ideas on how to handle it. She'd tried being friendly and helpful. She'd experimented with being icily professional. Teasing a flame out of the kindling, Olivia remembered she'd even tried to ignore Gabriella, but that was impossible, with them working in adjacent rooms in the same busy winery.

They'd gotten off on the wrong foot from the start, Olivia remembered, while she used the antique leather bellows to blow life into the fire. Being Marcello's ex-girlfriend, Gabriella would have been jealous of any single woman that he hired. The fact that there had been a spark of attraction between Marcello and Olivia hadn't helped.

After she and Marcello had agreed not to take things further romantically, as it might compromise their working relationship,

Gabriella had picked up on this and been friendlier for a while. Olivia had made a point of mentioning her new boyfriend when Gabriella was around, hoping it would contribute to world peace. It had briefly done so, but then Gabriella had found a different reason to be angry. She'd started resenting Olivia's status as head sommelier, and her increased responsibilities.

Her growing role was a blessing, Olivia thought. At least it meant she could work independently. Imagine if Gabriella was her boss! Life would be unlivable.

Heading back into the tasting room to start the next fire, Olivia saw that her young assistant, Jean-Pierre, had just arrived.

"Good morning! Er, I mean, *buon giorno!*" Jean-Pierre's friendly greeting derailed her gloomy thoughts.

"*Buon giorno,*" she replied, thinking how funny it was that she, an American, and Jean-Pierre, a Frenchman, were doing their best to speak as much Italian to each other as they could, both determined to improve their language skills.

In halting, careful Italian, Jean-Pierre spoke again, tugging his unruly brown bangs thoughtfully. "It is a lovely morning, though frigid. Can I help you with your arson?"

Smiling encouragingly even though he'd used the wrong word, Olivia handed him the bellows.

"Please! It is tiring to use these. You can take over and I will go and remove the wine bottles, ready for the guests."

Jean-Pierre looked confused as he took the bellows.

Walking back to the tasting counter, Olivia replayed what she'd said. Her pronunciation had been clear, hadn't it?

"Darn it," she said under her breath. Her pronunciation had been perfect, but she'd used the wrong word. Instead of *rimuovere*, which meant "remove," she had used *rompi*. She'd just confidently told Jean-Pierre that she was about to smash the bottles! No wonder he was glancing around nervously as she headed through the side door into the storage room.

Learning a new language certainly was a journey, Olivia decided, feeling thankful that most of the winery visitors were from other countries, even in winter when tourism dropped.

She checked the printed tasting sheets, setting out some bottles of the sangiovese red wine, the winery's famous Miracolo red blend, the new red blend that Nadia the vintner had recently created, and two white wines—the vermentino and the chardonnay—as well as La Leggenda's Metodo Classico sparkling wine.

The rosé she'd made had been an unexpected success despite Olivia's lack of experience in wine blending. In fact, it was selling so well it had been removed from the tasting menu as stocks were getting low. Next season, Nadia promised, they were going to make triple quantities of it, using Olivia's selfsame recipe.

That made her feel very proud, and a few steps closer to her goal of becoming a successful winemaker with her own wine label.

Voices from outside signaled that the day's first guests were arriving, and Olivia pulled her attention back to work. The Spanish tourists who entered the winery were clad in ski jackets, clearly here to enjoy the snowy slopes to the north.

"Welcome, and *buon giorno*," she greeted the guests as they headed toward the counter, thrilled that they'd taken time from their outdoor activities to visit La Leggenda. "Would you like to enjoy the full menu, or three selected wines?"

"Just three, *por favor*," the woman in the front of the group said, smiling.

"Red, white, or a mixture?" Olivia asked. As she spoke, she was reminded all over again of why she loved her job. Introducing new enthusiasts to La Leggenda's quality wines was pure joy.

Briefly, Olivia cast her mind back to her previous life as an advertising account manager in Chicago. That had been the opposite, especially when catering to the majority of the clients, who had champagne visions, beer budgets, and threw epic tantrums when the results didn't match their expectations.

"I think we should focus on your reds," the woman said, to nods from the rest of the group. "We are red wine lovers, and have heard about your Miracolo blend. It is famous!"

"A great idea," Olivia enthused.

As she poured their first tasting portions, footsteps thudded outside and Marcello rushed in. The dark, handsome winery owner looked stressed. His phone was pressed to his ear as he rushed down the corridor.

"Our first wine is the sangiovese red," Olivia said, wondering what had happened to upset Marcello. "Our winery's sangiovese is classic. Earthy, with a flavor profile of black cherries, it is oaked for a few months in order to give it the spicy, peppery tones that add so much complexity to this delicious wine."

As she poured, Marcello rushed up the corridor again, this time speeding out of the winery. From the parking lot, she heard faint shouts.

Smiling at the guests as she watched them savor this delicious, traditionally Italian red, Olivia suppressed a flare of worry. She hoped there wasn't a crisis. Marcello was usually very calm. The only time Olivia saw him run was when his evening jogging route led him along the service road she and Erba used to walk home.

"Next up is the wine you have been looking forward to, our Miracolo red blend," Olivia explained. "It was originally formulated by mistake, by Mr. Vescovi, the father of the three siblings who own the winery today."

As she spoke, there was a clatter of feet from outside, and in charged the three Vescovis she'd just told the guests about!

Marcello led the way, followed closely by the lean, dark-haired Antonio who, from the look of his muddy boots, had been working on one of the nearby vine plantations. The petite Nadia brought up the rear. She was much shorter than her brothers, but as she sprinted across the tiled floor in her high-heeled shoes, she looked fiercely determined to keep up with them.

A couple at the back of the group looked around curiously at the commotion. Olivia glanced at Jean-Pierre with her eyebrows raised, but her assistant shook his head and gave a tiny shrug. He, too, had no idea what was happening.

Keeping her calm smile glued in place as if nothing at all was wrong, Olivia continued with her story while pouring the Miracolo.

"Mr. Vescovi senior thought he had made a terrible mistake, as he used wines from the wrong vats when blending it. He realized that a large amount of wine would be wasted, which was a terrible blow for the small winery that La Leggenda was then. However, he luckily decided to taste the wine before he threw it away. He knew straight away that he had accidentally created something outstanding, which would make La Leggenda's name famous. That is why he called the wine Miracolo, as its existence was a miracle!"

Her guests looked enthralled by this story, which was the part of La Leggenda's history that she enjoyed telling the most. It was incredible that such a great result had come from a catastrophic error.

Thinking worriedly about catastrophes, Olivia could hear raised voices coming from Marcello's office. It seemed like an argument was erupting.

She struggled to keep focused on the guests, pleased by their nods of approval as they sipped the award-winning Miracolo.

"I will take a case of this, please," the nearest guest told her. "This is magnificent! Made for apres-ski!"

"I will also take a case," the woman at the back of the group said. "We need to have enough of this to enjoy on our vacation, and take home!"

Pleased that this group was placing good orders, Olivia passed the sheet to Jean-Pierre, who hurried away to prepare the cases.

"Our final red wine of the day is a brand new blend created by Nadia, our head vintner," Olivia said. From the office, she could hear that very vintner shrieking, "No! Absolutely not! No!"

Olivia poured the third blend. "In line with international market trends, this new blend is primarily cabernet sauvignon, with a little merlot, a splash of sangiovese, and a small amount of local Barolo grapes. When creating this wine, Nadia imagined that it would be the perfect drink for enjoying by a log fire, and so this wine is named Focolare, or Fireside, Blend."

She saw nods of agreement from the group as they sampled this wine, which was Nadia's pride and joy.

"A case of this, too, please," one of the group said. "We will be enjoying a fire every evening in our chalet, no?"

"Our assistant sommelier will ring up your purchases." Olivia smiled, and Jean-Pierre stepped forward proudly.

As soon as the guests' attention was on him, Olivia rushed from behind the counter. There must be a crisis erupting! How could she help? As she ran through the side doorway, Marcello strode purposefully out of his office, with Nadia and Antonio close behind him.

"Olivia, are you available?" he asked, sounding anxious.

"Yes, I am."

"We must have an urgent meeting immediately! Come to the restaurant! Jean-Pierre, join us as soon as you can."

With a twinge of guilt, Olivia remembered the strange woman's visit and her failure to ask proper questions about it. It couldn't be coincidence that something had happened to stress Marcello out, so soon after that surprise inspection. Had she made a terrible mistake in allowing it? She had a strong premonition that this meeting spelled trouble—if not for the winery, then for her.

CHAPTER THREE

Olivia hustled into the restaurant together with the Vescovis. Antonio looked angry. Nadia's eyes were sparkling and her chin was set in a way that Olivia knew meant she was ready for a fight. And Marcello looked uncharacteristically edgy. His deep blue eyes were narrowed in thought, and he stood by the table, tapping his fingers on the chair as he waited for the others to be seated.

With tension tangible in the air, she was becoming more and more certain that she'd caused this catastrophe, whatever it was, and that it was related to what had happened this morning. Instead of calling her into his office to speak about it privately, Marcello was going to discuss it in front of all the Vescovis, as well as her assistant vintner!

After seeing the tourist group out with a friendly "*Ciao*," Jean-Pierre ran in to join them.

"Gabriella!" Marcello called, and Olivia tensed. Not her, too?

Gabriella appeared from the kitchen, wiping her hands on her apron. Olivia was surprised to see that her demeanor was friendly and cooperative. There wasn't a hint of the combative and frankly bullying attitude she'd shown to Olivia.

"Is there a problem?" Gabriella asked sweetly, and then, once she had everyone's attention, she glanced meaningfully at Olivia. "Has someone caused a crisis?"

"Sit down, sit down," Marcello ordered impatiently. To Olivia's relief, he didn't immediately agree with Gabriella and, in fact, looked fed up with her sniping.

Chairs scraped as they hastily obeyed his request.

"What is happening?" Jean-Pierre asked, looking confused.

With her mind spinning, Olivia waited breathlessly for Marcello to speak.

"We have just been offered what I can only describe as the opportunity of a lifetime!" Marcello announced.

Olivia felt her heart speed up. She'd expected bad news, but this sounded like the opposite. What could it be?

"Tell us more!" Jean-Pierre gasped, clearly as anxious as her.

"At the last moment—the last possible instant—we have been nominated to join an exclusive event; one that is invitation-only," Marcello explained. "The event is known as the Platinum Tour."

Now it was Olivia's turn to gasp. She'd heard it mentioned in her old life. Although she didn't know many details, marketing people spoke of it in hushed voices. Marketers could spend their entire careers trying to get companies and clients involved. She listened, fascinated, to Marcello's description.

"The Platinum Tour is an extremely popular and sought-after event. It is a by-invitation-only, limited-numbers luxury tour for the wealthy elite—business leaders, international CEOs, celebrities, billionaires, and other influencers. It takes place seasonally, and one of the tour's chapters is the Tuscany Chapter. As part of their travels, the group visits a small number of highly exclusive wine estates."

There was a breathless silence in the room. Olivia saw her own amazed hope reflected in Jean-Pierre's eyes. Was Marcello going to say they were part of it?

"The wineries chosen usually remain consistent, as the tour prefers to deal with places the guests know and enjoy. However, yesterday, a catastrophe occurred at Vino Montagna winery."

Another familiar name. Vino Montagna was a leading winery in the area. Olivia had visited it recently. It was co-owned by an Oscar-winning movie star and one of Italy's most prominent designers, and frequented by many celebrities.

"An electrical short caused a severe fire in the tasting room," Marcello explained. "As a result, Vino Montagna is closed for the rest of winter while renovations are done. We have therefore been approached by the Platinum Tour organizers as an alternative venue."

The puzzle pieces were falling into place for Olivia. This must be why the strange woman had made her rushed visit earlier in the day. As if confirming her thoughts, Marcello spoke again.

"They have a very stringent checklist of points. The tour organizer, Stella Markham, did an inspection first thing this morning. After walking through the winery and examining all the facilities, she said we just meet the necessary standard," Marcello said.

"So that was who she was!" Olivia blurted out. Thank goodness she'd arrived early, she thought, glad that her premonition had been wrong.

"Did you let her in?" Marcello asked. "That was fortunate, as she had a list of other venues if we were not available. Well done, Olivia."

Olivia felt a surge of relief. Thank goodness her actions had saved the day, and not been as foolhardy as she'd feared.

"However, we now need to make a decision," Marcello continued, looking serious. "The tour is the day after tomorrow. It is a make-or-break event. We will have to exceed all expectations in terms of our service, our environment, our food. Everything must be perfect if our guests are to be happy, but we do not have much time to prepare. Are we up to it, or should we decline?"

Olivia felt like jumping up and down in her seat with excitement. Surely yes was the obvious answer? But Antonio was shaking his head, and she saw Gabriella frowning.

"I say no," Antonio said. "It is too short notice and our winery is not looking good enough. Tiles need replacing in the tasting room. The planters outside are looking ugly. Even the paving in the parking lot is damaged from cold. We cannot afford to risk disappointing such high-caliber customers. We would be the laughingstock of the area."

"Do I get a vote?" Jean-Pierre asked. When Marcello nodded, the young Frenchman cried, "Yes, of course! What an opportunity! Surely the small details do not matter? After all, it is a place full of history and they are here for wine."

"I agree. Our wines will win them over. Never mind a few cracked paving stones. We must take the chance we can do it and push ourselves to the limit. I say yes," Nadia emphasized, banging her fist on the table.

Gabriella folded her arms. "No. I am against it for the same reasons as Antonio. If we do not succeed, it will damage our reputation. My restaurant chairs need reupholstering and the walls must be repainted. Billionaires will scorn the place if it looks shabby."

Marcello looked at Olivia, and she felt her stomach flip-flop.

There were two votes for, two against, and now it was her turn.

Knowing that she'd make even more of an enemy out of Gabriella, but forcing herself to have the courage of her convictions, Olivia nodded.

"I think we must accept it. I've been to Vino Montagna and their paving wasn't perfect. Nobody expected it to be. We had a great time there anyway. It wasn't only the wines, but also their amazing knowledge of them, and the way we were treated. That was what made the difference for me," Olivia said, remembering the outing with a fond smile, as it had been her and Danilo's second date.

13

"You do not have the same taste as a billionaire," Gabriella hissed at her with narrowed eyes.

Olivia studiously ignored her baiting. They were now three to two in favor of the tour. The deciding vote rested with Marcello. If he said yes, the tour was on. If he said no, then she guessed his word would be final.

A tense silence descended on the room as everyone waited in expectation to see what he would say.

CHAPTER FOUR

Marcello gave a decisive nod.

"I am not participating in the voting. It is not necessary," he said, to Olivia's shock. She heard Gabriella gasp in outrage, but didn't dare glance in the affronted restaurateur's direction. "I can see that we have a majority. The majority has decided, and we will accept the tour. I will call Stella back immediately and tell her our decision."

Marcello stood up and marched back to his office, and only then did Olivia look at the others. Antonio seemed even more worried. Nadia was triumphant. Jean-Pierre looked excited, and Gabriella was searing Olivia with a furious glare.

"So, we are all going to be put to huge stress and inconvenience for a stupid once-off?" Gabriella hissed.

Nadia leaned threateningly across the table. "How do you know it will be a once-off? Emergencies occur. Other fires happen! We might become the official tour reserve. Perhaps they will even decide to use us again!"

"Even a once-off would benefit us, surely?" Jean-Pierre said. "If the billionaires enjoy the place, they will come back and tell their friends!"

"If they have any," Gabriella muttered.

"I think it is a great opportunity," Jean-Pierre concluded, pretending not to have heard Gabriella. "I have always wanted to meet a billionaire."

Olivia agreed. She felt thrilled that they'd been chosen, and wasn't sure what all the negativity was about.

"We must work as a team. If we all pull together, this will be the best experience that these people will have on their tour," Olivia said, feeling like the group cheerleader, even though nobody else was cheering. All the same, unity was essential. If everyone was fighting with each other, it would be a disaster, and she could already see that Gabriella and Nadia both wanted to fight.

Antonio stood up. "I will attend to the damaged paving immediately," he said, and strode out.

"I will go and rearrange all my plans for the next two days. Let us hope none of our booked patrons are inconvenienced by this idiotic tour. If anything goes wrong, which I am sure it will, it will all be your fault, Olivia," Gabriella spat, scraping her chair back and stomping into the kitchen.

*

By five p.m. when Olivia left, the evening had turned dark, cold, and misty. Stepping outside the tasting room, she looked back, appreciating the golden glow that streamed from the doorway, bright with the promise of firelight and hospitality.

Then, to her surprise, a familiar silhouette materialized in the doorway.

A moment later, Marcello joined her, pulling on a jacket. His dark hair looked rumpled from the stressful day he'd clearly had, but his gaze was warm, and so was his smile.

"Olivia. I am glad you have not yet left. I was delayed in my office, making arrangements for the Platinum Tour. I had hoped to speak to you earlier."

Curious, Olivia said, "What is it?"

She was certain that this would be something to do with the tour, but Marcello's next words left her feeling surprised.

"Can you travel with me to Chianti tomorrow? We will need to leave early, at eight-thirty, and should be back by mid-afternoon. I have something important to discuss with you."

Important? What was so important that Marcello had to travel into the Chianti region to tell her?

Olivia's mind raced. Impatience overwhelmed her and suddenly tomorrow seemed much too far away. Why couldn't Marcello tell her now? She felt tempted to plead with him to give her at least a hint. Then she decided not to. It would be pushing their professional boundaries too far.

"Can we spare the time away before the tour?" she asked, thinking of what a whirlwind tomorrow would be.

"Yes. I have confirmed with Nadia and Jean-Pierre that they will handle the wine tasting as well as the preparation," Marcello reassured her.

"In that case, I'd love to go with you. What a treat," she enthused, seeing from the mischievous gleam in his eyes that he'd sensed how curious she was, but wasn't about to set her mind at rest.

Sometimes Olivia wished that she and Marcello weren't so much on the same wavelength. It was disconcerting how easily he could read her. It occurred to her that she and Marcello thought along similar lines more often than she and Danilo did. Were you supposed to be more in tune with your boss than your boyfriend? Olivia wasn't sure about that!

"I look forward to our journey," Marcello said with an enigmatic smile.

Olivia racked her brains for other leading questions but couldn't think of any. She couldn't ask how she should dress. She was going on an outing with a winery owner, in the Tuscan midwinter. It was perfectly obvious what her ensemble should include for smartness, warmth, and elegance.

"Have a good evening," she said reluctantly, abandoning her fruitless quest for information.

"And you, too. Are you sure you do not want a ride home?"

This was another traditional question, which Marcello asked whenever he saw her outside at closing time.

"I love the walk," Olivia said, and even on a cold, misty night it was absolutely true. The stroll along the quiet roads, shrouded in fog and with fine water droplets caressing her face while she gazed at the outlines of trees just visible in the darkness, felt like an adventure every time. It brought her no less of a thrill than when she walked the route in bright sunshine, enjoying every detail of the hills, forests, and patchwork fields that made up the rolling landscape.

"I will see you tomorrow," Marcello confirmed, before heading back inside.

With curiosity still fizzing inside her, Olivia headed up the service road. She knew that even in the mist and darkness, Erba would hear her footsteps and be waiting. Sure enough, the moment she crested the hill, Olivia heard the patter of hooves from the goat dairy where Erba spent her daytime.

Strolling along in the misty darkness, Olivia remembered that she had a special evening ahead with Danilo. Tonight, she would hopefully uncover one of the biggest mysteries in the old and previously dilapidated farm she'd bought.

It had seemed like a crazy idea to invest in a twenty-acre piece of rugged, disheveled real estate in the hills of Tuscany, but Olivia had fallen in love with the farm. She'd since discovered it had been used for wine production long ago, before being abandoned and falling into disrepair.

Olivia had been enthralled to discover an old, locked storeroom hidden in the forested hills. For months, she had searched for the key, unwilling to force the lock to find out what was inside the small, secluded building.

Recently, Danilo had uncovered an old, antique-looking key. He'd found it near the bottom of the pile of rubble which had dominated the barn before Olivia had repurposed it as a winemaking room.

Tonight, Danilo was coming around after work. They planned to hike up to the storeroom and see if the key worked. Olivia was nervous about what they might find inside, and felt glad that Danilo would be there so that they could open it together. At least, if it proved to be empty, they could cheer each other up afterwards.

So far, her farm had yielded two incredible finds. The first was an unopened antique bottle of wine, which was currently at a specialist store for the label to be restored, and the second was a far more ancient shard of glass, identified as being from a priceless bottle originally from a local winery.

What further treasures, if any, were hidden away? Olivia was excited to find out.

She couldn't wait to see Danilo again! How lucky was she to be dating a man who was handsome, kind, funny, and great company? And, although they'd only been on a couple of dates, she was starting to realize Danilo was also very romantic.

The downside was that their time together had been limited. In fact, it had been a full week since they'd seen each other, which Olivia hadn't expected at the start of a new relationship. But Danilo, a carpenter and woodworker by trade, had recently been snowed under with urgent orders. Yesterday, he'd told her that his in-tray was finally clear and everything had been delivered.

What to do first? Mulling over her evening's plans, Olivia stopped for a moment to admire the small vine plantation near the driveway. The young plants were thriving, despite the colder weather, and thanks mostly to Danilo's help and advice. Thinking of him, she smiled.

Would Danilo want to see the small batch of wine fermenting in the barn? Even though there wasn't much to see, Olivia was sure he'd be interested in the progress of the ice wine she'd made after harvesting the grapes that had been frozen on her farm's wild vines. It was her very first vintage as an independent winemaker, and she felt a mixture of excitement and nerves whenever she thought about its progress.

They could go past the barn on the way to the storeroom, inspect the fermenting wine together, and then come back to the farmhouse for food.

In which case, dinner was her next priority. Olivia had better get cooking!

But, as she opened the front door, her phone beeped with an incoming message. Quickly, she grabbed it. Was Danilo going to arrive early?

As she read it, her heart plummeted into her shoes.

"Sorry! We will have to postpone tonight, I cannot make it. D," the terse and unloving message read.

Staring at the words, Olivia let out an anguished sigh as discouragement filled her. Why could Danilo not make it? He knew how important tonight was. It was no ordinary dinner date, but the night that they were going to try out the key!

He hadn't even given a reason in that short message, Olivia realized, feeling uncertain about things all over again. What was the reason? Why wasn't he telling her? Why hadn't he called? Or, at the very least, added a row of X's or a heart emoji? Perhaps she had gotten the wrong impression of him, and he didn't have romantic feelings about her at all.

Olivia had been cheated on in the past, and she had trust issues. Logically, she knew that a relationship couldn't progress from "friends" to "deeply committed" in one wild leap. But in her heart, she feared that the unexpected cancellation meant things weren't working out.

Perhaps she was fooling herself, and this wasn't a real relationship, Olivia thought despondently, trudging into the kitchen.

Her adopted black-and-white cat, Pirate, jumped onto the counter, meowing excitedly. He didn't care that Olivia's plans were canceled. All he cared was that she should serve him his dinner immediately.

Despite herself, Olivia felt better. It was impossible to remain downhearted around Pirate. He was always doing something entertaining. But as she reached for the kibble container, ready to pour some into his bowl, Olivia changed her mind.

She had to try again to get Pirate into the carrier. As a previously wild ex-feral, he was unneutered and hadn't had his shots. Taking him to the vet was becoming an urgent priority. The problem was that Pirate didn't want to go to the vet. Or get into the carrier.

It was confusing how such a gentle and affectionate feline could turn into a deadly people-shredding machine in an instant, but Olivia had seen it happen. Never mind that, she'd personally experienced the results! She still had the Band-Aid on her wrist to prove it.

"Come, Pirate!" she said, trying to infuse her voice with calm authority.

Hoping that her gentle but firm touch would soothe the cat, she picked him up.

Pirate draped his light weight in her hands, purring vigorously. Olivia felt hopeful that this time, her efforts would succeed.

"What a beautiful kitty you are," she cooed, jouncing him gently in her grasp as she headed purposefully across the kitchen to the carrier.

Why did they make the doors so small? she wondered, kneeling down and trying to keep Pirate's paws off the floor while she aimed him at the narrow doorway.

"In, sweet kitty! Nooo!"

With a hiss, Pirate reverted to his feral roots, wriggling out of Olivia's grasp and swiping angrily at her. She snatched her hand away just in time. She really didn't want another flesh wound. They stung!

Growling, Pirate ran into the living room. Olivia grabbed the kibble bag and ran after him, shaking it enticingly even as frustration surged inside her.

"Foodies! Foodies!"

But Pirate had changed his mind, clearly deciding freedom was more important than dinner. He darted into the hallway and headed upstairs, his paws thudding on the wooden steps. There, Olivia knew from experience, he would take refuge under the bed with his back against the wall. She would have to crawl under the bed if she wanted to try and grab him again, but Pirate's strategic position would mean he could stay safely in place, while delivering devastating right hooks with his claws bared.

"All right," Olivia capitulated. "You win."

Discouraged, she returned to the kitchen and poured the kibble into his bowl. She knew he'd sense she'd given up and would be back in no time at all, munching contentedly as if the dramatic capture scene had never played out!

As she put the bag away, her phone started ringing. Hoping that Danilo had changed his mind, Olivia grabbed it. It wasn't Danilo, but she was comforted to see that the caller was her best friend, Charlotte, from back in the States.

"Hey," she greeted her.

"What's up?" Charlotte asked immediately, clearly sensing Olivia's mood.

"Everything's good." Olivia pressed her lips together in annoyance as she watched Pirate trot confidently down the stairs again.

"I meant, what's wrong?" Charlotte said patiently.

"Nothing! I've just gotten in and I'm about to enjoy a lovely evening at home," Olivia said, deciding to put a brave face on her lonely predicament. There was no need to burden Charlotte with her relationship worries.

"Oh. I thought you sounded sad."

"Not at all," Olivia said firmly.

"Well, I just got back from the hairdresser. She put more red highlights into my hair and I'm loving it."

"Send a picture! I want to see," Olivia said, feeling better as she thought of her cheerful friend's russet-hued locks.

"I will. Are you preparing dinner now?"

Olivia glanced at the fridge. It was packed full of delicious ingredients, and she'd bought fresh gnocchi yesterday. She could make a garlicky tomato sauce to go with it, and cover it in grated Parmesan for a decadently delicious result.

Firmly, Olivia told herself to have some discipline. It was too early to start preparing food. Instead, she decided to spend an hour on a tedious but necessary chore.

"Pirate's eating his dinner after refusing *again* to go into the cat carrier," Olivia updated her friend with a sigh. "But mine will have to wait. For now, I'm heading upstairs. I'm busy tiling the bathroom walls, and I need to get it finished."

"I remember they were in a horrific state. I thought you'd have to pay someone to fix them up. And you're doing it all yourself?" Charlotte's voice rang with admiration.

The original bathroom, though spacious, had been badly plastered and then, at some stage, somebody had glued thick blue wallpaper onto the walls. In a bathroom! The place had been filled with peeling fronds of paper and crumbling plaster, and Olivia had grown used to bathing in what felt like a building site as she'd scraped and chiseled layers of the old coverings off the walls.

Now, section by section, she was retiling the walls in a soft cream shade, with a few mosaic tiles providing a sparkly green highlight.

Olivia didn't fool herself that she was in any way talented at the task, but she was proud of her homemade efforts.

"I'm not a natural tiler, and it's very hard work," Olivia admitted. "Still, I'm saving money, and it's something to do in the evenings. There's only so much studying Italian a girl can do."

She switched her phone to speaker and put it on the edge of the bath, before adding water to the dry mix that was waiting in the container. Mixing it well, she picked up one of the smooth cream tiles and pressed it into place, enjoying the clayey smell of the mortar.

"Talking of studying Italian…" Charlotte's voice dropped, sounding curious. "Have you studied any good Italians lately?"

Olivia snorted with laughter.

"If that's a question about my love life, the truth is that it's not much different from when I was single," she admitted sadly, placing another of the cream tiles carefully into its spot.

"What about Danilo? I was imagining you'd be preparing a lovely dinner for him."

"I was supposed to, but he canceled on me." Olivia knew Charlotte could pick up on the disappointment in her voice.

"So that's why you sounded sad. Don't worry. I'm sure he must be busy this time of year," Charlotte soothed.

"I'm wondering if I rushed into this." Olivia scooped up another chunk of mortar and pressed another tile into place. She was well over halfway now. It wouldn't be long before this tedious task was behind her.

"Of course you are. You wouldn't be you if you weren't. Being in a new relationship isn't easy. So much uncertainty. You must be wishing you could skip ahead a little while, to when things are more settled."

"That's exactly how I feel." Charlotte had summarized all Olivia's angst. She felt comforted that her friend knew her so well. "I was thinking thirty years might do it."

"Thirty years? You'll miss out on all the fun parts. Be brave! Remember from what you told me, he's also been on his own awhile, and probably doesn't want to rush or crowd you."

"You're right. I just have to try not to panic," Olivia agreed reluctantly.

"And Marcello? Is he still single?" Charlotte's tone was loaded with meaning.

"Yes, but we have an agreement, remember. No romance in the workplace." Olivia chose another sparkly green tile for contrast. They were her favorite. She always felt excited when it was time for a green tile.

"Hmmm. Does Marcello know about Danilo?"

"I haven't had a chance to tell him. I mean, what am I supposed to do? Walk up to him and say I'm dating someone? If Danilo and I are actually dating. We've only been on two dates!"

Scraping up more mortar, Olivia knew she sounded defensive. Another "Hmmm" from Charlotte didn't help at all.

"We're going on an outing tomorrow," she said.

"You and Danilo?"

"No. Marcello is taking me out. I'm not sure where. It's a business trip, but he said he has something important to tell me. Not that a business trip is any hardship, as it's likely to be to a vineyard," Olivia said.

"Have you thought that he might have romantic intentions? Perhaps that's the something important? What if he confesses that you've made him rethink the whole no-more-dating-staff rule?"

Olivia almost clapped a hand over her mouth in horror. Just in time, she remembered her fingers were smeared with gray, sticky mortar.

Charlotte could well be right, she realized. In which case, tomorrow's outing would become an embarrassing disaster.

Suddenly, Olivia was dreading it.

CHAPTER FIVE

As Olivia headed to the winery the following day in the cold but sunny morning, she was brimming with mixed emotions. On the one hand, she was worried that Charlotte's hunch was right, and Marcello was going to tell her he'd changed his mind, and romance was on the cards.

On the other hand, she felt relieved that today would include an outing, and a chance to get away from the mad preparations for the Platinum Tour that everyone at La Leggenda would be embroiled in.

When she rounded the corner and joined the path that led to the front of the winery, she saw Marcello was already there. He was examining the flower beds that flanked the entrance door. At this stage of winter, the beds contained mostly greenery, but Marcello was gazing hopefully into them.

"I see some buds," he told Olivia, turning and smiling. "Perhaps spring is not as far away as we think! Around the corner, new energy will bloom. I love spring!"

Olivia found her heart fluttering at the use of that word "love," and not in a good way. Her fears surged again. It felt as if Marcello were setting the tone upfront for this trip, or even foreshadowing its purpose.

He greeted her in the traditional Italian manner, with a kiss on each cheek. As he bent forward, a lock of his hair brushed hers, gently tickling. She smelled the fresh scent of shaving gel, and the woody aroma of his leather jacket.

"You are always early. Knowing this makes me try to arrive sooner," he told her in complimentary tones.

Smiling, Olivia guessed she'd identified the problem. They were both aiming to be earlier than the other. She guessed that meant they shared a similar mindset, or at any rate, a passion for the wonderful business they worked in.

Normally, the thought of qualities in common with her boss would make her feel positive, but now it gave her an uneasy twinge.

As Erba scampered off, eager to join the herd at the goat dairy, Olivia climbed into the passenger seat of Marcello's SUV.

"Where are we going?" she asked, but he shook his head.

"It's a surprise," he said.

She was perplexed to pick up a hint of nervousness in his voice. It was very unlike Marcello to be nervous, and this was another warning sign.

As they headed out of the main gate, Olivia reminded herself to remain professional and calm, no matter what surprises were in store.

Marcello liked to play classical music or opera on his road trips, and this morning, Nessun Dorma filled the car at a volume that was comfortable enough for conversation, but also meant there was no uneasy silence. It was one of her favorite arias, and always filled Olivia with emotion.

Staring out the window, Olivia admired the winter tapestry that surrounded her. At this time of year, the heavy rain had turned the grass and fields deep green. The branches of the hazel trees were bare of leaves, but festooned in yellow catkins which added color to the deep, dark, rain-soaked landscape.

Whenever Olivia headed out of town on a road trip, she felt elated to have restarted her life in this beautiful, historic area where she instinctively felt she belonged. Who would have thought that an impulse vacation could have led to such a huge, yet rewarding, life change in this incredible part of Italy?

They were driving toward Florence, but before they reached the city, they joined the highway and headed into the rolling terrain of the Chianti district.

Where were they going? She recognized the turn-off that led to the celebrity-owned wine farm where she and Danilo had enjoyed a wine tasting and sumptuous dinner as their second date. Staring at the signpost, Olivia remembered what a perfect outing it had been. The wine tasting had provided an afternoon of laughter and conversation in a gorgeous setting, and the dinner had been the perfect opportunity for them to become closer and talk more intimately. They'd headed back to her farmhouse for coffee, and Danilo had stayed over for the very first time.

The next day, Olivia had felt she was floating on air with happiness. But now, she was worried that he hadn't thought the evening was as perfect as she had. Perhaps she'd been too clingy? She'd tried very hard not to be clingy at all! Or had Danilo expected more of a commitment? she wondered. Surely it had been too soon for talk of permanence, or declarations of love?

On the other hand, maybe Danilo had decided that after that date, things were moving too fast. Was he feeling trapped after expecting something more casual? she fretted with a frown. Only when Vino Montagna was out of sight did she manage to put her troubled thoughts aside.

Beyond that winery, this part of Tuscany was completely new to her. It seemed unspoiled, and more remote than the area where La Leggenda was located. Only the occasional quaint village, with stone church spires reaching to the sky, punctuated the rolling panorama.

"And here, we turn again," Marcello said, sounding deeply contented as he swung the SUV onto a quiet road.

This was clearly a familiar route to him. He hadn't even glanced at his satnav, despite being a fair distance from La Leggenda. This was the heart of the Chianti Classico area, Olivia knew, and given the worldwide fame of these wines, she was excited that this was their destination. But where, exactly, were they heading?

Increasingly curious, Olivia waited until Marcello headed along another narrow, winding lane which led into the scenic town of Greve.

As Olivia took in the shops, their signage so understated and pretty compared to the louder, more in-your-face retail displays in the States, she noticed a discreet sign announcing: *Castello di Verrazzano Wine Store.*

"We're going to Castello di Verrazzano!" Olivia exclaimed. It was among the most famous organic wineries in Italy. She longed to know more about their farming methods, especially when she heard Nadia or Antonio bemoaning the difficulties of growing wine within these strict, but rewarding, parameters. Nadia in particular would march into the tasting room yelling, "Bugs! I hate all bugs!" when her vines were challenged by the local insects.

Her guess was right. Marcello nodded, looking satisfied.

Just outside of town they headed up the hill toward the winery. The imposing castle, flanked by rolling hills covered in vine plantations, was visible from the moment they crested the hill and Olivia gasped in awe.

This was one of the stateliest and most gorgeous castles she'd ever seen. It looked perfectly preserved, as if time had washed gently over its high stone walls and elegant towers, doing nothing more than imparting a weathered richness to its veneer.

"What an amazing place," she breathed.

"It is one of the most beautiful buildings I know," Marcello agreed, his voice filled with emotion.

Glancing at him, Olivia saw his face was alight with happiness. Clearly, Marcello did have a history with this place, and clearly, he loved it.

Olivia craned her neck as they neared the vine plantations. These vines looked sturdy and healthy, and she was surprised by how lush the plants looked. The amount of sheer hard work that it must take to maintain such massive fields boggled her mind. Did they use mechanization? she wondered. Hopefully there would be a chance to ask questions.

They climbed out of the car and Olivia stared up at the high walls, and then swiveled around to take in the panoramic view of the vineyards they had driven past. In the distance, she could see the golden stone of Greve town, nestled among the hills.

What a magnificent venue. She couldn't have asked for a more regal setting for the no doubt excruciating scene that would soon play out between her and Marcello. Luckily, the strong building behind her felt supportive, and her nerves abated, replaced by a rush of positive energy.

"Shall we go in?" Marcello said softly.

They walked into the cool, high-roofed hall. Inhaling an appreciative breath, Olivia thought she picked up a complex mix of history, wine, and the subtle aroma of food. Crispy dough, baking tomatoes, and a hint of garlic teased her senses with their barely-there presence.

Instead of following the directions to the well signposted tasting room and restaurant, Marcello nodded a greeting at the smiling young receptionist before he turned the other way. Olivia walked alongside, but fell behind as Marcello headed through a doorway and up a steep, spiral staircase.

Cool grew colder, and dim grew darker, the only light emanating from the faint globes overhead. This was a true castle experience! No doubt, these hidden stairs had been the domain of servants, but probably also of trysting lovers. Who knew, Olivia thought, with yet another stab of doubt.

"We are about to enjoy the most beautiful view," Marcello continued, blithely unaware of Olivia's internal conniptions. "Looking out over Chianti, from the battlements of this ancient castle, is an auspicious way to start this very special day. This castle has a good energy."

Marcello was setting a brisk pace, and Olivia was so out of breath from the winding stairs that she couldn't do more than murmur in assent, although her trepidation was growing with every step.

Scenarios collided in her mind. Turning down her boss was not something she had ever imagined doing!

Worse still, she couldn't suppress her fears that Danilo wasn't serious about her. If she rebuffed Marcello, believing herself to be involved with another man when in fact she wasn't—well, it would be the most terrible decision of her life. She would have lost out in every possible way.

After what seemed like a long climb, they exited the stairway and headed along a corridor with heavy wooden doors on the left, and on the right, the occasional high view from tall, narrow windows.

At the very end of the corridor, the wall had been dismantled and a waist-high wrought-iron balcony installed. Olivia caught her breath as she stared out over the view, thrown into dramatic relief with the low winter sunshine.

It was an enticing combination of order and chaos, Olivia realized. Wild, tangled forests at the borders of the estate were curbed by the edges of the massive vine plantations, which combed their curving lines over the hillside. Stately cypress trees lined the driveway.

"It's magnificent. *Magnifico*," she said.

Marcello nodded, and yet again, Olivia was surprised to see he looked unsure.

"I have brought you here for a reason," he said. "A very important reason." He turned to face her, his dark eyes wide and serious.

Olivia felt her mouth grow dry. Her worst fears were realized. Unable to speak, her heart hammering with expectation, she waited for the bombshell to land.

CHAPTER SIX

"Olivia, I—" Marcello began.

And then, from behind them, a joyful bellow broke the moment.

"Marcello Vescovi! There you are!"

Both of them swung around to face the speaker. Marcello's face was filled with expectation and joy. Olivia felt weak with relief that the moment she'd dreaded had been postponed by this fortunate encounter.

The stocky, silver-haired man approaching them had strong features and wore an air of authority as easily as he wore his stylish Gucci coat. She guessed he must be the estate manager or in charge of the winery. And clearly, Marcello was his long-lost friend. Beaming from ear to ear, he wrapped the tall Marcello in a bear hug, greeting him in rapid Italian which Olivia was pleased she could get the gist of.

He was berating Marcello for not having visited more frequently, and congratulating him on the quality of the La Leggenda wines, and expressing excitement about some future venture that sounded important. That was the essence of the conversation, combined with much arm-waving and gesturing and cries of *"Mio Dio!"* and *"Strabiliante!"*, and Marcello's laughing responses.

Switching to English, Marcello placed his arm around Olivia's shoulders. The touch gave her a frisson of worry. Was she going to be announced as his girlfriend-to-be?

"I am being rude. I should have introduced Olivia Glass, our head sommelier, immediately. Olivia, this is Sergio Elmo, the general manager of this estate. He is in charge of the wine growing and has pioneered their journey to organic."

"It's an honor to meet you," Olivia said, relieved that Marcello had referred to her purely in work terms. More exciting still, this man was an icon of the Tuscan wine industry. She felt as if she were greeting a movie star as he grasped her hand warmly in his own.

"The pleasure is mine. Marcello has spoken very highly of you," he said with conviction.

Olivia felt breathless at the compliment. How kind of Marcello! Although, given today's circumstances, she couldn't help worrying about exactly what he'd said.

"Now, firstly, you will want to tour our vineyards, I am sure," Sergio invited.

"I'd love to!" Again, Olivia glanced out over that exquisite view. She couldn't wait to learn more about what it took to produce these world-renowned wines—and organically, too.

With Sergio leading the way, they headed back down the narrow staircase. Descending in the gloom, she was glad of the sturdy wooden rail that circled the outer wall.

Sergio headed out of the main entrance, past a large group of tourists, and then hugged the castle's walls, leading them along a paved path and then turning into the verdant fields beyond.

"Our estate has occupied this same area of Chianti for more than a thousand years," Sergio told her, following a sandy track that led between two plantations of tall, healthy vines.

A thousand years? Olivia found it difficult to comprehend that an estate could have remained stable and established for that vast amount of time.

"How large is it?" she asked. "And how much of it is planted with vines?"

"The full estate is two hundred and thirty acres. Of this, approximately half is planted with vines. Our soil here is stony, but rich in limestone."

Olivia felt encouraged. Her farm was stony, too. Look how productive Castello di Verrazzano's fields were. Hopefully she could coax her farm into greater fertility in less than a thousand years. She was already thirty-four, after all.

"We renew our vineyards periodically, and according to a specialized schedule. This keeps the average age of our plants at around twelve years," Sergio explained further.

"How do you divide up your plantations?" Marcello asked.

"We aim for each type of grape to grow on the ground most suited to it. This might look like one estate, but to a vine, it is not. It is a thousand different places, each with its own qualities and microclimate. Our job as caretakers of these precious plants is to choose where each one will grow and thrive to its best. The soil type, combined with the way we manage the growing and harvesting, as well as our mainly east exposure, is what imparts a unique taste and quality to all our wines."

Olivia felt inspired by this information. She was in awe of the mastery it took to provide a signature quality to every wine produced in this estate. Would she ever have the expertise to do this? Her thoughts turned with hope to the small batch of ice wine busy maturing in her barn.

"Do you grow mainly sangiovese grapes?' she asked, guessing that this would be the most popular type in the heart of the Chianti region.

"Yes. Different varietals of sangiovese are, of course, the heroes of the red wines that we are known for. We also grow merlot, canaiolo, cabernet sauvignon, and colorino, and we have small plantations of white grapes also."

As they walked in between the vines, Olivia was impressed all over again by how healthy and well cared for they looked. It amazed her to think that this could be done using completely organic fertilization and maintenance.

"We weed mechanically. After all, a human has limits, and weeds are tenacious," Sergio laughed. "But all our grapes are harvested by hand."

"You practice grassing, don't you?" Marcello asked.

As he said the words, Olivia realized what was so different about these plantations. Grass was growing everywhere, even under the vines. They were walking along one of the only clear pathways she could see, and it was decidedly narrow. She'd never seen this done before, although recently she had noticed that the La Leggenda plantations looked untidier than usual. Perhaps this was something they were introducing?

"In traditional wine farming, pesticides are used to clear this space, but we believe that is old thinking and we can work better with nature. Grassing enables this. If correctly done, it has so many benefits," Sergio enthused. "Of course, our main aim in everything we do is to encourage the natural health of the vines and reduce the need for pesticides, in line with our fully organic status. Grassing promotes so much biodiversity among the fields, leading to better health of the vines. It actually reduces unwanted vine growth, as now there is competition for the soil under the plants. It prevents erosion and it means that water does not evaporate as fast."

Olivia's mind was buzzing as she took in this wisdom. She wanted an organic farm, too. Perhaps this meant an end to her backbreaking sessions of trying to weed out all the grass and other growth around her vines, which had always been a discouraging job, and which she'd abandoned completely when work was too busy or the weather was bad.

31

"Shall we go to the cellar now?" Sergio turned left, joining another of the rare paths, this one leading back to the castle.

Olivia glanced at Marcello, who looked as excited as she did to absorb this incredible knowledge. This could transform what they did at La Leggenda and take their farming to the next level.

She couldn't believe what they had learned in just a few minutes of strolling through this magical property. Imagine what they could pick up if they had a full day here, or even a week.

They followed Sergio around the side of the castle. At this early hour, the underground cellars were not yet open to the public, but as soon as the smartly dressed attendant spotted Sergio approaching, he quickly unlatched the creaky iron fastening and swung the enormous door wide.

"The cellars date back to the sixteenth century," Sergio said. "Our barrels are placed along the internal corridors, to better protect them from any fluctuations in temperature."

This was one of the most atmospheric cellars she'd ever seen, Olivia thought. Following Sergio into the gloomy depths, she breathed in the complex scent of oak, maturing wine, and the feeling of deep history that pervaded the air with a subtle musty tinge.

She wished she'd known earlier how unique this place was, so that she could have planned a trip with Danilo. It would have been a memorable experience for them to share. As it was, she feared that embarrassing memories might end up being made here!

"This way." Sergio led them along a sloping corridor. The lighting was subdued, perhaps to provide a stable environment for the maturing wine in the massive oak barrels that punctuated their journey, standing like guards along the way.

Sergio unlocked a steel gate, his keys clanking in the latch. He swung it open and they entered a small, vault-like room, with a long wine rack placed along the back wall.

"This is our most exclusive storage area. General visitors are not permitted inside; we open it only for very special guests. In here, we keep bottles of our best vintages, ever since 1924."

Olivia gazed raptly at the rows of wines. But Sergio had another treat in store. Moving to one of the huge barrels that served as tables, he took a wine from the closest side of the rack and opened it.

"This wine is not historic. It is part of our vintage from two years ago, which we are very proud of. Please, have a taste of one of our most successful Chiantis."

Olivia felt as if she were enjoying an out-of-this world experience as she swirled and tasted the magnificent Chianti, still stunned by the fact that she was able to engage with this wine while in the depths of one of Italy's most historic cellars.

What a magnificent aroma, Olivia thought admiringly.

She met Marcello's smiling gaze. His face looked warm, and there was an intense expression in his eyes as he stared at her. Or was she imagining that? Olivia worried, hastily glancing down at her wine.

Thankfully, Sergio broke the awkward moment with some conversation. "You are Americano, no?" he asked.

"Yes, that is correct," Olivia admitted.

"Your country has a distant connection with this castle. In fact, Giovanni da Verrazzano, who navigated to the bay of New York in the fifteenth century, was born here in 1485. The Verrazzano Bridge in New York is named after him."

"Really?" Olivia was enchanted with the information. This day was expanding her knowledge in every direction.

"Thank you for this experience," she said, putting her glass down. Sergio was looking toward the door, and she guessed that in a few minutes, the hordes of daily visitors would start to arrive. No doubt, he wanted this special room with its store of priceless wines to be safely locked up.

"See you next week," Sergio said to Marcello, as they headed back down the passage. At the gate, they clasped hands warmly, before Sergio rushed in the opposite direction, heading up another concealed stairway to disappear into the labyrinth of the castle.

Now, Olivia was alone with Marcello once again.

He moved away from the lines of tourists that were forming outside the cellar entrance, and uneasiness rekindled inside her. She'd been so captivated by the experience they'd just had that she'd all but forgotten what lay ahead.

"I have something important to tell you, Olivia," Marcello said.

Her misgivings rushed back as she waited for him to speak.

CHAPTER SEVEN

Marcello's face was set and determined as he stared down at Olivia. His eyes were sparkling. He seemed positive and excited, though still strangely tense. As for her, her insides felt like a tumble dryer. She stared back, trying to keep a cool and competent demeanor and hoping that her stomach wouldn't let out an audible growl of nerves.

"I have been offered an amazing opportunity. The chance of a lifetime, in fact," Marcello told her gently, and Olivia felt the coil of tension inside her loosen. This didn't sound like the beginnings of a declaration of romance. It sounded different—and, in fact, more serious.

"What opportunity?" she asked.

Suddenly, she felt apprehensive for an entirely different reason. What if Marcello was going to sell La Leggenda or make a huge life change? Olivia started to fear that the foundations she loved and relied upon so much might be dissolving as he spoke.

"Sergio has invited me to spend a few months here, doing an intensive mentorship with him. He has seen the need to guide other wineries in the principles of organic growing, and he has noted how we have succeeded on a smaller scale at La Leggenda."

Olivia gasped. This wasn't just a phenomenal opportunity, but also a huge compliment to Marcello. No wonder he'd seemed so excited and nervous. She'd been completely wrong in her guess.

But then the full implications struck her.

Marcello would be away from La Leggenda! Could the winery cope without its leader? There were so many day-to-day decisions that had to be made, some on the fly, some with careful forethought. All required the wisdom and judgment that forty-year-old Marcello had acquired during a lifetime of experience on his beloved estate.

He would be away from operations, not just for a few days—a weekend fishing trip with friends was the longest vacation she'd known him to take—but for months.

"I can see from your face that you are thinking the same as me," Marcello said. "It is an opportunity I never thought would come my way, but every opportunity means a sacrifice."

"I understand," Olivia said solemnly, appreciating the weight of the decision.

"It is truly a life-changing offer. When Sergio made it to me a week ago, I was delighted beyond words. But, at the same time, I thought carefully about it. After all, our business has to come first, even when the quest for growth and learning is calling."

"Absolutely," Olivia agreed.

"Making the right decision with so much at stake is never easy. And I could not have accepted this offer—which I have done—without the privilege of having such a dedicated and driven team at La Leggenda. You yourself, Olivia, are so valuable to our business. I admire the speed at which you have learned, embraced all responsibilities and looked for more, and your passion for the winery."

"Thank you," Olivia said, feeling ten feet tall at the compliment. Marcello's encouragement made the fire inside her burn so bright!

"I have booked a table for us for an early lunch," Marcello said. "This is to thank you for what you have done for us, and also to talk about your role in the next few months. The restaurant here is superb. Shall we go?"

Olivia suddenly realized she was starving. Turning away from the cellars, she walked with Marcello to the restaurant. Except they didn't go directly into the restaurant. Instead, Marcello headed for some nearby outbuildings, nestling on a hilly slope.

"There is so much more to Castello di Verrazzano than wine alone. The property is home to wild boar, they farm honey, make balsamic vinegar, and manufacture a huge selection of cheeses on site. It is incredible. Before we eat, I wanted to explore with you, to see where the meats are cured, and visit the cheese room."

After opening and closing a screen door, they were in the cool interior, with a spicy, gamey aroma. Olivia stared in amazement at the hundreds of curing meats hanging from the ceiling on the other side of the counter. The air was redolent with their heavy, spicy flavor. She'd had no idea that the winery produced them on this scale.

"Where are they sourced from?" she asked.

"From this farm, as well as neighboring farms. All local," Marcello explained, as the white-aproned attendant greeted them with a friendly "*Buon giorno.*"

Olivia nodded in admiration. How fitting that the production of these tasty-looking meats carried through the same ethos as the rest of the winery. She breathed in the smell again, rich, sumptuous, and satisfying.

"And, if we exit now, I will take you to the building I love even more."

When Marcello had said "cheese room," Olivia had never expected to walk into a characterful hall that was packed with cheeses of all shapes and sizes, placed on shelves and in alcoves that lined its long, high walls. There was a gigantic round of Parmesan that she fell in love with instantly. She wanted to take it home—if it would have fit in her car! Gazing at their massive, curved sides and breathing in the rich, sharp aromas, Olivia was reminded why the smell of cheese was, to her, one of the most evocative scents of Italy.

"These are all manufactured on site, obviously," Marcello said.

"I see there are some goat cheeses," Olivia observed, pleased that this was an area where their winery could improve immediately, thanks to La Leggenda's goats.

"Yes. They have a large herd here, and also use local dairy produce, as well as buffalo which are farmed nearby, to make the mozzarella."

Olivia wondered if La Leggenda would be the right place to keep buffalo. She hoped Marcello would be able to find out more about what it took. She had a feeling they might not be as easy as goats, but surely it would be worth it? She adored buffalo mozzarella!

"Now, we eat," Marcello said, practically having to drag Olivia out of the cheese room. She wanted to chain herself to the counter and never leave.

Seeing these rooms inspired her that at La Leggenda, they could also make more of their other offerings. Cheese tourism! The thought excited her.

When they walked into the luxuriously furnished restaurant, the manager showed them to a cozy corner table next to a brightly burning fire. After being out and about in the breezy cold, Olivia felt grateful for its blazing warmth.

The waiter brought them a small salad that was subtle and mouthwatering, made with fresh greens, spicy arugula, and white beans, with a dressing that Olivia knew she could try to replicate for years and never achieve the exact herbal tang.

"I thought, with our starters, we could enjoy this estate's rosé," Marcello said.

As the waiter poured the wine, Olivia gazed at it in awe. It was a paler, peachier color than the one she had created, but the aroma was incredible.

"It smells as if summer has landed in the glass!" she exclaimed, and Marcello laughed.

"Yes, summer in a glass is the perfect way to describe this wine," he agreed.

She sipped, smiling. Yup, it tasted of summer, too. Fresh, fragrant, and with a playful fruitiness. What a triumph. When she thought back to the magnificent Chianti she'd tasted in the cellar, Olivia realized that although this wine could not be more different, it still possessed similar qualities, and that subtle trademark flavor that the winemaker had explained the estate strived for.

Her salad disappeared in only a few bites, which proved to be just as well, because almost immediately, the waiter set a generously piled plate of antipasto on the table.

Staring hungrily down at the finely crafted salami, the perfectly cured ham, the creamy slices of cheese, and the crusty ciabatta bread, Olivia was thrilled to be actually tasting what she'd seen earlier, and appreciating the results of all the effort and expertise that had gone into their creation.

Setting about her task methodically, she tried a small piece of everything on the plate individually. The spicy, peppery salami had to be her favorite meat, she decided. But then she tried the delicate, wafer-thin Parma ham and wasn't sure anymore. They were neck and neck runners!

"This is superb," Olivia said, breaking the silence that had been filled with appreciative munching. "Marcello, I can see exactly how valuable this opportunity will be. There are so many aspects to this place that make it unique, so many factors we can learn from. And the wine growing alone—this could take us not to the next level, but several rungs up the ladder!"

"Exactly. Which brings me to my next decision, which is how I assign the responsibilities in my absence," Marcello said, and now his face was serious again.

"Of course," Olivia agreed, wondering how he would divide up the tasks.

"That is why I have brought you here," Marcello said, and her heart quickened. So this discussion would reveal the real purpose of the visit?

"Why is that?" she asked.

"I have decided that we need one person to take over my responsibilities. One person who is capable, competent, experienced, a hard worker, and who will be able to take over the day-to-day running of the business and fill my shoes in that regard."

Olivia nodded. This conversation was veering in a direction she'd never expected. She didn't dare to hope what he might say next, as she asked him, breathlessly, "Do you have any idea who the right person would be?"

"I have a difficult selection to make," Marcello told her, and now his face was as serious as she'd ever seen it. "My choice is between you—and Gabriella."

Olivia stared at him wordlessly, feeling as if a bomb had just landed on the white-clothed table.

CHAPTER EIGHT

Olivia had no idea what to say in response to Marcello's devastating announcement.

He was choosing between her and Gabriella?

Gabriella?

Fighting hard to keep her tumultuous emotions from showing on her face, she nodded in a considering way, even though she could feel her right eye had begun twitching uncontrollably. She hoped Marcello didn't notice. After all, she needed to prove, from this instant onward, that she was calm and mature, capable of handling the personalities in the winery as well as its day to day running. Inwardly, though, she was panicking. This wasn't a simple case of transferred duties. It meant the difference between career enhancement and career disaster.

"I am hugely proud and honored that you're considering me, and obviously it would mean the world to me if I could accept this position," she began, wishing her eye would stop convulsing, and that her voice sounded less shrill.

She had no doubt that if put in charge of the winery, Gabriella would make her life unbearable.

Was there any way, she wondered frantically, that she could influence Marcello?

Olivia knew that this was a make-or-break moment. She had to handle this sensibly. She could not do what she wanted to, which was to burst into tears, lie down on the floor, cling to Marcello's ankles, and beg him not to put that poisonous witch of a restaurateur in charge of the whole place!

"I know both Gabriella and I have qualities that would add value to this transitional time, and I can see why it's a difficult decision for you to make, as we both bring different strengths to the table," Olivia said. "From my side, I hope that moving all the way from the States to live in the local area has shown my passion and commitment to my new career in wine. This opportunity would take my growth to the next level and I'd be really grateful for it."

In the stressful moment, she realized she'd been transported right back to the boardroom table at JCreative in Chicago, where she'd spent innumerable hours racking her brains for ways out of untenable situations. A hundred times, she'd been forced to utter calm words while her brain was screaming at her in panic. Each of those times, Olivia had somehow found a way to make good on her impossible promises.

It sure hadn't been easy!

She'd thought those days were behind her, but perhaps the experience she'd gained in these nerve-shredding sessions might stand her in good stead now.

"You are right," Marcello agreed after a pause. She thought he sounded surprised. Perhaps that was good. Or maybe not? Should she have taken the emotional approach, gone all-in and wrapped herself around his ankles regardless?

Did Marcello believe that passion was more important than common sense?

Olivia's stomach wrenched as she realized she might have handled this pivotal moment, which was her only chance, completely wrong. She'd forgotten that she was not in snowy Chicago, but in blustery Tuscany, where Mediterranean passion ruled the day.

Nothing she could do now! She was committed to her path. In a reasonable tone, thankfully with less shrillness, she continued.

"What would you say are the most important aspects of stepping into your role?"

It had been drilled into Olivia to always ask the client questions. She remembered the thousand times that her ex-boss James had screamed at his team, "Assume makes an Ass out of You and Me!"

Now it was Marcello's turn to look calmly thoughtful.

"I feel that the person I choose needs a deep knowledge and experience of the winery," he said.

Olivia had to stop herself from biting her lip. She fell short here, through no fault of her own, but simply due to her limited experience at La Leggenda. Gabriella had been there for two years, and Olivia had to grudgingly admit that, though highly unlikable, her opponent was both intelligent and perceptive. Like a sponge, she absorbed information, even if she then used it in damaging ways. In addition, she had the advantage of having spent a lot of off-line time with Marcello. He might have let slip essential hints about the winery's workings during pillow-talk, Olivia thought in frustration.

"Absolutely," she agreed, as if appreciating the important and weighty information that had been imparted. Again, she thought Marcello looked briefly startled. "What else?" she asked.

"A willingness and ability to learn. An enthusiasm and passion for wine," Marcello said, sounding brighter.

Well, she hoped she was a frontrunner in both those categories. Olivia realized this felt like a job interview. Her first interview at La Leggenda had been a shoo-in compared to the pressure of this one.

"Yes, I can see those would be vital. What else?" she probed.

"I work long hours," Marcello confessed with a rueful grin. "Whoever steps into this role will need to be prepared to work an average of twelve hours a day. I know it is not ideal. I keep telling myself that I need to step away, to delegate, or simply to relax in the evenings, but especially since we now have distribution channels within the States, there are sometimes urgent matters that need to be addressed late in the night."

Olivia felt she might have a narrow advantage here. After all, she was *from* the States. And the number of times her mother had called after midnight, "forgetting" the time difference because she wanted to tell Olivia about an amazing job offer back home, or a condo in their neighborhood that had just come available for lease—she knew she could keep her temper, and be reasonably coherent, no matter the time of day.

"I'm a night owl myself," she shared, hoping Marcello wouldn't deduce from her morning arrivals at the winery that she was really more of an early bird.

"Then there is the question of dealing with all our local distributors." Now, Marcello sounded regretful, and Olivia felt the delicious food curdle in her stomach as he continued. "Many of them are born and bred Italians, from local towns and villages. We need to be able to continue our relationship with them seamlessly."

Olivia felt her heart hit the floor. Of course, dealing with so many local individuals, speaking Italian would be essential. Sales and distribution was all about relationships. Olivia wished she'd studied Italian at school. In fact, she started wishing she'd been born in the country. This was a major setback. Even the Platinum Tour organizer had picked up her lack of language prowess in one simple greeting.

Regret filled her that this might be the deciding factor, but yet again, she did her best to conceal it.

"Marcello, there are so many angles to consider. You must be torn trying to decide who would be the better caretaker of your business. I know you will choose the best person. Of course, I would be hugely complimented if it was me, and I will do my best to live up to your standards and to work on the areas I need to improve."

Even though she'd done her best, Marcello was still looking doubtful, as if realizing what a huge obstacle the language issue would be.

Gritting her teeth, Olivia plowed ahead to voice the unthinkable.

"I'm a team player," she said, even though in this instance, she was anything but! "If you decided it would be better for us to share the responsibilities, I will gladly work with you and Gabriella to divide them up. We can do it. It's all about what's best for the winery. When will you make your decision?" Olivia asked, feeling slightly sick.

"As soon as the Platinum Tour is over, I will announce my choice," Marcello told her gravely, and Olivia felt tension twang inside her.

Clearly, Marcello was going to use the tour which she had voted for to influence his final decision. Suddenly, the pressure on her shoulders felt like a lead weight. This was going to be a make-or-break event for her personal career, as well as for the winery.

Her future at La Leggenda now hinged on its success.

CHAPTER NINE

Olivia had never dreamed that her outing would end on such a frazzled note. By the time she and Erba arrived home, as darkness was falling, her nerves were shredded.

Finally, she could allow herself to roll her eyes and shriek helplessly, the way she'd been wanting to ever since Marcello had announced the choice he was making.

"Noooo!" Olivia yelled to the skies, feeling grateful that there were no neighbors within earshot of her agonized cry.

Her insides were churning with the knowledge that the next couple of months would either be the most rewarding challenge of her life, or else a torturous episode that would make her wish she was back in Chicago. And the final decision was only going to be made after an event that hadn't yet taken place, and over which she didn't have full control.

"Erba! What am I going to do?"

Erba didn't seem to care. She was blithely heading toward her Wendy house, expecting Olivia to feed her.

Olivia complied, hurrying around the farmhouse behind her goat and tugging out a chunk of hay and a sliver of alfalfa for her to enjoy.

As she headed into the house, her phone buzzed. Danilo had sent a message.

"Hey Olivia. Are you up for pizza tonight?"

Was she ever! It had been far too long since she'd sat down at her local restaurant to enjoy what, in her opinion, were the best pizzas in the whole of Italy.

"In an hour?" she messaged back, and was pleased to receive a thumbs-up from Danilo.

Although, as doubts crept in and she reread the invitation, she was concerned that it seemed to be too friendly, and not romantic enough.

Was Danilo really serious? What did this relationship actually mean?

As Olivia headed to the kitchen to feed Pirate, she found herself consumed by conflicting emotions.

43

It was as an afterthought that she decided to place Pirate's food bowl in the cat carrier. The idea came to her suddenly, and while she didn't give it any chance of success, she hoped that if Pirate saw food being placed inside, he wouldn't fight quite so hard next time he was placed inside.

To her astonishment, Pirate peered suspiciously at the open wire door, sniffed the doorway, and then slowly leopard-crawled in!

"Pirate!" Olivia breathed.

She lunged forward and snapped the door shut even as the outraged cat exploded backward.

Olivia couldn't believe it! After this super-stressful day, she'd managed to solve a problem that had been consuming her with worry for months.

"I'm so sorry," Olivia said, snatching her hand out of the way as an enraged paw swiped at it through the door, with claws out like knives. "We're going to the vet right now. Right now, do you hear?"

She picked up the basket, which was wiggling furiously thanks to the struggling cat inside. Kibble spilled from the overturned bowl and scattered on her kitchen floor. As Olivia hustled back to her car, she felt relieved that she was meeting Danilo at a restaurant tonight. Offering up a homecooked meal in a tidy kitchen would be beyond her powers now.

Luckily the vet was close by, on her side of the village. Olivia always loved driving into the local village in the evening. The lights of the houses and apartments twinkled in the dusk, and the ruined castle at the town's entrance was subtly lit by spotlights, making the ancient stone seem to glow from within.

This time, Olivia had little chance to appreciate the scenic beauty of her surroundings. She was deafened by angry caterwauls from the back seat, and fretting that Pirate might somehow force his way out. If he managed to escape the carrier and make a run for it, she'd never see him again!

She parked outside the vet, grabbed the basket, and rushed inside.

"I need to book Pirate for a neuter," she told the assistant, who was dealing with the last customer of the day.

The friendly assistant beamed at her. Having sold Olivia flea remedy, wormer, and cat food, she knew Pirate's story.

"You have managed to catch him at last?" she praised.

"I'm so relieved," Olivia admitted.

"We will keep him overnight. The vet has two other surgeries to do early tomorrow, so we can add this to the list. If all goes well, you should be able to fetch Pirate after nine."

That was just before she was due to go into work.

"I'll see you tomorrow. Thank you!"

Olivia handed over the basket, feeling her insides wrenched by the now-pitiful sounds emanating from within. Pirate had given up on threatening and had now resorted to begging! She felt terrible for him, having to spend a night in such an unfamiliar and scary place. As an ex-feral, he would never have been to the vet before.

Squaring her shoulders, Olivia reminded herself to be firm. Pirate needed neutering! She didn't want him roaming around, fathering generations of kittens who would grow up to be homeless, just like he'd been. And, furthermore, he was overdue for the shots he needed.

One night in the warm back room of the veterinary clinic was a small price to pay for a safe and healthy life, Olivia thought, hoping that if she focused on the positives, it would tamp down her anguish at hearing those forlorn yowls.

*

Arriving at the pizza restaurant just a few minutes later, she saw Danilo's car was already in the parking lot. He was taking his jacket out of the trunk, and she was pleased to see that he was wearing the black knit top she'd bought him, which fit perfectly over his broad, muscular shoulders.

His hairstyle changed continually, which Olivia knew was thanks to the attentions of his hairdressing apprentice niece, and not due to any real interest on Danilo's part. Today, his dark hair was in a crisp side-part, with a knife-sharp edge to the short, faded, and super-trendy cut.

Feeling stressed and disheveled and aware she didn't look her best, she approached him, feeling awkward.

"Olivia. Is everything all right?"

Clearly reading her face, Danilo looked concerned. That only added to Olivia's angst, because instead of enfolding her in the warm embrace she'd been hoping for, he stood back, frowning worriedly.

Where to start? Recent events seemed like a good place.

"I've just dropped Pirate at the vet," she confessed.

"You got him into the carrier? That is amazing! Well done!"

"I feel so guilty," Olivia admitted. Danilo still hadn't hugged her. Well, to be fair, she hadn't hugged him either.

"Do not be guilty," Danilo emphasized. "He will be the happier for it. Come, let's sit down. You need a glass of wine, I am sure."

He hadn't said why he canceled yesterday, Olivia fretted, as they walked into the restaurant. There, the welcoming aroma of fresh, crispy pizza crust, garlic-infused tomato, and melted cheese made her feel better.

The smiling owner had kept a corner table for Danilo, and her older son, who usually waited on them, immediately brought glasses of their favorite wine. Olivia appreciated the perks of being a regular. You never had to order drinks—they just arrived! Her choice at this restaurant was the local sangiovese, and Danilo's was the vermentino white.

They clinked glasses and Olivia took a grateful sip.

"What happened yesterday evening?" she asked, deciding to cut to the reasons for Danilo's last-minute cancellation.

"Oh, I am sorry about that. Another urgent job came in yesterday morning, and I had to send a quick message to you as my youngest nephew was borrowing my phone for schoolwork."

Olivia blinked. This sounded plausible, but at the same time rather strange. Were those good enough reasons for canceling a date with only a terse text? She wasn't sure. Her brain was telling her to be calm, but her heart was yelling in fear that this relationship might go the way of her others.

Which would mean with a break-up and a massive public fight, if her track record was anything to go by.

A public break-up in the anonymity of a big city was one thing. In the intimate environment of their local village where everyone knew everyone else's business, it would be a thousand times worse.

"We were going to open the secret storeroom. I was disappointed that we couldn't do that," she pressured him.

"We can do it next time," Danilo said. "Yesterday was a horrible night, in any case, cold and rainy. It would have been unpleasant up in the hills. Leaving the mystery for a few more days will only make it more exciting."

Olivia felt miffed that Danilo was using calm logic in his argument. She'd been looking for a chance to vent her emotion.

"Shall we order? I'm starving," she said, deciding to abandon the discussion. "I'll have the Parma ham and rocket pizza, please," she said to the waiter.

"The same for me," Danilo said.

He reached out his hand and as his warm palm touched hers across the table and his fingers laced with hers, Olivia felt better, and her fears subsided.

"What else happened? You still seem distracted."

Olivia felt like rolling her eyes. How could Danilo be so perceptive about her mood, and yet at the same time so unaware of how his callous cancellation had affected it?

"Marcello is taking a few months' sabbatical to be mentored at Castello di Verrazzano," she explained. "In his absence, he needs someone to run the winery."

Danilo's eyebrows shot up.

"And that is you, Olivia?" he asked, sounding hopeful.

She made a face. "No. He's still deciding. Between me and Gabriella!"

Clearly, Danilo didn't understand the serious power-play between them. He smiled in a sympathetic way.

"Hopefully he will choose you," he reassured her.

Olivia didn't feel up to the task of describing the full horror that Gabriella would unleash if she was put in charge. Even so, she had to share the important event that Marcello would use to make his final call.

"We're hosting a special tour tomorrow, for a group of billionaires. It looks as if he's going to make the decision on which of us to choose based on how we handle the tour," Olivia shared, feeling nervous all over again.

"Billionaires? Is that the Platinum Tour?" Danilo asked.

"Yes, it is. Do you know much about it?" Olivia was eager to get more information on what tomorrow might bring. Perhaps it would give her an advantage over Gabriella.

"I know some people in the restaurant world who participate in it. They own a fine-dining restaurant in Florence, with a Michelin star. They say the tour is extremely hard work, and the delegates on it are very difficult, but it brings them great rewards. It leads to referrals throughout the year, increased media exposure, and other opportunities. The owner told me last time I spoke to him, it was the single biggest influencer for the success he had last year."

"Oh, really?" Nervousness uncoiled inside Olivia. This indeed sounded like a make-or-break event. And they were on trial, as a last-minute addition to the prestigious tour. What would happen if one of the guests didn't like the winery, or found some other problem with their experience?

"What do you mean, difficult?" she asked carefully.

Their food arrived, and Danilo passed her the salt, grinding black pepper over his pizza with a look of happy anticipation.

"The very rich who attend this tour are peculiar people," he explained. "They can throw temper tantrums over nothing. My friend said that they live in a different reality from normal folk. Their wealth can procure them almost anything, so they expect everything and can be easily offended. And they demand an extremely high level of service. Super-service, is what he called it. Even though they already are Michelin-starred, he and his team practiced super-service in their restaurant for weeks before the first tour arrived, to be sure of getting it right."

Olivia bit into her pizza, feeling worried. This super-service didn't sound easy, and the team at La Leggenda didn't have time to rehearse protocols! The billionaires would be subject to her own basic Italian, Jean-Pierre's habit of gesticulating wildly and spilling wine on the floor when he got excited, and Gabriella's restaurant service—when she was in a mood, she'd bang the dishes down on the table and whoosh irritably away. Not to mention how Nadia, when a wine wasn't working out, would march through the tasting room, glowering at everyone.

Olivia was sure Gabriella would be in a mood tomorrow. Marcello would also have told her that he was deciding between them. Most probably, the mere idea that she was in competition with Olivia and not being automatically placed in charge would have set her temper at hurricane-level!

The friction of all the different personalities added liveliness to the winery. It was all part of the expressive Italian culture. But it seemed that the billionaires wanted super-service and not expressive culture.

Olivia wondered if Gabriella and Antonio might have made the right call with their no-votes, and she, Jean-Pierre, and Nadia were being irresponsibly hotheaded.

"You are looking anxious," Danilo observed.

"I'm feeling stressed," Olivia admitted. She dug into another piece of pizza. Thank goodness carbs always calmed her.

"La Leggenda is a unique destination winery," Danilo said firmly. "I cannot think any billionaire would not love their experience."

"But we haven't practiced super-service," Olivia said, hearing the plaintive tone in her own voice.

Danilo looked unsure. "That was for a restaurant. A winery is a different place, no? A different atmosphere! Restaurant service brings out the worst in people as there is so much conformity in the industry. Wine tasting is a more individual experience." He took a sip of wine and suddenly spluttered with laughter. "Perhaps you can get Gabriella to do a belly dance. That would provide something memorable!"

Olivia choked on her wine, tears streaming from her eyes as she simultaneously tried to swallow and breathe. What an image that was! Gabriella's furious face atop her curvaceous, gyrating body was enough to send anyone into hysterics. She'd misjudged Danilo. She had thought that he didn't understand how conflicted the dynamic was between her and Gabriella. But this snarky comment showed he did, only too well!

Then Danilo took Olivia's hand again, pressing his warm fingers onto hers.

"You are amazing at what you do. Your personality shines as soon as you walk into a room—it is like the sun coming out. You will be brilliant at hosting this tour. And I am confident Marcello will choose you. You are the right person to lead the winery. Anyone can see that."

Olivia felt her heart melt with happiness and relief. She was thrilled by his support, which gave her renewed confidence in their relationship as well as in her own abilities. That was just as well, because she found herself dreading the tour even more after what Danilo had said.

Now that she knew the sky-high standards these privileged guests would expect, she realized how many things could go horribly wrong.

CHAPTER TEN

The next morning was drizzly, gray, and windy. Olivia felt worried as soon as she woke, aware that something was missing.

With a nasty jolt, she realized what the missing element was. Pirate! She'd become so used to his warm yet light weight pressing on her toes, and the disgusting sounds as he began his personal grooming routine before sunrise. Yet, somehow, even the grossest noises had become reassuring to Olivia. After all, they were all part of how her shiny cat kept his coat so scrupulously clean.

Now, she felt a gaping hole in her life as she stared at the empty duvet, thinking of Pirate. Traumatized and alone, he would have endured the worst night of his life in the veterinary clinic.

Olivia decided to get ready and then take a quick trip to the vet to collect her cat. After making sure that Pirate was healthy and well, and recovered from his ordeal, she could hustle to La Leggenda to start the winery's make-or-break day.

She showered and took some time with her hair before dressing in a beautiful knit top with a pattern of blue and gold, paired with cream-colored pants and beige boots, and her turquoise coat. With her hopefully stylish and billionaire-friendly outfit complete, Olivia headed downstairs, grabbing her purse off the hall table.

She rushed to her car, scrambled in, and zoomed out of the farmhouse, breaking all land-speed records as she headed to the vet.

Hurrying inside, Olivia greeted the receptionist. She didn't recognize this woman, who clearly worked in the mornings.

"I'm here to collect my cat. He's just been neutered." She beamed at the woman in relief. "Was he well behaved?"

The receptionist gave her a strange glance.

"We had no males neutered this morning," she said, and Olivia's heart stopped.

Something must have gone terribly wrong. Had Pirate managed to escape the basket, and run wild out of the vet?

"What happened to my boy?" she gasped, feeling tears prickle her eyes.

The receptionist stared at Olivia, looking just as horrified.

"What is your cat's name?" she asked.

"Pirate. He's black and white. I brought him in yesterday evening." Olivia had started hyperventilating. She'd never imagined she'd land in this nightmare.

To her astonishment, the receptionist started smiling.

"Ah, Pirate! Yes, Pirate is ready," she said. "*She* bit the vet, but *her spay* went well, and *she* is in good health and has had *her* shots."

Olivia's mouth fell open with shock as she absorbed this latest twist in the tale—or rather, tail.

Pirate, a girl?

Never had Olivia dreamed that her feisty black-and-white feline was a female! Of course, in retrospect it made sense. Pirate's petite frame. The elegant way she crossed her paws. Her thorough attention to hygiene. Her strong opinions. Not to mention her high intelligence! At last, all the facts fell into place.

"I'm so glad it all went well," Olivia said, still feeling blindsided by the gender-reveal. A spay was twice as expensive as a neuter. She paid the first bill for her new, high-maintenance girl cat, and then waited.

A furious yowling signaled that Pirate was on her way. The sound increased in volume as the harassed-looking receptionist carried the basket from the back room.

Then, to Olivia's surprise, the yowling stopped.

Pirate was gazing at her through the bars, out of wide yellow-green eyes, and for the life of her, Olivia couldn't work out whether her silence meant she was pleased to see her owner, or whether she was plotting a terrible revenge!

"Thank you so much," Olivia said again. Joy filled her as she grasped the basket's handle. Finally, Pirate was safe from any unwanted kittens, and would live out her life as a healthy cat.

She carried the basket carefully to the car and placed it in the back seat. The yowling started up again as she drove out, but it was more muted this time.

Olivia tried to drive carefully. She didn't want to upset Pirate's delicate feminine emotions. She eased through the intersection and idled her way gently through the stop signs. A tentative ascent of the hill, and then she was back at the farmhouse, parking in her place with a sigh of relief.

She hadn't realized how much Pirate's neutering—or rather, spaying—had been weighing on her mind. Now it was done, and she felt profoundly thankful that she'd been able to do the right thing for her cat.

She decided to release Pirate in the bedroom, so she could be cozy and warm. Carting the carrier upstairs, Olivia placed it on the bed. She opened the door, dreading the explosion of fur and claws that might follow, and worried that Pirate might dart down the stairs and vanish forever. But to her surprise, Pirate crawled out hesitantly, gave Olivia a resentful glance, and then jumped off the bed and crept underneath it.

Sounds of diligent grooming followed. Pirate was cleaning the smell of the vet off her as thoroughly as she could.

"You're such a brave, clever cat," Olivia praised her previously wild feline. "You must settle in and relax, and have a calm day. I'll see you later, my bo—er, I mean, girl."

It was time for her to head to work. The rain had eased up, so Olivia decided to walk.

"Work time!" she yelled to her goat as she closed the front door. "We're going in early!"

In a flash, with a drumming of hooves, Erba accelerated around the side of the farmhouse and they set off at a brisk pace.

"We have a busy day, Erba," she told the goat as they marched out of the farm. "I may end up working late. You must be good and behave yourself. We don't want the billionaires to have a poor impression of La Leggenda."

As she said the words, Olivia's stomach twisted with nerves.

This was going to be a huge day. Huge! Anything could go wrong, and there would be complex politics in play. During this pivotal day, she knew Marcello would be watching her carefully and assessing whether she was up to the job of running the winery in his absence.

The next eight hours were going to be critical for her, as well as for La Leggenda.

*

Before she even reached the winery buildings, Olivia saw that preparations were frantically under way. Never, ever, in her months at La Leggenda, had she seen anyone scrubbing the tall, cream gateposts at the winery's main entrance. Especially since all the recent rain had washed their surfaces sparkling clean.

Or so she thought, staring in astonishment at Marcello who, armed with a bucket and brush, was energetically soaping them down.

He took a moment from his task to wave at her.

Perplexed, she continued to the winery. Given Marcello's activities, she wasn't too surprised to find Antonio on his hands and knees in the parking lot, plucking out the almost invisible shoots of grass and weeds that had crept between the solid stone pavers.

Erba detoured curiously toward Antonio, stared down at the small green mound, and ate it.

Antonio glanced up. His stressed expression dissolved into a smile.

"If only I could train her to do the whole job!" he said.

Antonio, at least, seemed in good spirits. Olivia didn't think she'd get the same warm reception from the other no-voter.

Heading into the winery, Olivia heard the furious scrape of a scrubbing brush. Wearing overalls, Nadia was on her hands and knees, scouring the life out of the lobby tiles, which had been efficiently mopped the previous night by Jean-Pierre, Olivia remembered.

"*Buon giorno!* Nadia greeted her breathlessly. "Olivia, you are tall. Will you please polish the brass lettering behind the tasting counter? I have left a step ladder there."

Olivia was beginning to wish she'd worn her shabbiest jeans to work and brought along her smart clothes in a bag! Especially when she saw Jean-Pierre on an even bigger ladder, brandishing a long feather duster to chase nonexistent cobwebs out of the corners of the high ceiling.

As Olivia started working through her list of chores in the tasting room, she sensed storm clouds were gathering in the restaurant. Banging noises and furious shrieks came from the kitchen and as she watched, Paolo, the head waiter, fled out, heading at top speed for the bar area, armed with a handful of cloths and a disinfectant spray.

Then Gabriella herself marched out, flinging her tawny, immaculately waved hair back. She glared furiously across the restaurant.

"Olivia!" she yelled. "There you are! Come here at once!"

CHAPTER ELEVEN

Olivia traipsed reluctantly in Gabriella's direction. Inwardly, she was smoldering. What right did the restaurateur have to bossily demand that she trek the whole way across the tasting room, while Gabriella herself simply stood and watched with her hands placed on her curvaceous hips?

"I trust that your wines are ready? You must bring bottles through here to go with the snacks. I will show you where to place them so that this event can run according to plan."

With a shock, Olivia realized what this strategically timed scene was all about. Marcello had just walked into in the tasting room, with the bucket and sponge still in his hands.

Clearly, Gabriella wanted to show Olivia that she was in control, and that her efforts would make the event successful. The significance of the Platinum Tour must also be at the top of her mind.

"The wines are all prepared. We discussed the choices after the meeting, and Jean-Pierre set all the bottles aside yesterday," Olivia said, managing to stay calm and not rise to the bait. Then, deciding to give Gabriella a taste of her own medicine, she added, in loud and concerned tones, "But what about the food? You seem to be running late! Can I help you with the preparation, seeing I'm on top of things in the tasting room? Or can I send Jean-Pierre across to assist?"

Gabriella glowered at her and turned away, stalking back to the kitchen.

Olivia kept carefully expressionless, but inside, she was giggling that her rival's attempt to undermine her in front of Marcello had failed.

*

Before Olivia knew it, it was time for the tour to arrive. Checking the clock with a pang of nerves, she dashed to the restroom for a final freshen-up. There had been no time to do so much as tidy her hair in the feverish rush of preparation.

As she hurried back, she heard the powerful purr of a motor outside. As she exchanged nervous glances with Jean-Pierre, they both crept to the winery entrance and peeked around the door.

A gleaming, sleek, black minibus had pulled up outside. It looked as if it was a special edition, designed by Ferrari. It was huge and chrome-lined, and the windows were heavily mirrored. Perhaps even armored? Olivia wondered, fascinated to see the style in which ultra-wealthy groups traveled.

The front doors opened, and two uniformed men climbed out and headed around to the side door.

Olivia felt something tickling her neck. Looking around, she saw that Paolo and Nadia were clustered behind her, peering around her shoulders, not wanting to miss the moment when the first pair of billionaire feet touched down on La Leggenda soil.

At that moment, with a powerful roar, a silver Range Rover accelerated into the parking lot and pulled to a stop beside the bus.

Out climbed the tour organizer, Stella Markham, with her dark hair perfectly styled and wearing a red power suit.

"Welcome, all," she called, as the attendants opened the bus's sliding door.

With a scamper of feet, the La Leggenda group fled back into the tasting room.

Olivia had only just taken her position behind the counter when, with a clatter of heels, Stella led the way inside.

"Good afternoon," Marcello greeted her.

Olivia gasped as she saw how smart her boss looked. Just a few minutes ago, he'd been covered in soot after a chimney had chosen the worst possible moment to block up. Now, he was wearing an exquisitely cut black suit and a crisply starched white shirt. His hair was tamed back and a smile warmed his handsome face.

"Afternoon, Marcello," Stella announced in ringing tones. "It's my pleasure to introduce to you our esteemed guests on this year's Platinum Tour. I must add that we always use the feedback of our honored customers to decide on our program for the following year. If the group enjoys the experience, you will be invited to participate again."

Olivia felt doubly excited at this news. All they had to do was to impress every one of the powerful, wealthy moguls in attendance, and they might become a regular destination.

But as the tour members strolled into the tasting room, Olivia couldn't help gawking. They were not what she'd expected at all.

She'd anticipated a group dressed to the nines, just like Stella was. Designer suits, gold brocade, thousand-dollar haircuts, and shoes she could spend her whole life trying to afford.

The motley crowd that sauntered in, gazing casually around, didn't look like that at all. Apart from the tour guide, only one other guest was wearing a suit, Olivia realized, perplexed. The billionaires were astonishingly dressed down. In fact, they were remarkably shabby-looking, she thought with concern. She was seeing worn jeans, ancient jackets, torn T-shirts, and scuffed shoes. Not to mention hairstyles that looked as if they'd been cut by themselves at home!

Glancing at Jean-Pierre, Olivia saw he, too, looked flummoxed, as if he was worried that they'd gotten the wrong tour group in some kind of administrative mess-up. She felt the same.

Perhaps these visitors were so well-off that they didn't need to wear designer brands, she guessed. They could look disreputable and bring ancient clothing on vacation, simply because they were so phenomenally wealthy, they didn't care what people thought of them.

"Marcello, this is Sid Murray. He's a regular guest on our tour," Stella enthused, introducing the large, ginger-haired man wearing a badly fitting khaki safari suit paired with ancient trainers. Only one detail clued Olivia to his billionaire status, and that was the gigantic Rolex flashing on his wrist.

"Hello, mate," Sid replied in a strong Australian accent.

"Drake Rafter. Bernie Cooper. Rupert Curren. Chico and Aldo Bocelli, who are brothers and the only Italian guests on our tour this time. Jose Ramos. Hamilton Mackay. Carmody Cole. And another of our valued regular supporters, Sashenka Davydov."

Trying her best to remember the first and last names of each guest, Olivia couldn't make out who was who from her vantage point as the ill-dressed group crowded around Marcello, whose warm exclamations of greeting rang out.

"Our tour operates on a strict schedule," Stella explained. "They have an hour and a half to spend at your winery. Then they will be bused to Florence for a private art and fashion show, during which time our two celebrities will entertain them." Stella gestured toward the two men standing at the back of the group. "The renowned Tomas Dittman, who I am sure you have heard of, will be performing a piano recital, and our youngest celebrity, Instagram idol Ferdie Tooley, will be thrilling them with some brilliant magic tricks. Then our day concludes with a sumptuous dinner at the Michelin-starred Osteria di Massimo."

Was that the restaurant Danilo had been talking about? Olivia wondered. She guessed it must be.

Tomas, the pianist, was the only guest wearing a well-cut suit. The young Instagram idol was wearing a screamingly loud jacket covered in hearts, diamonds, clubs, and spades. He looked extremely nervous.

It was time for her to meet her first customer. A stern-faced man, with short hair that had been bleached white-blond a few weeks ago and grown out since then, strolled over to the tasting counter.

He wore a peeling bomber jacket, which Olivia guessed was at least a decade old, over a gray T-shirt with actual holes in it. Not designer rips, real holes! She glanced at his shoes, hoping they might redeem him.

Nope, not this time. He wore unraveling leather moccasins that looked the same vintage as his jacket.

Even so, this was her first encounter with a high-caliber Platinum Tour individual. Giving it her all, Olivia smiled widely.

"Good afternoon and *buon giorno*," she greeted him breathlessly. "I am Olivia Glass, and I'm going to guide you on your tasting journey."

As she spoke, the man frowned.

"You're American?" he asked, in a not-very-pleased Southern drawl.

Olivia's heart sank. Her nationality had landed her in trouble before. What was she going to do if having an American sommelier at La Leggenda proved to be the deciding factor that ruined the tour?

Out of the corner of her eye, she saw Gabriella peeking gleefully across from the restaurant. Olivia knew that she had only a moment to come up with an answer that might satisfy this influential guest and save the day.

CHAPTER TWELVE

Olivia smiled humbly at the billionaire guest.

"I'm fully bilingual," she fudged. "I have spent some years in America, yes. What an amazing country it is!"

Approximately thirty-four and a half years of her life, to be exact. But this white lie allowed her to head trouble off at the pass. The billionaire seemed to accept her explanation and he nodded approvingly at her praise of the country that was in fact home to both of them.

"Are you giving the staff uphill, Drake?" A solid, dark-haired man in worn jeans and a sagging gray sweater that was unraveling at the elbows strode over to the table. He was also American, Olivia realized, bemused.

"No, Bernie, I'm trying to get a drink. Seems the wine flows like concrete here."

Hastily, Olivia filled some glasses with the vermentino white. This wasn't the way she'd planned the tasting to proceed. Instead of an expressive introduction to the wines, this felt more like a bar service. Oh well, she thought, as they downed the contents without seeming to take any interest in what the vermentino was all about.

Two more men walked over, conversing together in Italian.

"*Buon giorno.*" Olivia smiled. "May I offer you the vermentino white? It is—"

"*Si, si,*" the first man said impatiently.

The other smiled. "Ah, an Americano. Nice to meet you. I am Chico. My brother's name is Aldo. We own Chi-Aldo Luxury Cosmetics."

"That's wonderful!" Chico seemed the first friendly face she'd met on the tour so far and at least he didn't seem to mind that she was American. Despite his casual attire, Olivia saw that he and his brother were wearing heavy gold chains around their necks.

She hoped to tell them about the wine, but they, too, took their glasses and continued circulating. There was a buzz of conversation. As she listened in, Olivia surmised that this was the start of the tour. She wondered if the billionaires would all get along, or whether everyone was engaged in subtle one-upmanship to establish a pecking order.

"So, Tomas, tell me more about your recent concert in Berlin," the safari-suited Australian, Sid, asked the pianist as they headed to the tasting counter.

"It was the biggest concert event of the year," the aquiline-featured man replied in German-accented tones, gesturing extravagantly with a slim, long-fingered hand. "I kept an audience of ten thousand enraptured for two hours. Including the prime minister, the king and queen of Denmark, and the Monaco royalty. They all said it was their most uplifting musical experience ever." Tomas turned to the tasting counter and selected the fullest glass of wine. "For me, though, it was simply another day at the piano, and another chance to reveal my incredible talent to the world."

One-upmanship, Olivia decided.

Sid nodded in solemn agreement. "I've always loved music myself. I guess my hero's Justin Bieber. Have you heard him on the keyboard? Got a lot of talent in the way he plays."

Tomas's nostrils flared angrily. Grasping his wine, he gave the Australian a haughty glare before stalking away.

Game and first set to Sid, Olivia thought with a flicker of amusement.

Her next guest was a large, balding man with a scruffy beard, wearing a creased white kaftan paired with Gucci leather sandals.

"I am Carmody, and I would like a glass of water," the man demanded in plummy British tones. "Filtered, please, no ice, no lemon, and in a simple tumbler. After my experience in the mountains of Tibet, I have learned that alcohol corrupts the chakras and interferes with the process of spiritual enlightenment."

Olivia stared at him in consternation.

He was on a wine tour! How was he going to enjoy himself? She'd seen Gabriella smothering her braised beef in the cheap rough red wine she bought in bulk and used for marinating. Would that damage Carmody's chakras? Maybe he didn't eat meat either, Olivia wondered.

"Water coming up," she said with a forced smile

But Carmody had turned away and was drawing a state-of-the-art cell phone, ringing loudly, from the folds of his kaftan.

"Yes, Martha?" he answered sharply. "No, we cannot offer a discount. Must I remind you, we sell luxury furniture? I don't care if they're a charity. *We* are *not* a charity."

Stabbing the disconnect button, he put the phone away and swept back to the counter for his water, staring at it critically before sipping.

A gray-haired man wearing a shapeless black tracksuit cleared his throat irritably. Olivia whipped around, smiling apologetically for her nanosecond's delay in attending to him.

Remembering what Danilo had said about super-service, Olivia decided he hadn't been exaggerating.

"Welcome. Would you like to try our vermentino white wine?" she said.

"Vermentino?" he asked. He also sounded British. From London perhaps, Olivia guessed.

Finally, someone who seemed interested in her description! Olivia glowed with the prospect of trotting out her carefully rehearsed chitchat.

"That's right," she began, but got no further.

"What a dreadful name. The word *vermentino* makes me think of vermin."

Oh dear. And she'd thought he was a wine enthusiast! Reminding herself not to prejudge, Olivia continued explaining.

"The vermentino grapes are Italian in origin, but have recently become more popular around the world. I believe they are grown in California today."

"Hmmm," he said, looking at Olivia with narrowed eyes as if he suspected her of lying.

Behind him, a short man with red hair, wearing a tartan jacket that looked as if it had been picked up from a thrift store, poked him in the back. "Hey, Rupert, you're in retail goods. Which major store chain in the United Kingdom does the biggest annual turnover?" he asked in a strong Scottish accent.

The gray-haired man glanced around. "I'm busy, Hamilton," he snapped.

At least Olivia knew Rupert's name now, as he turned to her again.

"This is a rather sharp wine. Sour, in fact. We own a bottling business as one of our subsidiaries so I know what I'm talking about. And to me, it tastes off."

Rupert's voice resonated around the room. A few people turned to look. A couple of them glanced suspiciously down at their own glasses.

Olivia felt her heart rate triple. Just one unhappy customer might influence the whole group, especially since their wine knowledge appeared to be on the sketchy side of nonexistent! Those who were even drinking wine, she thought, glancing at Carmody, who was now grimacing at his water as if it, too, was incorrectly bottled.

What to do? She couldn't say Rupert was wrong. Perhaps he found the vermentino too dry, she thought.

"Can I offer you the rosé? It has a complex flavor and a lovely fruity aroma," she said, quickly taking a bottle from the ice bucket. She poured it into a fresh glass, hoping it would appeal to this fussy customer. He sipped, and with a twist of her stomach, Olivia could see he didn't like this wine either.

Luckily, he was derailed by Hamilton, who strutted up to the counter.

"You dishing out pink wine now, lassie? Give me a glass, will you?" He turned to Rupert. "You need to come and resolve our argument. Or else, just say I'm right!"

Jean-Pierre tugged at her sleeve.

"We must arrange the carafes at the food table," he reminded Olivia.

"I'll go and do it. You put some glasses on a tray and continue circulating," she said. She didn't dare to leave these guests unattended for as much as a moment.

As she hurried around the counter, she almost collided with the only woman on the tour, a tall, broad-shouldered blond. Her hair was tied back in a messy ponytail and she was wearing a shapeless floral-print dress that looked like a curtain, but Olivia was sure the massive diamonds that sparkled in her necklaces and rings were real.

"Excuse me!" Olivia said, hoping the woman, who must be Sashenka, wasn't going to be angry.

"I see they are harassing you already," she observed in amused tones with a flavor of Eastern Europe. Perhaps she was Russian, Olivia thought. She smiled politely, unsure what to say or if she should agree.

"These men all have big egos," Sashenka explained. "Most, bigger than their business acumen. So few are self-made. He inherited from his father. Him, too. He married into the business and his wife runs it. He got lucky when a business partner sold out."

She pointed a clear-varnished nail in various directions as she spoke, but the only problem was that Olivia was facing her, and didn't dare to look around as Sashenka trashed the credentials of most of the tour guests. She was worried that if she did, they might see her and know that Sashenka was gossiping with her.

"Really?" she said, wishing she knew who was who.

"I myself am self-made. Today, my vodka exporting empire is the biggest in the whole of the northern hemisphere. I started at the age of eighteen, smuggling just one bottle across the border!"

"Wow," Olivia said. That was a serious achievement.

"We will speak later. I can open many doors for your winery in Eastern Europe, Ukraine, and Russia."

Delighted that the tour was finally bearing fruit, Olivia hurried to the restaurant.

They'd already uncorked the red wines that would accompany the food to allow them breathing time, and after much discussion, had decided to serve them in crystal decanters. Olivia thought it had been a lucky decision, as it would hopefully prevent further negative comments about the bottling.

She poured out the first red wine, admiring how deep and rich its color looked in the spotless crystal, and then the second.

When it came to the third, Olivia hesitated.

This wine had a strange smell.

She leaned closer, inhaling the aroma. It was rough and sharp, not what she'd expected at all.

What was going on? Mystified, Olivia checked the label.

She felt like clutching her forehead in consternation. This was the Miracolo red, La Leggenda's premier blend. And it didn't smell right at all!

She poured it into the decanter, realizing as she did so that the wine was lighter in color. This wasn't the original Miracolo—or if it was, something had been added to it.

Olivia stared around her in panic. Without a doubt, this wine had been sabotaged.

Who could have done this, and why?

Sniffing the wine again and trying to think in a calm and logical way about this shocking find, Olivia found her suspicions focusing on one particular person.

CHAPTER THIRTEEN

This was the restaurant, Olivia reminded herself. She'd left bottles uncorked. And her rival had been prowling around unchecked, while the wine team had been fussing over the billionaires in the tasting room.

Olivia felt convinced that Gabriella had tried to sabotage the wine, hoping to ruin the tasting experience and trash Olivia's reputation. She must have done so by substituting her cooking wine for the contents of the Miracolo bottle.

Glancing around at the kitchen, she saw no sign of Gabriella. Olivia was certain she was hiding away.

She was appalled that Gabriella would stoop so low as to risk the success of the whole Platinum Tour, just to score a cheap victory. Becoming the manager in Marcello's absence was clearly more of a priority than the winery's future success.

Blindsided by this realization, Olivia had to acknowledge they were not a team, and Gabriella didn't care about her at all. If the restaurateur was put in charge, she was quite sure that she would either force Olivia to leave, or get her fired.

At least she'd picked up on this problem and could do some hasty damage control.

She decided to start by carrying all the carafes into the tasting room. She couldn't risk leaving any unopened bottle unattended. They must be safely stashed behind the counter until everyone sat down for the food.

After completing this emergency maneuver, she took the faulty bottle and poured it down the sink, wrinkling her nose at the sharp aroma that billowed out. This was almost as bad as the undrinkable Valley Wine that she'd been forced to market back in Chicago.

Seething with anger at Gabriella's irresponsible actions, she returned to the tasting room, where Jean-Pierre looked to be run off his feet.

Now that everyone was drinking—except Carmody—the atmosphere was more congenial, Olivia saw, as she carried around a fresh tray of glasses.

Sashenka was discussing music with Tomas, the pianist, who finally looked happier.

"I have a Steinway in my second home. I do not know how to play it, but it looks beautiful in the entrance hall, below the chandelier," she said.

"A magnificent piano," Tomas agreed. "After my successful tour in Tokyo last year, the organizers gifted me a Steinway which I keep in my apartment and play daily. Every day, I receive letters from the other residents, who tell me how my playing changes their lives. Some of them say they are in tears after every recital."

"May I offer you some more wine?" Olivia asked. She hoped that Sashenka was enjoying the La Leggenda products she'd so generously said she would promote.

"I am impressed with the quality of your offerings. So this is your red blend?" Tomas held his glass up to the light and peered consideringly at it.

"Yes, it's our most famous wine." Olivia felt herself glowing at the praise.

"It is excellent," Sashenka agreed, which made Olivia feel more positive. Perhaps, now that everyone was relaxing, there would be no more hitches or nastiness.

She turned away with her tray and found herself facing the nervous-looking youngster in the too-big jacket.

"Can I offer you some wine?" she asked.

He smiled tentatively at her.

"Can I show you a card trick?" He produced a pack of cards from his pocket with a flourish, drawing three of them out of the pack.

"Sure," Olivia said, putting her tray on the counter. She loved card tricks. Ferdie must be an accomplished magician to be such a huge Instagram celebrity.

"Choose one, please, pretty lady," he invited her in quivering tones.

"Okay, I choose the middle one. The seven of hearts."

"Seven! Always a lucky number. Now, I am going to place all these cards upside down and I want you to try and track the card you chose."

Olivia watched intently as he shifted the three face-down cards around.

"All right! Where is your card?" he asked triumphantly.

"It's there." Olivia pointed at the card on the right which she'd easily been able to keep track of. She knew it wouldn't be the same one, of course, but that was all part of the fun.

With a flourish, Ferdie turned over the card.

It was the seven of hearts.

"Well!" Olivia said, staring down at it in surprise. She'd never had that outcome before! Ferdie looked crestfallen.

"Was that supposed to happen?" she asked.

"No," he said miserably.

"It must be pre-match nerves. Have some wine," she soothed him, and waited while he took a glass. She wished she could spend more time with him, as he seemed in need of support, but her other guests were waiting.

Determined to seize the initiative, Olivia approached Drake and Rupert, who were discussing fast-moving consumer goods. Wine was a fast-moving consumer good, wasn't it?

"Can I introduce you to our red blend?" she asked. "It's La Leggenda's most famous wine."

"Sure," Drake said. His snappy mood seemed to have lifted. He took the glass from her and held it up to the light, admiring its color.

"This is a fine wine. A lot like a merlot. Just a bit more complex," he said thoughtfully, after tasting.

"How would you know?" Rupert asked. "You know nothing about wine."

Olivia felt her smile wobble. It hadn't sounded like Rupert was joking. He hadn't spoken in a teasing way. It had sounded more like an insult, as if Rupert was out to pick a fight or perhaps settle an old score.

"And you have any knowledge?" Drake said, with aggression evident in his tone.

"I know enough to be sure that these aren't good wines," Rupert said, staring condemningly at Olivia. "The first one I had was sour. This isn't any better. This winery wasn't advertised in the tour brochure. I think that one of the good places dropped out, and they chose this place at the last minute and without a proper vetting."

She felt taken aback by the accuracy of his guess, even though they had been vetted by the organizer herself, and their wines had a stellar reputation.

"I think this is a great wine," Drake said. "I'm a fan of reds."

"You're ignorant, and clearly don't have a palate at all," Rupert retorted, as Drake's eyes flashed with anger.

"Did you come on this tour just to insult other people?" he snapped.

"I came on this tour to drink good wines. I'm still waiting to be served any. Hopefully I'll have the chance at the restaurant tonight, which I know well. They, at least, have a decent wine list," he said contemptuously.

With the torrent of abuse she was getting from Rupert, Olivia was wishing she had some super-service protocols to fall back on. He was being impossibly rude, and she had a horrible feeling he was out to get her personally. Would he stop if she started crying?

No. Olivia feared his behavior would get worse. Her only hope was to remain calm.

"We also have a different red blend, and a plain sangiovese," she said, trying to sound helpful and not as if she was on the verge of panicking.

Rupert glared at her. "You can stop trying to sell me your wines. Trust me, lady, you're wasting your time," he said tersely.

"Don't be so rude to her," Drake snapped. "She's just the waitress. If you have an issue, why not take it up with the owner? Look, he's over there."

He pointed to Marcello, who was standing at the lobby's entrance.

As Drake spoke, Marcello raised his voice for an announcement.

"My friends, it is a fine afternoon, and the day is now at its warmest. Please will you accompany me on a short tour of our grounds, followed by a walk through our winemaking building."

There was a murmur of anticipation from everyone except Rupert, and the group headed for the exit where three six-seater golf carts were parked. Antonio and Nadia were already behind the wheel of two of them. Olivia was thankful that with such roomy golf carts, there was lots of space for the fussy guests to spread out. Drake and Rupert got into separate carts. She hoped that by the end of the tour, they would have forgotten their differences with her, and each other.

As the carts rattled away, Olivia's shoulders sagged in relief that the first part of the tour was over. It had been chaotic! She hadn't felt in control of the situation for one minute. It hadn't been like a normal wine tasting at all, or in any way how she'd imagined it.

Rushing back into the tasting room, she started tidying up the used glasses, piling them onto trays for Jean-Pierre to carry through to the kitchen. At least quite a bit of wine had been drunk, even though Carmody's water was barely touched.

"Those rich people were very difficult," Jean-Pierre stage-whispered to her.

"They were!" Olivia agreed. Apart from Sashenka, she didn't know if any of them were impressed enough with La Leggenda to tell their friends about the winery.

Feeling despondent, she carried the wine carafes back into the restaurant, resolving to stand guard over them until the tour returned, to prevent Gabriella from getting up to any more mischief. As Gabriella and Paolo carried in the steaming plates of snacks, Olivia toyed with the idea of grabbing a saltshaker when Gabriella's back was turned, and doctoring the food to be inedible.

What a sweet revenge that would be, she thought meanly. It would be a fitting retribution, and Gabriella deserved nothing less after her own underhanded actions. Quickly, Olivia reached for the salt.

CHAPTER FOURTEEN

For a long moment, Olivia weighed the full, heavy saltshaker in her hand, fantasizing about strewing it over the food. She could feel triumph glowing within her at having avoided Gabriella's sly attempt to destroy her, and retaliated with a brilliant counter blow.

Then, sighing, she replaced the salt on the table and turned away from the steaming platters. The idea of sabotaging Gabriella's spread was tempting, but she knew she could never go through with it. At heart, she wasn't a nasty enough person to do it, even though she wished she was! In any case, she knew a bad dining experience would reflect badly on the whole winery, not just the restaurant.

Remembering Carmody's need for pure water, she rushed back to the tasting room and placed a few bottles of still and sparkling aqua minerale on the table.

With the wine bottles arranged by the carafes, the water bottles, the shining glasses, and the sumptuous plates of snacks, the long table looked magnificent.

Olivia couldn't help ogling the snacks. Gabriella had outdone herself. She was sure the moguls would be delighted by the mounds of smoked salmon and caviar atop cream cheese bruschetta, the tiny individual pots filled with rich, slow-roasted Wagyu beef, and the porcelain spoons of chopped cherry tomato, mozzarella, and basil with a drop of pesto that Olivia knew would be bursting with flavor.

Then there were the mini game pies, made from exquisitely fine and crunchy pastry with a wild boar and red wine filling, the tablespoon-sized truffle risottos, and the salmon and strawberry brioches.

She noticed that Gabriella was hovering protectively around the plates. Perhaps she was anticipating a revenge move. Deciding to toy with her, Olivia reached casually for the saltshaker once again, and saw Gabriella tense immediately.

Feeling satisfied, and now giggling inwardly, Olivia put the salt down and headed to the fire. She was sure the guests would be chilly after their ride in the open golf carts.

Stoking the fire produced a comforting rush of warmth that made her feel more positive still. After a fascinating tour, with more fine wine and mouthwatering snacks in the coziness of the restaurant, Olivia couldn't see how any of the guests would remain unimpressed.

Even Rupert.

She'd only just finished preparing the fires and tidying up before the rattle of golf carts outside signaled the return of the group.

She hurried to the lobby, arriving at the same time as a flush-faced, enthusiastic Bernie and Jose.

"What a winery! Never have we seen such a magnificent winemaking facility," Jose enthused.

"It was wonderful to hear the story of the Miracolo," Bernie added.

Olivia felt delighted to see that, at last, the guests' mood had turned, and they'd settled into a positive, appreciative vibe.

"It was very authentic. It gave me an insight into the reality of wine farming, and winemaking. And it was amusing in parts," Sid agreed.

Marcello followed the guests, looking pleased with the success of the outing.

"I think our visitors enjoyed the tour," he said to Olivia. "They were fascinated by the plantations on the steeper slopes, and by the goat dairy, because Erba was perched on the roof."

"The roof?" Olivia blanched in horror. The goat dairy building was so tall it was almost double story. "How did she get up there? How will she get down again?"

Worry for her goat filled Olivia.

"I am sure she will find her way," Marcello reassured her.

At least Erba had managed to delight the guests, which was more than Olivia had yet done. Even if she was starting to think she should take out pet insurance for her wayward animal.

Remembering her role, and that super-service must continue, she raised her voice.

"Please join us in the restaurant. We have prepared carafes of our favorite red wines, together with snacks from our tasting table."

Olivia headed to the restaurant, quickly pulling out seats as the guests arrived. Once comfortably seated, they wasted no time in attacking the food. In fact, they seemed so hungry that Olivia was wondering whether they would have noticed if she had poured salt over it.

Sid wouldn't have noticed, she guessed. The fussy Drake would have. Hamilton, not so much. Carmody would have said the salt was interfering with his spirituality. Tomas would have said that a grateful audience member had gifted him a mountain of salt!

Olivia had to stop herself from laughing aloud as she immersed herself in her fantasies. And then a real live angry cry jolted her out of them.

"This beef is tough!"

It was Rupert again. This time, he was loudly complaining about the melt-in-your-mouth Wagyu. Olivia had no doubt it was perfectly cooked, and in any case, the high fat content of Wagyu contributed to exceptional tenderness no matter how it was prepared.

"What, are your teeth rotten?" Drake asked playfully. Olivia bit her lip anxiously, knowing the comment would not be well received.

"My teeth are fine," Rupert snapped. Rummaging in his pocket, he took a tablet from a pill box, poured a half-glass of mineral water, and swallowed it down.

"If your teeth are fine, why are you popping painkillers?" Drake probed.

"It's not a painkiller. It's prescription medication for my ongoing health." Rupert glared at Drake. "I'll have you know I am a very health-focused person. Comes from being a national triathlete, all the way up until I was in my forties and stepped into the business full time. That's why I still don't have a paunch. Unlike you."

Pulling his stomach in and sitting up straight, Drake looked angry at the personal jibe, and Rupert used the moment to further his argument.

"I don't know why this winery bothered with inedible snacks to go with the undrinkable wine. We are heading to a fine dining restaurant. This tour is not the standard it used to be. Maybe we should just stop off at a McDonald's or Burger King."

"Burger King? Is there a local one?" Picking up on the conversation, Sid looked eagerly around.

At that moment, Olivia saw Gabriella was standing behind Rupert—ironically, carrying a fresh plate of the Wagyu braised beef mini-casseroles.

She must have heard his criticism, because she was staring at him with narrowed eyes as if she had decided they were now lifelong enemies.

Mesmerized by the conflict that was playing out, Olivia waited for the situation to explode.

Gabriella's curvaceous chest rose and fell heavily, as if she were taking several calming breaths. Her plump lips clamped together and

Olivia could see it was taking immense control for her to suppress the vengeful shrieks that she wanted to unleash.

Fascinated, she watched as the tawny-haired woman managed to summon up the vestiges of a smile.

"I apologize that the beef displeases you," she said. "It is made according to a local recipe. Highly authentic; a humble stew that has been made in this region for centuries. Our recipes seek to provide flavor, while also paying homage to history and the traditions of the generations before us."

She smiled charmingly at Rupert, who looked blindsided by her master-move. Olivia, too, felt in awe of Gabriella's comeback. How had she thought up that response on the fly?

Amid murmurs of approval, everyone tucked into the Wagyu mini pots, apart from Rupert, who was scowling again. Now that he'd been bested by Gabriella, he returned his attention to the wine.

"This is as substandard as the last lot of wines." He sighed impatiently. "And don't give me cultural stories about the humble origins of past generations." He gestured expansively to the table. "If I want to live like they used to a hundred years ago, I can research the lifestyle. It's not what I pay top dollar for on vacation. I want good food, top wines, and to be treated accordingly. Not patronized."

He roared out the last words and Olivia felt herself shrink back in horror. It was as if Rupert was deliberately spoiling for a fight.

Gabriella, displaying a level of self-control Olivia hadn't dreamed she possessed, was nodding sympathetically, saying, "Absolutely. Absolutely, signor."

Nobody else was taking the slightest bit of notice. Ferdi had taken out his pack of cards and was shuffling them nervously while glancing at Jose on his right. Jose hadn't noticed the cards and was deep in conversation with Carmody. They seemed to be discussing travels in Tibet.

Aldo, Chico, and Bernie were having an animated argument about which investment cars held their value the best. At least, Olivia thought so from the words "Maserati," "Ferrari," "retail price," and "customer appeal" she heard resounding around the room.

The only person who appeared to be listening to Rupert was Tomas the pianist.

"I am from humble origins," he said proudly. "My talent took me all the way to the top."

With a frustrated snort, Rupert glanced at the clock.

"We're due to leave in five minutes," he announced. "I'm going to wait in the bus."

Five minutes? Olivia couldn't believe how the time had flown. For better or worse, the Platinum Tour would soon be whirling away in their dark, polished minibus.

As Rupert stomped out, Olivia hoped fervently she'd seen the last of him. He was nothing but a troublemaker, she decided.

"More wine?" she asked Drake.

"I'll have some more of the pink wine," he agreed, before continuing his conversation with Bernie. "Yes, I drank that exact brand of tequila with Richard Branson a few years ago, and also found it nicer with orange than lemon."

Fascinated, Olivia leaned in, trying to overhear more of their discourse. But movement caught her eye, and she turned, seeing to her dismay that Rupert was storming back into the restaurant again! He looked florid-faced and smoldering with wrath.

"If you thought we were heading on to better things, you would be wrong," he announced angrily to the room. "There's a problem with the bus and it won't start. We are now stuck in this hellhole—probably for the rest of the night!"

CHAPTER FIFTEEN

Horrified by Rupert's news, Olivia rushed to the door, arriving neck and neck with Gabriella. They glared briefly at each other before the restaurateur shoved her way through first. Since Olivia wasn't wearing ridiculous heels, she caught her up and passed her before they reached the lobby.

Olivia burst out to find the uniformed driver and tour guide peering worriedly into the engine. Marcello was already there. He must have been getting ready to bid farewell to the guests. Now, he was handing the driver wrenches, his hands covered in oil.

"Is everything all right?" she asked. "Marcello, should I call Antonio?" He was the most mechanically minded of the Vescovis.

"No, no, *grazie, signorina*," the driver said. "The problem is minor but it requires a small spare part to fix. We have already called the mechanics in Pisa, and they are on their way with the part."

"I have had a look," Marcello confirmed. "The part is essential, so we can only wait."

"How long will they take to get here?" Olivia fidgeted worriedly. This would throw out the carefully planned schedule. Stella would be furious.

"Half an hour, they promised," the driver told her.

Olivia exchanged a glance with Gabriella, who looked as appalled as she did. Half an hour seemed like a lifetime in this situation.

"I will organize some sweet treats. We have milk and dark chocolate truffles in the fridge," Gabriella said, and rushed away.

With Marcello still managing the bus repairs, and the tour guide and driver both frantically holding lights and working inside the engine, Olivia guessed the job of confirming the duration of the delay fell to her. She took a deep breath as she walked back into the winery.

"Attention, esteemed guests," she called, standing at the restaurant door. "We have a minor mechanical issue to fix. The bus requires a spare part, which will take half an hour to arrive. Luckily, we have some delicious chocolates for your enjoyment. And, of course, more wine and spirits from our bar. Please ask Paolo and Jean-Pierre to serve you."

The two young men leaped into action, circulating among the guests. To Olivia's relief, the murmurs of dissatisfaction were soon drowned out by the loud, enthusiastic calls for drinks.

After making sure that everyone was content, Olivia hurried back outside. Antonio had arrived, and was lying under the bus while Marcello knelt beside him, passing screwdrivers and hammers. Olivia saw the gleam of a flashlight. She hoped that the mechanically minded Antonio might be able to fix the problem without needing to wait for the spare part.

Antonio spoke in muffled tones, so rapidly she couldn't pick up what he was saying.

Marcello, however, looked horrified.

"There are more problems," he said, sounding as distressed as Olivia felt. "It is not just a single part that needs replacing, but a section of the exhaust pipe also, and some welding must urgently be done."

"Can we do it here?" Olivia asked.

Marcello nodded. "Yes. We will make a plan. Antonio is going to jack up the front of the vehicle, and we can then raise it onto bricks to allow enough room for welding. It will not be easy, but it is possible. The challenge is that it will take more time."

It was already getting dark, Olivia realized. What if the group missed out on the art exhibition and piano concert? Olivia dreaded that they might be angry at the winery, simply because the breakdown had occurred while the bus was parked here.

"Shall I call Stella and let her know?" she asked. Explaining the problem to the tour organizer would be an ordeal, she was sure, but at least one less issue for poor Marcello to deal with.

Marcello glanced at her gratefully.

"I spoke to her just before you came out here. She is busy rearranging the schedule. The concert can be moved to tomorrow and the group will go straight from here to the restaurant. It is unfortunate, but there is no other solution."

"I'll check on the guests again," Olivia said.

She'd only been outside for a few minutes. But yet, back inside, the situation was degenerating at an alarming rate. The hubbub of voices was so noisy she could barely hear herself think. Paolo and Jean-Pierre were rushing around with trays of drinks. Gabriella had disappeared from sight completely. Someone had knocked over a chair. And following the trail of upended furniture, Olivia stared in horror at the scene in the middle of the restaurant.

Rupert and Drake were facing each other in a combative stance. They looked ready to have a stand-up fight. In fact, Rupert was rolling up his sleeves as he shouted insults at the other man.

"You're so small-time," he taunted. "Just a little IT techie who got lucky and rich. You're never going to make it in the big leagues. Everyone's laughing at you, and you don't even realize it."

"Take that back!" Drake roared. "I won't stand for your bullying a moment longer. The only reason you're on this tour is to insult and belittle as many people as possible. Why is that, I wonder? Don't have enough to do at work? Business not going as great as you make out?" he yelled.

Hamilton and Bernie, who were watching, nodded supportively, making Olivia worry that this would end up as a three-against-one punch-up. What could she do?

As Olivia was agonizing over how she could prevent a full-on fist fight, Jean-Pierre clumsily inserted himself between the soon-to-be-brawling duo.

He dropped his tray loudly. It clattered to the floor and a water bottle bounced off it, landing sharply on the tiles and spilling everywhere, but not shattering.

"Oh, I apologize!" the Frenchman said. "I am so very uncoordinated today! Please excuse me while I tidy up the mess."

Olivia was filled with admiration at Jean-Pierre's quick thinking and how he had saved the day. Drake and Rupert were both backing away from the spreading pool of water.

"Who would like some sparkling wine?" Olivia invited loudly.

There were a few bottles of Metodo Classico in the restaurant fridge. Quickly, she assembled some flutes and handed them out. By the time everyone had a glass, Rupert had disappeared. Hopefully he'd realized how obnoxious he was being and had slunk away to calm down, Olivia thought.

Glancing across the table, she saw that Carmody and Jose were deep in conversation. Both were sipping amber-colored liquid from simple tumblers.

Was it apple juice? Olivia wondered briefly.

She didn't think so. Olivia was pretty sure that those glasses both held strong whiskies. Feeling shocked, she guessed that the stress of the afternoon had overridden Carmody's Tibetan learning, and besmirched his spirituality.

She heard raised voices from outside and rushed to the door.

When she saw Rupert there, she stopped abruptly in the doorway. He clearly hadn't calmed down or thought better of his earlier disgusting behavior. Rather than picking on his fellow travelers, he was now bullying the poor tour guide who'd sneaked away for a quiet cigarette.

"This is all your fault," he yelled. Olivia realized he was slurring his words and sounded very drunk. Clearly he'd managed to choke down a lot more of their inferior wine than he'd admitted to doing.

"You can't even organize a working bus. How'd you even manage to get this gig, I ask you? Did you falsify your papers? Do you even know what the word 'falsify' means, or are you too stupid to understand it? Thanks to your incompetence, our trip is ruined. Don't think for one moment that I will let this go."

"*Signor, signor*, I am sorry." The tour guide had turned pale. He looked horrified by this tirade, as if his world was about to end. Olivia felt a rush of sympathy for him. It wasn't his fault the bus had broken down. And it was completely wrong that he should have to take a storm of unfair abuse from one of the guests.

Olivia clamped her lips together angrily, knowing one word from her would only trigger Rupert all over again.

"I'm going to get you fired," Rupert sneered, staggering slightly. "Trust me, the organizers will do it as soon as I ask. You're just a wretched little menial worker, of no importance in any of our lives, and you don't deserve better."

Olivia felt her temper rising. How could Rupert treat an innocent and defenseless human being so heartlessly while using his wealth as a weapon?

"Please, don't take it out on him," she beseeched Rupert, knowing that she might only make things worse. "Can I call Marcello, and he can handle your complaint?"

Rupert turned, and Olivia realized she was right. Her intervention had only made him angrier.

"What do you think you're doing, butting into my conversation?" he yelled at her. "You are just as bad as this idiot. You're incapable and incompetent. You've given me poor service the whole afternoon and misrepresented your wines so badly that I could take legal action against you. I'm going to get you fired, too."

Olivia took a step back, feeling as if he'd smacked her in the face with those horrible words. She'd never expected such an aggressive attack.

She knew she should bite her tongue and walk away, but she found she couldn't. Instead, seething with anger, she leaned close to Rupert. Of course, she couldn't risk upsetting the entire tour group by yelling. But she could hiss like a snake. In fact, like Gabriella. Channeling the restaurateur at her worst, Olivia narrowed her eyes, hoping she looked as intimidating as Gabriella could when she did the same.

"I don't care how wealthy you are, or how much influence you have, or how many times you have bullied people before. I do care that your behavior is toxic and unacceptable. And I want you to know that if I hear one more word of threats from you at this winery, there will be consequences. One. More. Word. And. You. Will. Suffer. Those. Consequences!" Olivia stabbed her index finger at the astonished billionaire while she spoke.

"How dare you say such a thing!" Rupert spluttered angrily, but he staggered back a step, clearly rattled by her heartfelt words. Behind her, Olivia sensed someone brush past. She didn't dare take her eyes off Rupert, as it would show weakness. All the same she felt a flicker of guilt that her threats, meant for his ears only—and the tour guide's, of course—had been overheard by one of the other billionaires.

"Well!" Rupert was the first one to drop his gaze. He turned and stumbled angrily away into the darkness.

Olivia turned away, letting out a deep sigh of relief. She'd broken all the rules of super-service, but she didn't care. Bullying was unacceptable and she refused to put up with it one moment longer. Quickly, she hurried back into the winery, hoping that her hissed threats would keep Rupert's behavior in line until the bus was fixed.

She was comforted to see that in the restaurant, the atmosphere was becoming more festive. Someone had turned on the music. Jean-Pierre and Paolo were circulating nonstop with a variety of drinks, and Gabriella had whipped up a round of grilled panini sandwiches with Parma ham and provolone cheese.

"Next year, the tour should include a full meal at this restaurant," Sid praised, biting into the crusty treat as cheese oozed out.

"Yes, I think so, too," Sashenka agreed. "They have done us proud. After all, we have overstayed our welcome here, but all they offer is more hospitality." She laughed raucously.

Olivia went out to the parking lot to check on the progress of the repairs. She was encouraged to see they looked nearly complete.

"Can you hold this for me?" Marcello handed her the flashlight and crawled under the bus to support the pipe while Antonio did some final hammering. Meanwhile, the driver was tightening something under the hood. Carefully, he closed the hood. The tour guide wiped it down as Antonio and Marcello wriggled out from under the bus.

Then the driver washed his hands in a bucket of soapy water somebody had placed near the bus door, dried them carefully, and climbed in. This was the moment of truth, Olivia thought, as he pressed the starter button.

Everyone sighed in relief as the engine purred into life. The heater began humming gently, warming the leather-lined interior.

"It is time to go. We can call our guests outside," Marcello said, heading to the bucket to wash his hands as well.

The timing couldn't have been better, Olivia thought. The guests were merrily drunk and would hopefully leave with fond memories of La Leggenda, even if they were too full to do more than pick at the Michelin-starred dinner that awaited them.

Going back inside, she felt happy to be announcing the positive news, but she was concerned to see that although she'd only been outside for about ten minutes, the restaurant looked emptier than it had. The guests had wandered away to explore the winery. Where had they all gone?

She saw Sashenka had walked out, and was admiring the gardens by the light of her phone's flashlight. Chico and Aldo were reading the posters on the walls in the tasting room. Drake had found his way into the restaurant kitchen, hoping to scrounge more snacks from a pleased-looking Gabriella, while Hamilton was opening the fridge and peering inside.

"Any more of those choccies?" he asked Gabriella, who giggled in delight. Clearly, different rules applied to billionaires interfering in her domain.

Only Carmody and Jose looked rooted to their chairs, with a noticeably emptier whiskey bottle between them.

"Please, can you all go back to the bus?" Olivia called, repeating the words over and over as she stood in the restaurant doorway, hoping she was speaking loud enough to be heard by all the scattered visitors.

Gradually, they all headed back inside, drifting through the tasting room to the lobby. Even though managing a group of moguls felt like herding cats, they were at least moving in the right direction.

"We should do a head count," Jean-Pierre said, as they followed the guests outside to the waiting bus.

"A head count. Good idea," Olivia said. It was dark, people were milling around, and the last thing they needed was for anyone to be left behind.

She counted on her fingers as they entered the bus.

Olivia ran out of fingers just before the last person, Sashenka, stepped elegantly inside.

"Eleven," she said.

She turned to the driver.

"Are we one short? How many guests were there when we arrived?"

"Twelve, *signora*," the driver said.

Olivia peered through the tinted windows, anxiously looking at the group sitting quietly within.

Quietly! At that moment she realized who was missing.

Rupert must have stumbled off into the darkness after having his fight.

"Excuse me. I'll go and find the missing person," she said.

Running back through the winery, she felt furious that Rupert was causing so many problems. Even in his absence, he was creating mayhem, because the bus couldn't leave. Where could he be?

There was a powerful flashlight on a shelf near the restaurant's side door. She grabbed it before heading out into the dark.

Hastening through the restaurant gardens, she called loudly, "Rupert? Rupert! Where are you? It's time to go!"

She worried that he might have passed out, and she'd end up falling over him.

"Rupert?" she yelled again.

Gazing into the gloom, she was encouraged to see a faint shape ahead, near the pond.

But, as Olivia neared the water, she observed the shape was shrinking in size. It definitely wasn't human sized. It was smaller. In fact, goat sized!

Erba was standing on the opposite edge of the pond.

"Well, hello," Olivia greeted her goat, pleased that she'd managed to get down safely from the dairy roof.

But Erba didn't acknowledge her, seeming fascinated by something in the water.

With dread beginning to prickle her spine, Olivia stepped forward, training her flashlight at the shape that was barely visible in the dark waves.

It was a person, she saw, feeling her heart accelerate. A person with limbs splayed, lying face down, the outline of the dark tracksuit only just visible in the cold, lapping water.

Olivia gulped in a huge, shocked breath.

This was unmistakably Rupert.

Worse still, he was undoubtedly dead.

CHAPTER SIXTEEN

Olivia clapped her hand over her mouth in horror, but a faint squawk emerged from between her fingers. Her mind was racing, her brain illogically trying to convince her that maybe everything was okay and he'd just gone for a swim.

"Erba, go back to your friends," Olivia said in a shaky voice. Her goat was too young to face the harsh realities of death.

What had happened? she wondered frantically, as Erba, obedient for once, turned and trotted away. Had he slipped and fallen in?

Olivia had no idea. At the back of her mind, a little voice was protesting that he couldn't possibly have slipped and fallen in, but Olivia wasn't sure why that voice was so sure of itself.

She backed away from the chilly, unpleasant waters, shivering as she heard the wavelets lapping against the pond's muddy edges.

Trembling from shock, she gasped again as she realized she would now have to go back and tell this elite group that a catastrophe had occurred. Marcello would have to call the police, and she was sure the police would insist that nobody leave until they investigated the scene!

As she imagined the vitriol that would be vented by these privileged guests, she broke into a panicked run. They would be furious at this further delay.

She arrived back at the bus in a shocked rush, with the flashlight's beam dancing unevenly ahead of her. As if sensing her distress, Marcello appeared, striding toward her.

"Olivia, what is it?" he asked in a low voice. "Has something gone wrong?"

The next moment, he enfolded her in his arms and Olivia found herself sobbing into the soft wool of his smart jacket.

"It's Rupert. He's in the pond. He's drowned, Marcello!"

"Drowned?" His voice was low and horrified.

"He's face down in the water. Not moving."

"Oh, *mio Dio*, how can such a tragedy happen here once again? On this important tour, and to us?" Marcello whispered, echoing Olivia's own thoughts.

Grabbing the flashlight in one hand, and Olivia's hand in the other, he raced through the gardens toward the scene.

He stumbled to a stop as he reached the paved pathway surrounding the pond. Then, walking round to the side where the pond was shallower, he splashed carefully into the water, wading out until he reached the body.

Olivia closed her eyes and turned away. She didn't want to look.

A minute later, Marcello was back, with water streaming from his clothing and flooding from his shoes.

"Without a doubt, he is dead. He is icy cold and has no pulse. We must call the police immediately. Olivia, are you all right? Do you need to sit down in my office for a while?"

"No. I'll manage. I'd rather stay and help, if I can," Olivia said bravely.

"I will make the call as we walk. Then we will have to break the news to our guests."

It was dark, so she couldn't see Marcello's face, but he sounded grim, as if he was dreading the reaction that this would trigger.

Squelching his way back to the parking lot, Marcello dialed, speaking briefly and tersely before disconnecting.

"They are on their way. Now to explain this to the group," he said, with quiet resolve in his voice.

He pulled open the door of the bus.

Conversation and laughter billowed out of the leather-scented confines.

"I am sorry to say there has been a tragedy," Marcello began.

"The bus won't start again?" Sid quipped, to general laughter.

"We're out of wine?" Drake suggested, chortling.

Marcello continued in somber tones. "One of the group has been found deceased. It appears that Rupert Curren has drowned in a pond near the restaurant gardens."

There was a short silence. Olivia steeled herself for the tirade of acrimony and blame that these billionaires would vent at Marcello, and her.

"Dead?" Sashenka asked, leaning toward the bus door from her position in the front seat and gazing curiously past Olivia as if she might be able to see the body from the parking lot.

"Unfortunately, yes," Olivia confirmed. "We need to wait for the police to arrive before the bus leaves." Her voice trembled as she spoke, expecting a storm of abuse.

"Well, there is no reason to stay on the bus while waiting," Chico declared. "We have a comfortable restaurant right here."

There were murmurs of assent from all the other tour guests. Olivia moved in front of the open doorway, feeling even more worried. This wasn't what she and Marcello had planned at all! But already the billionaires were on their feet and heading purposefully toward the door, leaving her with no choice but to let them climb out.

"Come this way," she said, hoping that if she showed calm leadership they would at least follow her straight into the restaurant and not wander off around the grounds, trying to see where the body was and most probably contaminating the scene.

Contaminating the scene! Olivia felt a chill as she realized she was already suspecting that there might have been foul play.

She marched into the restaurant, where Gabriella was clearing glasses away. Jean-Pierre, who was mopping the floor, glanced up in confusion as he saw the group trooping in again.

"Our valued guests will be spending a little more time with us due to a tragic event. One of the group has passed away. We hope that our new friends can find some comfort *in the restaurant* while we wait for the police," Olivia announced, emphasizing the relevant words as she made a beeline for the side door, which she closed firmly.

Jean-Pierre's face was a picture of consternation as, with a scrape of chairs and a wave of convivial banter, the group sat down.

"Reminds me of the time I flew to Singapore last year," Bernie started telling Sid. "I don't usually use commercial flights but this time I had to. Anyway, the man across the aisle from me in first class choked on his boeuf bourguignon and died right there. They couldn't save him. He had a preexisting condition apparently. Something to do with his heart. More wine, please," he called to Jean-Pierre.

Abandoning his mop, the young assistant rushed to fulfill the request.

"Aye, when it's your time, it's your time," Hamilton confirmed. "Talking of food, what are the chances of another round of those excellent grilled cheese and ham paninis?"

Gabriella had been hovering in the kitchen doorway, looking at once appalled, curious, and fearful. The request for food sent her scurrying back inside. Olivia hoped she'd be able to rustle up something else delicious, because after what had happened, she doubted the guests would make their Michelin-starred restaurant booking.

"More whiskey, please, barman." Carmody snapped his fingers at Paolo, who rushed behind the bar to do his bidding.

So it had been whiskey, Olivia realized. Carmody sounded decidedly tipsy, but fortunately he didn't seem to be a mean drunk like Rupert.

Gazing around the room, which was filled with a festive ambience, Olivia was concerned that the group in general seemed to be regarding this as an interesting event, and nobody seemed overly upset by Rupert's death. Were none of them feeling the same shock and worry that she was? Or were they just hiding it, not wanting to show vulnerability to their peers?

Or could there be another reason? Olivia thought, with a twinge of anxiety. Rupert hadn't made himself popular with his fellow travelers, and had in fact gone out of his way to taunt and belittle the others.

Even though she forced her mind away from these rising suspicions, Olivia couldn't get rid of the little voice that was nagging at her, telling her there was something highly irregular about this death, and that she was forgetting an important detail.

As she carried a tray of glasses around, she overhead Carmody, now deep in conversation with Jose. He, too, sounded as if the drink was taking effect.

"You shee, these Tibetan monks, they knew about the shircle of life. You have to accept it because it's all part of the great plan." His arms flailed in a vaguely global gesture, knocking Jose on his ear. Neither of them seemed to notice.

There was a short silence while Jose took in this wisdom.

"The shircle," he echoed, battling to focus as he gazed down at his glass.

"It's all connected. Beth and dearth." Carmody blinked, looking confused. "I mean—I mean the other way."

"Dearth and beth," Jose agreed wisely.

"Yes. No." Carmody swayed in his seat.

"I undershtand the wisdom. This has been a shpecial day. Highly aushpicious, in fact life changing. I feel reconnected with my own shpirituality in a very deep way. Oh, look, food."

Putting his glass down, Jose grabbed the plate of mozzarella and salami paninis that Gabriella was offering.

As Gabriella handed out the platters, the excited conversation was tamped down to a convivial murmur as the now mostly-very-drunk guests piled into the paninis and grilled cheese delicacies that she had managed to magic up at short notice.

And then Olivia's stomach twisted as she heard the distinctive sound of a small Fiat pulling to a stop in the parking lot.

The way the brakes squeaked impatiently clued Olivia that the driver was already in a bad mood. Tiptoeing to the door, she peeked outside.

A coroner's van was following close behind the Fiat. As soon as it stopped, Marcello rushed over to help the team unload the equipment, which included a stretcher, Olivia noted uneasily.

Then the Fiat's door opened and Olivia felt her stomach sink all the way into her shoes as she saw Detective Caputi climb out.

The detective was wearing plainclothes—a warm black jacket and elegant yet sturdy low-heeled boots. Her shiny, gray, bobbed hair gleamed in the outside lights as she opened the trunk and took out a bulky equipment bag. Slinging it over her shoulder, she snapped out instructions at her fellow officers.

Why her? Olivia wondered. She'd harbored a faint hope that the unpleasant detective might have been promoted after her excellent work on the recent murder case that Olivia had been caught up in.

Clearly the detective was a feet-on-the-ground person with no aspirations to ascend the dizzy heights of the police career ladder—whatever they were, Olivia hazarded.

She turned to Jean-Pierre.

"Please make sure nobody leaves the room," she told him. Much as she wanted to stay here in the warmth, among the comforting aromas of food and wine, she knew she couldn't.

Gathering up her courage, Olivia stepped outside to meet her nemesis again.

CHAPTER SEVENTEEN

"Er—*buon giorno*," Olivia greeted the detective tentatively.

Caputi spun round, glaring at her.

"You again? Why am I not surprised to find you in attendance here!"

Her gaze raked Olivia, as if the detective was holding her personally responsible for the entire murder rate in greater Tuscany.

"I think a guest has died of natural causes," Olivia said politely, not wanting to stoop to the detective's angry level, while aiming to plant the seed that most probably this was the case.

"Natural causes? With you around?" The detective snorted irritably.

To be fair, Olivia guessed she must be getting tired of having her evenings interrupted by urgent call-outs to La Leggenda, even though none of them had been Olivia's fault!

She trailed behind the group as they made their way through the gardens, led by Marcello, who hadn't even had time to change out of his dripping clothes and drenched shoes. The fresh smell of herbs permeated the air as the officers' boots scrunched over leaves of rosemary and wild mint.

"Stay back," Detective Caputi ordered. "My team must examine the scene."

"What are they examining?" a curious voice asked from behind her.

Olivia spun around to see Sashenka standing there. She was munching on a grilled cheese panini and holding a wine glass in her other hand.

"You need to go back inside!" Olivia said.

A glint of orange caught her eye. Behind Sashenka, Erba stood, waiting expectantly in the queue of rubberneckers.

"We all need to go back!" Olivia said firmly. "Come on."

Sashenka turned reluctantly and spied Erba.

"Oh, what a pretty goat! Isn't she adorable? Does she like grilled cheese?"

Olivia decided not to point out that Erba was probably hoping for a sip of Sashenka's wine.

"You can try," she said.

86

Sashenka gave the goat the rest of her panini. She guzzled it enthusiastically.

Then, to Olivia's relief, Sashenka turned away from the scene, where Detective Caputi was supervising while large spotlights were set up.

With a billionaire to look after, Olivia felt justified in heading back to the winery, glad that she didn't have to spend more time watching the morbid body retrieval at the pond.

"Look, everyone," Sashenka announced, pushing the restaurant door wide. "I've brought us a goat."

"No!" Olivia protested, but it was too late. Erba trotted confidently inside as if she were on the top-ten of the VIP guest list. She made her way to the fireplace and settled herself down on the rug.

"She's so cute! Is that the one who was on the roof?" Chico asked.

"Let me see. We can compare it to the photos," Aldo said.

The brothers, together with Sid and Hamilton, crowded tipsily around the goat, scrolling through their phones.

"Definitely the same one," Chico confirmed. "What a friendly animal."

Olivia saw Gabriella watching from the kitchen, her arms folded and her lips pressed together in disapproval, as the brothers offered Erba another grilled cheese, which she ate with great enjoyment, and then a saucer of wine.

Apart from Carmody and Jose, who were now sitting in full lotus positions on the floor, with a whiskey bottle and two glasses between them, every single one of the billionaires filmed Erba lapping up the wine.

Olivia couldn't help feeling glad that she'd gotten to see their human side. It had taken a broken down bus, a large amount of wine, and an unexpected death to show her that these moguls were, at heart, real humans, with normal emotions.

Although that raised other concerns, because Olivia knew how powerful emotions could be, and what humans were capable of when they were angry with another person. Why would a billionaire go any less far?

Olivia noticed Ferdie, the magician, lurking on the outskirts of the group. As she moved away from the newly formed Erba fan club, he muttered to her, "Can I ask you something?"

"Sure. What?" Olivia turned to the young man.

"Is the evening entertainment off for now? The piano playing, and all that?"

"Yes. I don't know whether it's been canceled or postponed, though."

"Hopefully canceled," he muttered.

Olivia wanted to ask him more. She sensed there was a mystery of its own surrounding this youngster's presence on the tour. But before she could, there was a commotion outside the restaurant door.

Wheels rattled, lights gleamed, and she heard shouted voices as the stretcher was pushed along the paved pathway. Then Detective Caputi stalked inside.

"*Buon giorno*," she addressed the group, seemingly unimpressed to be talking to a room full of high-net-worth individuals. "We have retrieved the body from the lake. At this early stage, we are treating the death as suspicious. I will need to interview all of you. As an involved winery employee, who coincidentally found the body, you will be first."

Her voice rang with suspicion as she pointed an accusing finger at Olivia.

*

Five minutes later, Olivia was sitting uneasily in Marcello's office, which had been repurposed for the interview. The detective was sitting in the leather chair usually occupied by Marcello. Olivia felt disoriented by her stern presence in what she thought of as a safe place. Her arms were folded and she was staring at Olivia in a hostile way.

"I will be honest with you. Your arrival has spelled nothing but trouble for our local area. Ever since you came here, suspicious deaths have been occurring. I am going to get to the bottom of this, whatever it takes. I feel there is a bigger picture to be seen," Detective Caputi threatened.

Olivia stared at her in consternation, the more so when she realized that this had obviously been a personal, off-the-record warning. Only after speaking these words did the detective start her tape recording.

"When did you meet the deceased, Rupert Curren?" she asked.

Aware that her tape recorder was picking up every sound and nuance, Olivia did her best to reply calmly.

"He arrived at the winery with the Platinum Tour."

"Did you have any specific interaction with him through the evening?"

Olivia wished she could say no. But the problem was that other guests had noticed. She knew how the billionaires would feel, sitting opposite this scary woman in a one-on-one situation. Money and status would be flimsy defenses against her ferocious glare. They would say whatever it took to deflect her focus to someone else. Whatever it took, in this case, would include an explanation of how nasty Rupert had been to the winery staff, and Olivia in particular.

"Yes, he was a difficult customer," she admitted. Sure enough, the detective's gaze sharpened.

"In what way?"

"He complained a lot and was unhappy with the wines. He picked fights with the other guests. He was combative toward them. At one stage, he almost came to blows with Drake Rafter. Jean-Pierre was luckily able to defuse the situation. He also threatened the tour guide in a horrible way, saying he would get him fired."

Who had overheard her threatening Rupert? Olivia wondered. Somebody had. She knew with uneasy certainty that this information would come out. Probably, it would be better to tell the detective herself.

"I told him to stop being obnoxious and that his bad behavior would have consequences," Olivia confessed with a sigh.

Raising her eyebrows, as if this admission was a game-changer, the detective jotted a note in her book.

"Let us go back to before you started threatening the now-deceased guest," she said. "Was the group having dinner here? What was their program?"

"They were supposed to have a wine tasting and snacks. But because the bus wouldn't start and had to be fixed, it threw the whole schedule out and meant they stayed here longer than they should have. People were annoyed at first, but then most of them calmed down. They were drinking a lot. Gabriella prepared some food. Then, when it was time to leave, we couldn't find Rupert. I went looking for him and discovered him in the pond. Well, actually my goat found him. She was peering down into the water, and I went over to see what she was curious about."

Olivia hoped to goodness that this account cleared her. She had a very nasty feeling in her stomach—the feeling that you got when you weren't sure if you were going to go home, or straight to prison!

Hopefully, it would be home. Her cat needed her!

"Show me your shoes," the detective said, which surprised Olivia.

She twisted sideways in her chair and raised a foot above the desk, showing off her comfortable black leather boots. Olivia felt a little like a chorus girl as she stuck her foot in the air.

"No, no," the detective said impatiently. "Take them off."

Off? Why?

Now, she felt like Cinderella as she removed her boots and passed them across the desk. They were rather muddy, she saw. The tiles felt cold under her stockinged feet.

"I will give them back to you later," the detective said in uncompromising tones.

How much later? Olivia wondered nervously. She had to walk home and couldn't do it barefoot!

"That is all," the detective said. "You remain under suspicion of a probable crime and we will need to interview you again. Until this matter is resolved, you may not leave the area."

CHAPTER EIGHTEEN

As Olivia left the office, treading delicately over the cold floor in her stockinged feet, she wondered why the detective had been so fascinated by her footwear. Although the policewoman hadn't said, Olivia guessed that there must have been some evidence at the pond that had led her to suspect foul play.

That would mean footprints, Olivia surmised. So perhaps Detective Caputi was going to try to identify which tracks were Olivia's, and, if there were others, which were not.

She hadn't gone all the way up to the edge of the water, Olivia remembered, and that had been thanks to Erba. Her goat's odd behavior had spooked her, and had meant that she'd hung back, shining the light from a yard or two away, instead of on the brink of the water.

Would that make a difference? she worried. Were the footprints clear enough to see who had been where?

If they were, then Erba's presence at the scene might make all the difference between her owner spending the night in prison, and going back home again.

When Olivia stepped gingerly back into the tasting room, she found it was a whirlwind of activity. Stella had arrived, sharply dressed and immaculately groomed. Clipboard in hand, she was organizing the group.

"The police want you here until you have been interviewed. Once done, we will transport you back to your hotels. However, the police have asked that you do not leave the hotel premises and that you remain available during the course of tomorrow, as they may need to re-interview you."

The billionaires were standing in a group around Stella, looking mutinous.

"I want to go back to my hotel now," Chico protested.

"I was still hoping to make dinner at the restaurant," Drake complained.

"The restaurant meal has been postponed until tomorrow," Stella said firmly. "Tomorrow evening, the place has been exclusively booked out for us, and we have organized a meet and greet session with the chef."

That seemed to mollify the discontented billionaires, but only for a moment.

"I'm tired and want to turn in now," Sid said. "Why do we have to stay here? Can't the police come and interview us at our hotels?"

There was a murmur of assent from the group, who were clearly used to being pandered to.

From the corridor, a stern throat clearing, although not loud, seemed to pierce Olivia's eardrums.

The detective was standing, surveying the group. She held Olivia's boots in a plastic bag.

"Since the group is all staying in different hotels, we require that initial interviews be done here, on site. These will be brief. The only other option will be to remove everyone to a communal hotel for the night. The closest place is the three-star Collina Inn. There, they have informed me, six twin-bedded rooms can be made available."

She gazed at the group in a satisfied way.

The billionaires had suddenly gone quiet and were glancing at each other in horror. Olivia could sense the unspoken communication flashing between them.

"Three stars? What are three stars? Are there even pillows in the room or must you bring your own?"

"Hang on! Six rooms, and there are eleven of us? That—that means...!"

"I bet there's no room service there!"

"It sounds full of fleas!"

"This police detective looks like she means what she says!"

After waiting for the group to absorb the consequences of their choices, the detective pointed a stern finger at Sashenka.

"I will start with you," she announced.

Almost as an afterthought, she glanced down at the plastic bag and tossed it in Olivia's direction.

*

By the time everyone had been interviewed, and the driver and tour manager had ferried them back to their various lodgings, it was after ten p.m. Olivia felt exhausted. For once, her half-hour walk home felt like climbing a mountain, and she was grateful beyond words when

92

Marcello insisted, "We must close up now. Let me give you a ride home."

"Thank you," Olivia said.

She locked up, trudged out of the now-dark winery, and climbed into the passenger side of his SUV. Before she could close the door, there was a scamper of hooves as if from nowhere, and Erba rounded the corner at a run.

"Oh dear," Olivia said. She'd hoped that Erba would have gone back to join her goat friends for the night. Now she'd have to shoo her wayward animal all the way back to the dairy again, and hope she stayed there.

"She can ride with me, too," Marcello said kindly.

"Thank you." Relieved that she wouldn't risk the embarrassment of being publicly defied by her goat, Olivia opened the back door and Erba leaped lithely inside.

As Marcello watched the small goat nestle on the seat, Olivia realized this was the first genuine smile she'd seen from him in hours.

"I'm so torn up over what's happened," she confessed, as Marcello headed out of the winery. "I can't stop thinking—why us? Why here?"

Marcello nodded. "My thoughts exactly. This is a catastrophe. I cannot begin to think about what it will mean for our business and how far the negative consequences will reach. It is beyond a nightmare that billionaires, on a famous tour, arrive here and then one dies under suspicious circumstances. This could close us down."

"No! Surely not," Olivia protested, her stomach churning with anxiety.

Heading out of the winery, Marcello shook his head grimly.

"We need to find out what happened," Olivia said. "Maybe it was natural causes after all?"

"Until there is clarity, we are under suspicion and La Leggenda will be talked about in the wrong way. As the owners, our reputations will suffer along with the winery, and I know I will not be welcome at Castello di Verrazzano after this has occurred."

"No!" Olivia cried, aghast to hear him speak the words. The chance of a lifetime, and Marcello would have to turn it down?

Marcello sighed. "We will see what tomorrow brings. The winery will be closed for the day, as it is a potential crime scene and the police will need to search for more evidence."

"I'll come in anyway and help out," Olivia promised. "If there's anything I can do, I'll work on it in the morning. Perhaps we can release an official media statement."

"We will have to wait for the police to finish their investigation into the death," Marcello said. "They have already said they will return to the scene tomorrow and will be doing more interviews. I offered the driver and the tour guide overnight accommodation in two of our guest chalets. After fetching and carrying the group in all directions, they were exhausted, and the detective said she wants to speak to both of them again."

"That's so kind of you," Olivia said.

Marcello stopped the SUV outside the farmhouse.

Olivia climbed out and opened the door for Erba. She wanted to plead with Marcello to sleep on his decision to cancel the mentorship, but before she could say a word, his phone started ringing.

He made a frustrated face before answering it. As he drove away, deep in conversation, Olivia stared after him worriedly. From what she'd picked up, it had been a local calling to find out what had happened at La Leggenda that evening.

Word was already leaking out, and by tomorrow she was sure the whole village would be abuzz with the news.

Olivia fed Erba and then plodded into the farmhouse. What a terrible day this had been. She was too tired to eat, and it was too late to message Danilo. She'd have to call him tomorrow and explain the scale of the catastrophe. She hoped that Danilo would have some good ideas about how to handle it. At any rate, seeing as he would be one of the go-to people for village gossip, he might be able to help manage the situation.

She climbed the stairs wearily, and was met by the sight of Pirate, curled up on her bed and giving her a distrustful glance.

"Oh, Pirate." Gently, Olivia stroked her delicate, post-operative, high-maintenance girl cat. "You've had a terrible day. The worst day of your life. And so have I! We must both be hopeful that things will get better."

Pirate looked dubious at that wisdom. Olivia sensed her cat was taking it with a large pinch of salt.

After a quick shower, she wriggled under the covers, being careful not to disturb her discombobulated feline. She was sure that after the stress and exhaustion, she'd fall asleep in no time, but as her head touched the pillow, her mind started whirling. She couldn't stop

94

thinking about what had happened that day, or erase the moment she'd seen that dark, floating shape in the pond.

And then, Olivia realized the most disturbing fact of all.

She sat up in the darkness, breathing hard, her skin prickling with goose bumps.

It couldn't have been an accidental death. She'd just remembered what Rupert had said in the restaurant. He'd bragged to Drake that he'd been a national triathlete.

A strong swimmer could not have drowned so easily. It simply wasn't possible.

There had been foul play afoot. Olivia had suspected it at the time, and now she was convinced. Someone must have murdered Rupert.

Olivia shivered at the thought of his killer roaming free and the terrible consequences an unsolved crime would have for the winery.

""I'm going to have to investigate this myself, Pirate," Olivia confided to her cat. "This is a desperate situation. The winery's survival and Marcello's career are at stake. And, most importantly of all, Detective Caputi hasn't told me not to. I'm going to make a start first thing tomorrow—and I know who the first suspect is on my list!"

CHAPTER NINETEEN

The next morning, Olivia set off to La Leggenda feeling determined. As she drove, glancing occasionally into the rearview mirror where she could see Erba peering resolutely over her shoulder, she reviewed the available facts. Time was of the essence, so she would need to act fast and have her thoughts in clear order.

Rupert must have been pushed into the pond, she decided. But had someone hit him over the head first? Had a fight or struggle occurred at the edge of the pond and was that why the detective had examined her shoes?

It seemed likely. But no matter exactly how the scene had played out, Olivia knew who the biggest suspect was. Fortunately, thanks to Marcello's kindness, he was staying right here at La Leggenda.

The tour guide was her prime suspect. After all, he'd been the last person she'd seen speaking to Rupert before he'd wandered off to meet his fate in the pond. Rupert had angrily threatened the man and said he'd get him fired. The guide, therefore, had a strong motive for committing the crime.

Excitement flared inside her as she realized that if she handled this right, the case could be solved within an hour. That would solve so many problems and would make all the difference for the winery's reputation as well as Marcello's mentorship at Castello di Verrazzano.

If the crime was not solved fast, people would start regarding the winery as an unsafe place, and rightly so.

"So, if it isn't the driver, we take it in our stride and carry on to the next most likely person. We have a whole group of guests to question and the killer must have been one of them," Olivia told her goat, who was listening intelligently.

Olivia realized that she could play an important role in the questioning process. Perhaps even a critical role. After all, a group of billionaires would naturally be distrustful of the police, who were one of the few entities who had real power over them.

She, on the other hand, could approach the moguls in a non-threatening way. They might well open up to her more readily, especially since they knew her slightly now.

"And especially since Detective Caputi hasn't told me not to get involved!" Olivia reminded Erba triumphantly.

Her instructions had been clear and Olivia remembered the words well. All the detective had said was that she should stay in the area. She was sure that going as far as Florence would still count as "the area." Plus, there hadn't been any sub-clauses about not investigating. The fact Caputi had omitted to say this meant she didn't mind if Olivia stepped in. It might even be a cry for help, she decided.

Turning the car down La Leggenda's driveway, she didn't stop at her usual place in the parking lot but continued along the road, taking the turnoff that led into the hills and to the chalets.

Olivia loved the chalets, and marketing them was among the most enjoyable of her duties. The six well-equipped residences were nestled in a secluded, hilly part of the winery, each one with maximum privacy and gorgeous views.

The paved road wound through a grove of olive trees, and there, ahead of her, was chalet one. Admiring its stone walls, wooden detail, and sloped, tiled roof, Olivia was impressed by how well tended the chalet's small garden was. Its balcony was swept perfectly clean, and the only sign that it wasn't occupied was that all the blinds were down and the curtains drawn.

She carried on past chalets two and three, remembering that these were the larger, family-sized accommodations. It was more likely that Marcello would have assigned a smaller lodging to people staying on their own, and so it proved to be. One looked empty and the other had an unfamiliar-looking car parked outside.

In the carport outside the compact chalet four, she discovered the tour bus.

"If the bus is there, it must be the driver's lodging," Olivia deduced. So she needed to keep looking.

She eased the car around a neatly trimmed hedge, and on to the next building. Feeling nervous, she climbed out. Erba followed her, taking an appreciative look around, before trotting purposefully down the pathway that led to the goat dairy.

Olivia approached the front door and lifted the brass knocker.

Before she could second-guess herself that this might be a bad idea, she knocked loudly.

Olivia waited, feeling her heart pound hard.

Footsteps approached, and a moment later, the door opened.

"*Buon giorno*," the guide said, looking surprised to see her. He was a tall, lean man who was casually dressed this morning in blue jeans and a gray sweater that Olivia thought looked twice as stylish as the ancient and outdated clothing the billionaires had been wearing. "Are the police waiting already? Marcello said we should be ready at ten."

"No, the police aren't here yet. I was wondering if I could ask you a question. We met yesterday but didn't introduce ourselves. My name's Olivia."

Suspicion darkened his face for a moment, and then he moved back.

"I am Luca. Come in," he said, and Olivia stepped inside the chalet's plush, coffee-scented confines.

As he closed the front door behind her, Olivia's confidence evaporated. In its place, doubt and fear rushed in.

How had she managed to act in such a headstrong, irresponsible way? Not a soul knew where she was! If the tour guide had killed once, he could easily do so again. She felt a chill down her spine as she remembered there was another pond within an easy walk of this chalet.

She imagined herself floating in it, undiscovered for weeks or months, while Luca drove her car into the hills and abandoned it there.

"Coffee?" Luca asked from right behind her, and Olivia jumped so violently that her head nearly hit the high ceiling.

"Yes, thank you," she said, hearing the tremble in her own voice. At least making coffee would delay Luca for a moment while she worked out how to compensate for her own reckless actions. She headed to the small lounge. The curtains were open, revealing the large window with a view of the faraway hills and a plantation of sangiovese grapes. Framed paintings of lavender and geranium flowers adorned the opposite wall.

Olivia perched on one of the beige leather couches.

She had to message Danilo, she decided. It was something she should have done before she even left. Danilo needed to know where she was, and what she was up to.

Of course, her phone had hidden away at the bottom of her purse and it felt like eons before she found it. She pulled it out, aware that her hands were quivering with tension, which would make it difficult to write a quick message. Even so, she had to try.

"*Hey Danilo. Just in case you need to find me, I am in—*" she began.

And then Luca reappeared with two steaming cups on a tray.

Panic surged inside her. She hadn't finished her message. She was a few words short of being saved from a terrible fate. Although, perhaps she could bluff her way out of this.

"I was texting my boyfriend," she said with a smile. "I just sent him a message saying how scenic this chalet is. I've never been inside before. It's so pretty and well equipped. Not to mention, the cell signal is excellent. My message was delivered instantly!"

"It is an attractive place," Luca said. He was still looking at her strangely.

"You might be wondering why I'm here," Olivia said in bright tones. She put her cup down on the mahogany side table, deciding she needed to get to the point of her visit, and get out, as soon as possible. Something about the way he was looking at her was making her feel seriously uncomfortable.

"Why are you here?" he asked. Olivia felt her pulse accelerate as she realized he was looking specifically at her neck. She dreaded to think what nefarious thoughts might be running through his mind. She longed to abandon her questioning and flee the chalet, but she was committed now, and had to follow through.

"As you know, I saw Rupert having words with you outside last night, just before he disappeared," Olivia said, observing that Luca's eyes narrowed as she spoke. "Did you see where he went, or notice anyone else follow him out?"

Now Luca's expression tightened and Olivia knew he'd guessed the reason for her visit.

Instead of answering her question, he said in a low but commanding voice, "Be still!"

Olivia let out a terrified yelp as he lunged toward her with his hands outstretched.

CHAPTER TWENTY

Olivia cringed away from Luca as he surged forward. Frantic thoughts rushed through her mind. Was his dark-browed, frowning face going to be the last thing she ever saw?

But, to her astonishment, his hands clasped gently together as they reached her collar.

"A green stinkbug," he said. "I saw it on your jacket when you came in. I am sorry for not telling you. I was worried you would be frightened if you noticed it, and squish it. Then your jacket, and the chalet, would have smelled terrible for the rest of the day!"

"I—well, I might have been a little scared, yes," Olivia agreed, getting up on cotton wool legs and following Luca to the front door. "Thank you for removing it!"

"Let us allow this creature to fly free," he said.

Olivia pushed the door open and Luca stepped outside, opened his hands, and the small, bright green insect took wing into the chilly morning.

"Unusual to see them around in midwinter," Luca observed, as the insect vanished into the distance.

Olivia felt her shattered confidence regroup. There had been a reason for Luca's odd behavior, and from the episode that had just played out, he seemed like a kind person who loved innocent creatures, no matter their size or smell.

She followed Luca back inside and sat down again. This time, she felt calm enough to sip her coffee. Even though she didn't need the caffeine after the nerve-tingling incident that had just played out, the taste of the rich brew, with a dash of foamed milk, was soothing and delicious.

"So, you want to know about Rupert?" Luca asked, frowning as he reached for his own cup. "You are not the only one. The police, too, have been pestering me for information."

"Why is that?" Olivia asked.

"They wanted to know what had happened between Rupert and me. Did you tell them he had insulted and threatened me? That lady detective asked me a lot of questions, and said she would be back this morning, in case I had forgotten to tell her anything."

Olivia shrugged ruefully.

"Yes, I did tell the detective," she confessed. "I thought I'd better say everything I knew, as others might also have overheard. I explained to her that I threatened Rupert, too."

Luca sighed.

"I understand. Telling the full truth is always the best choice. As I said to the detective, I love my job! What a dream to manage a luxury coach touring the best parts of Italy, and to make sure that the guests on board are well looked after. Never would I risk my career, or the company's reputation, by committing such a terrible act. And if I had reason to suspect anyone had done it, I would tell the police, because I am worried that an unsolved crime like this might damage the business."

Olivia thought that Luca sounded passionate, and she appreciated the logic of his words and his desire to protect his job. She nodded, hoping that he would feel motivated to continue.

"I am used to guests complaining. Wealthy people can be exacting and any guest can become unreasonably angry if they are in the wrong mood. The management understands. If they can see I am doing my job well and getting good reports, they will not take action if one customer says he wants me fired."

"That makes sense," Olivia said. It seemed working with "exacting guests" who would vent their displeasure on whoever was nearest was an unavoidable part of the luxury tour business. How surprising to learn such behavior was not unusual.

Although it appeared Luca had no motive to commit the crime, Olivia didn't want to rule out her prime suspect without examining every angle. After all, he could have snapped in a moment of anger, and be lying smoothly to conceal what he had done.

"Where did you go after you and Rupert had words?" she asked.

"Marcello sent me to get a bucket of soapy water and a towel, so that everyone could wash their hands quickly after the repairs were done. I had a cigarette on the way, and then hurried into the scullery to do what he asked. When the bucket was filled, I took it straight back to the bus, and continued helping out until the guests boarded."

Olivia nodded. She remembered noticing the bucket which everyone had used for a clean-up. Plus, Luca had been at the bus when the repairs were wrapping up. Therefore, his time was accounted for and he would have had no opportunity to commit this crime.

"Who do you think could have done such a thing?" she then asked, hoping Luca would be willing to share his observations.

Luca tapped a thoughtful rhythm on his coffee cup. "I have not spent enough time with the guests to know them well. La Leggenda was only the second stop on the tour, after a visit to a designer menswear factory."

Olivia nodded thoughtfully. The winery had been the place where conflicts had escalated. Based on that, she knew who the next person on her suspect list was. But how could she find out his whereabouts?

Perhaps Luca would be willing to help.

"You fetched and carried all the guests," she said. "Would you mind telling me where they stayed?"

Luca looked horrified. In that moment, Olivia understood she'd made a huge mistake. Of course he wouldn't tell her a thing, if he thought she was going to rush off and harass his VIP guests.

It was just after eight a.m. and she'd already made her second strategic error of the day. Olivia felt like smacking herself upside the head. She had to stop being so impulsive. Thinking fast, she came up with a reason to reassure Luca.

"I'm asking because I need to do some PR," she explained in confidential tones. "Stella said that if the group enjoyed themselves, they might want to come back next year. But I'm worried they have been put off the winery after this death. I would like to visit their hotels and drop off a gift of wine for each of them."

Luca considered her words for a while and then nodded, to Olivia's relief.

"That sounds like a good idea," he agreed. "I can provide the hotel names. The room numbers, I am not sure of. I arrived at reception and they called the guests."

That put a small spoke in the wheel of Olivia's plans, but she thought she could handle it. After all, the moguls were confined to their lodgings while the police wrapped up their questioning. How hard could it be to find them there?

"That would be so helpful. We're all hoping they come back next year," Olivia said, even though she wasn't sure if she meant it.

"Shall I write the names down?"

"Please!"

Olivia waited while Luca thumbed through his phone, accessing his trip records. Interviewing the billionaires would be a tricky process, she decided. She would have to be careful what she said. If powerful people became offended, they could destroy the winery's reputation—but she reminded herself that an unsolved murder would be even more damaging for La Leggenda.

She'd be walking a tightrope, so it would be best if she really did arrive with gifts of wine and use this to start the conversation.

"Drake and Sid are staying at the Platino Toscana," Luca announced, scribbling on a notepad. Olivia nodded, glad to know the whereabouts of her biggest suspect. Drake surely had the strongest motive for murder. After all, he'd argued nonstop with Rupert during the wine tasting, and almost come to blows with him.

"Chico and Aldo are at the Gardens of Florence." Luca thumbed carefully through his list. "Bernie is at Villa Fiora. Carmody is staying with friends who own Villa Laggio. Hamilton is also in a private residence, Villa Tivoli just outside the village. Sashenka and Jose are at the Terrazzo Magnifico, and Ferdie and Tomas are staying at the Terrazzo Moderna down the road from the Magnifico. I think that's everyone."

He checked his list again before ripping out the page and handing it to her.

"I'll be glad to be able to give them a positive memory of La Leggenda. I appreciate your help," Olivia said.

At that moment, her phone buzzed with an incoming message. She checked it, alarmed to see it was from Marcello.

"Can you come in now? We are having an emergency meeting at eight-thirty."

"I have to go to the winery now." Quickly, Olivia stood up. "Thank you for the information. I hope your police interview goes well."

Luca grimaced. "I hope so, too."

As she headed out, Olivia's phone started ringing.

She grabbed it immediately, expecting that it would be Marcello. Instead, it was Danilo, and she felt a flash of guilt. She'd meant to call him, or at least message, first thing this morning, but she'd ended up rushing off on her urgent mission.

"Olivia!" Danilo's voice was filled with concern. "What is happening? People have been calling me since early this morning with awful news. They said there was another death at La Leggenda, and the whispers are that it is suspicious. Are you all right? I came around as soon as I could, but the only person at the farm is Pirate." Danilo paused and said, sounding curious, "He seems well, but why does he have a shaved triangle on his side?"

Olivia took a deep breath as she climbed into her car. There was a lot to update Danilo on. She wasn't sure which important news should take priority. In the end, she decided to go with the feline bombshell first.

"The vet discovered that Pirate is female," she told him. "She had a spay, not a neuter. They did keyhole surgery with dissolving stitches so that Pirate won't have to come back, which is very clever, seeing she bit the vet, and there's no guarantee of getting her into a carrier again!"

There was a brief, stunned silence. Then Danilo spoke again, his voice filled with wonderment.

"A girl! That is amazing, Olivia!"

She couldn't suppress a pleased grin. Danilo sounded as delighted as if he'd just learned the gender of his firstborn.

"Yes. It explains a lot."

"How well-mannered and loving she is. And her smaller, dainty size. Imagine all this time, you have had the care of a beautiful girl cat! Good, good kitty Pirate."

From Danilo's cooing tone, Olivia was sure he was gently petting the cat as he spoke. She felt her heart melt. It was moments like these that gave her hope that things could work between them.

"I'm glad you're there to visit her. She needs lots of sympathy from people who aren't me, as she's still angry with me," Olivia said, knowing that this would bring the conversation circling back to the reason for Danilo's arrival at her farm, and where, exactly, Olivia was.

"This death," Danilo said, sounding worried again. "Please, tell me."

Olivia turned the car around, driving back toward the main winery buildings.

"It was one of the Platinum Tour guests. The bus broke down yesterday so they had to spend longer here. They got very drunk. There was one man who was being obnoxious and fighting with the others."

Danilo drew in his breath. "And he was found dead?"

"He appears to have drowned in a pond," Olivia affirmed sadly, thinking again of how Rupert had bragged about his triathlon prowess.

"This is unbelievable," Danilo muttered. "Do the police suspect foul play?"

"They're still investigating, but I am sure they do."

"I guess you must be at work now? There must be so much to handle after a tragic event like this," Danilo sympathized.

"I'm heading to the winery now. I've been up at the chalets, asking the tour manager some questions."

"You are investigating?" Danilo's voice sounded sharp, and Olivia felt a stab of apprehension. It sounded as if Danilo wasn't pleased, but she didn't know if that was because he was worried for her, or because he disapproved, or both.

"I need to try and clear the winery's name. You can imagine what a disaster this is. We could all lose our jobs," she replied, picking up the defensiveness in her own voice.

"Yes, but—Olivia, you might end up in danger! And what if you get into trouble with that scary detective, because the police want to handle it without interference?"

Olivia felt astounded. Was Danilo insinuating she was incompetent? After he'd personally been there when she'd solved the previous crime she'd been caught up in?

"I'm just asking a few questions," she retorted.

"The police will think you are meddling!"

"They haven't told me not to," she tried.

"If you keep getting in their way, they will notice you," Danilo insisted.

"I'm not getting in anyone's way!"

"What will you do if you are arrested? I will have to come and bail you out of prison!"

Now Olivia felt her hackles rise. She knew that for the sake of their relationship she should answer diplomatically, but as an angry retort spilled out of her mouth, she realized this insult had stabbed too deep for her to pretend it didn't hurt.

CHAPTER TWENTY ONE

"Bail me out? What on earth do you mean by that? Are you saying I'm going to be arrested for trying to help solve this crime?" Olivia snapped at Danilo, aghast that their conversation had taken such an accusatory turn. Angrily, she continued. "Actually, don't bother telling me what you mean. I don't have time for this pointless discussion, since I'm very busy trying to fix things. I have to go into an urgent meeting now and won't have time to speak to you for the rest of the day. In fact, I'll be busy tomorrow, too!"

Dramatically, Olivia extended the timeline of her non-availability, hoping that this would show Danilo just how offended she was.

Huffing in outrage, she ended the call without saying goodbye, and turned her phone off.

She climbed out of her car feeling prickly all over, as if she'd been caught up in a fight she hadn't even seen coming.

Despite his wonderful attitude toward animals, she knew she was going to have to have strong words with her new boyfriend. Why was he not supporting her in her urgent mission to save the winery? And why did he think that trying to help made her guilty in some way?

Of course, a moment later, she started feeling terrible about what she'd done. Thinking back on the conversation, she suspected Danilo might not have meant exactly what he said. There could have been language nuances that had been lost in the brief phone call. She hadn't given him time to explain, or asked what he meant, but had just callously disconnected.

"Well, I was hurt," Olivia muttered, trying not to think about the fact that Danilo had rushed straight to her farm to check on her, and had ended up giving much-needed attention to her recuperating cat.

Thinking about how hurt she was didn't help. By the time Olivia entered the tasting room, she was feeling thoroughly guilty at not having heard Danilo out, or properly understood the gist of what he was saying. After the stern talking to she'd given herself about not rushing headlong into things, she'd gone and done the same again, this time to her boyfriend!

Her tempestuous outburst could have caused long-term damage to their relationship.

Sighing, Olivia headed inside, resolving to call Danilo later, after they'd both had a chance to calm down. Then she would apologize. There was no time now, because Marcello was already striding into the restaurant, where a table had been set up for the meeting. Gabriella was already seated, looking worried and wearing a somber black jacket, and Nadia was pulling out a chair next to her, grimacing in a stressed way. Running footsteps behind her signaled that Jean-Pierre was hurrying to take his place as fast as he could.

They glanced anxiously at each other as they sat. With an apology, Antonio rushed in. His hair was mussed and his boots were covered in mud.

Olivia saw Gabriella glance at the footprints absently, and guessed that she was too distracted to tell him off for dirtying her floors.

"We are unfortunately heading into a worse disaster than I expected." Marcello opened the meeting, speaking in grim tones. "Since last night, I have been contacted by many of our suppliers in the area, a few different news sites, and innumerable of our winery neighbors and friends. Nobody can believe that another murder has occurred here, and in far more serious circumstances. I cannot understand it myself."

He sighed. Looking at the stress etched on his face, Olivia doubted he'd had any sleep at all. He must have spent most of the night fielding the storm of inquiries.

Gabriella took a deep breath.

"I would like the reckless individuals among us to remember, it was I who said the tour was a bad idea!" she announced in triumphant tones. "Perhaps certain people attract these disasters?" she added helpfully, with a pointed glance in Olivia's direction.

Olivia stared down at the table, feeling ashamed. After all, the murders had happened since she'd arrived and what if she was bringing the bad luck? Worse still, her vote had been the deciding one for the tour. She had landed the winery in trouble again!

A thump on the table jerked her out of her somber reverie and she looked hurriedly up.

"We will not speak that way here! This is not the time for unhelpful comments that cause division," Marcello retorted in a voice close to a shout, glowering at Gabriella as he slammed his fist down on the table again.

Olivia had never seen him so smolderingly angry. Briefly, she thought that his relationship with Gabriella must have been impossibly stormy.

"There will be no blaming others! Not today, and not in the future!" Marcello glared at everyone as he reiterated his point.

A brief silence followed. Olivia exchanged a scared glance with Jean-Pierre and Nadia.

"What have you told the people who called?" Nadia dared to ask.

"I have advised them to wait for the police report. The death may have been due to natural causes." Marcello's voice resounded with disbelief as he said the words. Across the table, Gabriella nodded, clearly eager to atone for her earlier sniping.

"Exactly. It is very likely. Everyone has to die sometime, even billionaires," she said.

"Surely people in our village cannot jump to conclusions before the investigation is done?" Jean-Pierre asked.

Marcello sighed. "Unfortunately, they can and will. The longer this takes, the worse it will be for us. Our winery is already linked to this high-profile businessman's death. We must remain hopeful that this will fizzle out once the autopsy and toxicology reports are done."

Marcello looked deeply unhappy. His next words came as a shock.

"While hoping for the best, we must prepare for the worst. I have decided to decline the offer of mentorship at Castello di Verrazzano. It will be best if I withdraw with dignity at this early stage, rather than waiting until we are embroiled in scandal, when they may not be willing to have me there."

"No!" Olivia pleaded, feeling as if her world was imploding.

She was astonished to find that Gabriella cried out the same word, at exactly the same moment.

"Marcello, you cannot!" the other woman entreated. "This is your career goal! Memories are short. In a few weeks, people will have moved onto other scandals and not worry about who died here or why."

Olivia suspected that Gabriella was hell bent on getting the chance to manage the winery for a while, and that she was more concerned about being able to force Olivia out, than enhancing Marcello's career prospects. When Gabriella gave her a quick, sidelong glance, Olivia's fears were confirmed.

Even so, this was a chance for her to show team spirit by agreeing with her rival.

"Gabriella is right. The mentorship will provide valuable further education at a critical time when organic is becoming a huge selling point."

"Besides, your learning residence at the Castello shouldn't be influenced by events that happened at this winery," Gabriella added.

"I'm sure that if there was any foul play, the police will soon arrest the culprit," Olivia concluded.

She decided it would be better not to mention that she was trying to help with the investigation. After Danilo's negative reaction, she didn't want to stress Marcello any further.

She saw a strange expression flit across Gabriella's face, but didn't have time to wonder why the restaurateur looked momentarily haunted. She was too busy focusing on Marcello's reaction to her words.

"Even if the invitation stands, we will need to focus on damage control," Marcello continued in gloomy tones. "It will be touch and go whether our business survives this reputational disaster. I will not have time to do the mentorship, when my time needs to go toward saving our winery."

To Olivia's surprise, Nadia spoke next.

"We are all capable of answering a phone!" the fiery vintner exclaimed. "I deal with the suppliers as often as you do, in any case. They are the ones who matter. If we need to keep their business, I will be their go-to."

Olivia felt encouraged by her passionate support. She didn't think anyone would dare to cancel an order when Nadia was on the other end of the line.

"At the least, think it over for another day or two," Olivia entreated. "Imagine if you decline the invitation, and then the case is solved and the winery is cleared?"

Steely resolve filled Olivia as she fretted over Marcello's predicament. It was a race against time to find the culprit, and she needed results by tomorrow at the latest, given the groundswell of gossip that was building. Marcello's future was in crisis, and Detective Caputi was a busy woman. What if she was also dealing with other cases, and didn't have time to solve this one quick enough?

Olivia had already begun her questioning, and could fill her day with visits. After all, the winery was closed and she had nothing else to do.

Marcello sighed, glancing at Antonio. Olivia guessed he was hoping for support in his decision, but even Antonio looked reluctant to agree.

"All right. It may well be that I am thinking too emotionally in this matter," Marcello said. "I will wait one more day before deciding. In the meantime, if anyone asks, let us all stick to the same version. There was a death at the winery, a high-profile tourist passed away, and the police are investigating as a matter of routine."

That sounded good, Olivia thought. It was clear, factual, and didn't immediately spark any suspicion. Although she was sure everyone in the village would be imagining the worst, embellishing new details every time they met anyone.

As she got to her feet, she wondered again about Gabriella's strange expression.

Goose bumps prickled her spine as she recalled how furious the restaurateur had been when Rupert had criticized her Wagyu beef so rudely.

Perhaps she didn't even need to visit the hotels to interview the suspects.

The perpetrator might be right here, in this very room.

Olivia watched suspiciously as Gabriella hotfooted it into the kitchen. There was no reason for her to be in such a rush when the restaurant was closed today. She didn't have any urgent food prep to do.

Olivia rummaged in her purse, pretending to search for something, until the others had gone. Then she followed the restaurateur into her domain, feeling like a cat stalking its prey.

CHAPTER TWENTY TWO

As Olivia entered the tidy kitchen, she remembered with a flare of suspicion that Gabriella had already proved herself capable of switching good wine with bad. Who knew how much further her antisocial actions could have led her?

She let out a huff of annoyance when she saw Gabriella perched on the stool at the far end of the counter, scrolling through her phone. See? She hadn't rushed off to do urgent chores. She'd left so that Olivia couldn't ask her anything.

When Gabriella saw her, she put her phone away and summoned up her customary scowl.

"What is it? I am busy!" she snapped.

"I'm so sorry to interrupt your work," Olivia said sweetly. "However, I wanted to ask you something very important."

Gabriella folded her arms. Olivia noted the defensive body language.

"I do not have time," she said dismissively, climbing off her stool.

"Are you about to start some food prep?" Olivia said in an innocent voice, gazing at the empty counters.

"I am researching recipes," Gabriella said. "It is something I need to do in peace and quiet." She glared at Olivia.

"It's lucky you have the whole day to do it since the winery is closed," Olivia said, deciding to redirect the conversation where she needed it to go.

"I will not have the whole day, if people stand here taking up my time! Why are you even in this kitchen? Go and do something useful. Groom your goat!"

With every word Gabriella said, Olivia became more convinced that something was afoot. She needed to turn up the pressure, and hope she could shock the other woman into a confession.

"I came to ask you about Rupert. Did you kill him?" she asked sternly.

Gabriella physically recoiled in outrage.

"Me?" she squealed, tapping herself on the chest with a well-manicured finger. "Me, do such a thing? I cannot believe you are trying to accuse me, when I was being so loyal to the winery by saying nothing about the fact you clearly did it!" Now the same manicured finger stabbed the air in Olivia's direction.

"Me?" Olivia cried, waving her arms indignantly. She felt blindsided by the sheer cheek of the other woman's incorrect assumptions.

"Yes, you! It's obvious—to me, anyway. Paolo said that awful man was hounding you incessantly while the group was here. Then you magically go outside to 'find' him and you 'find' him dead?"

Olivia shook her head angrily. "I would never prejudice the tour, or the winery, that way," she said, hoping Gabriella picked up on the meaning in her words. "Unlike some people, I don't go around substituting cooking wine for the Miracolo blend, in the hope that I will get one of my co-workers into trouble. It's a small step from doing something like that to committing murder, and in fact it could even have been done using the same methods! I think I should call Detective Caputi this instant and explain everything to her."

She glowered at Gabriella, satisfied to see the other woman turn pale.

"Don't call the police. I am innocent!" she snapped defensively.

"You will have to sell that idea to me more convincingly," Olivia said, pleased to have her rival firmly on the back foot, and ready to confess to the crime.

"I didn't switch the wine to get you in trouble, I promise," Gabriella said fervently.

Olivia rolled her eyes, making sure Gabriella saw.

"Oh, really? Why did you do it?"

"I was angry at how they did not take us seriously. Those wealthy people did not want a wine tasting. They wanted servants to fill their glasses while they drank, and cared only about their own opinions. Switching the wine was my own private joke, laughing at these idiots who lack taste and who did not appreciate our wines. I doubt any of them would have noticed, but I would have giggled as I watched them drink."

Olivia didn't fully believe the story, but had to admit that the other woman did have a point. None of the moguls had been properly appreciative of the wines.

"Drake was a red wine lover," she countered in firm tones, needing to stay on the attack. "And that cooking wine smelled so vile, anyone would have picked up a problem. Does it dissolve the meat completely if you marinate it for too long?"

"It is not a bad wine. Rough and ready peasant wine. Here, taste!"

To Olivia's alarm, Gabriella turned to a large, gourd-shaped glass bottle on the counter, grabbed a tumbler from a cupboard, and poured a half-inch of the wine inside.

"I already smelled it," Olivia protested.

"It tastes better than it smells!"

Olivia sighed, raising the glass to her lips. This wasn't the way she'd intended this confrontation to play out. Drinking wine with Gabriella was not where she'd thought she would find herself.

"It does taste a little better," she had to admit.

"See?" Gabriella said triumphantly.

"You still had the opportunity to lace the food or drink with something harmful," Olivia insisted.

Gabriella sighed.

"Drink the rest of your wine! Perhaps it will help you to think clearly. By the time that odious man insulted my food, all the dishes had been prepared. How was I supposed to return to the kitchen, find a toxic substance, add it to a delicacy that most probably one of the others would have grabbed, and try to make sure he ate it?"

Olivia nodded reluctantly. Unfortunately, Gabriella's logic made sense.

"And no, I did not follow him outside and push him into the water. As you saw, I was very busy in the kitchen, right up until the police arrived. They were giving me no peace, with their demands for grilled cheese."

"Well, I was equally busy," Olivia said. "The guests were knocking back the wine, whether they appreciated it or not. I didn't have time to go roaming around the grounds in the hope that I might find Rupert near the pond, and then trip him up and push him in, after knocking him out with a weapon I didn't possess."

Gabriella gave a disappointed sigh. "Okay. True. I accept you didn't do it."

"Someone did, though, and I'm going to find out who," Olivia vowed. She put her glass down and left the kitchen, feeling determined.

As soon as she was out of sight of Gabriella, she detoured to the bar, where Paolo was replenishing the stash of whiskey and restocking the wine fridge.

This was the perfect chance to check Gabriella's version, she thought. Paolo had been working closely with her yesterday and would know if she'd disappeared for a while.

"*Buon giorno*," she greeted him.

Paolo looked suitably solemn. "Olivia, I am worried. Do you think they will find the killer? Everyone has been saying this might mean we have to close. And I love my job!"

"It's very concerning," Olivia said.

"I wish I had noticed more." Paolo gestured expansively toward the restaurant. "I was so busy, though! Running back and forward, carrying drinks, clearing glasses. I was only focused on my work. There was no time to observe."

"And Gabriella? Might she have seen something? Maybe she stepped out for a breath of fresh air?" Olivia asked casually.

Paolo shook his head, looking frustrated. "I doubt it. She was—how do you say—chained to the stove? She only left the kitchen to bring food through. Making those extra trays of food after the prepared snacks were finished was crazy work. She was not ready for it and had to rush around. In between my bar service, I fetched ingredients from the freezer room and cold room, to help her. The guests went mad for that food! You would think they had never eaten a grilled cheese panini before. We were all out of cheese by the time they left," Paolo said.

Olivia nodded. Paolo had confirmed what Gabriella had said. The two of them had, without a doubt, been busy throughout the evening and would not have had time to plan or commit the crime.

"I know the group scattered just before we called them to the bus. Do you know if any of them stayed inside, apart from Carmody and Jose?" she asked.

Paolo nodded. "The red-headed Scotsman helped clear the dishes. I thought it was really kind of him, although there was no need for it. He carried quite a number of plates and glasses into the kitchen. Then he started chatting to Gabriella and raiding the fridge, looking for chocolates!"

Olivia remembered that Hamilton had been peering enthusiastically into the fridge when she'd returned to say the bus was fixed. She felt pleased that she now had four suspects struck off her list, including Paolo. And the morning was still young.

Thinking of time, a new suspicion surfaced in Olivia's mind. If the tour bus hadn't broken down, everyone would have climbed on board and left the winery alive and well.

Had the breakdown been coincidence?

Or had it been sabotage, deliberately committed by the killer, in order to keep the group at the winery while he—or she—did the deed under cover of darkness?

With that thought in mind, Olivia climbed into her car and headed purposefully back to the chalets.

CHAPTER TWENTY THREE

Olivia hadn't figured that she'd be heading back to La Leggenda's chalets so soon. She felt relieved that the driver was on site, thanks to Marcello's kind offer of accommodation.

Had the bus been sabotaged?

Purposefully, Olivia headed to the chalet where it was parked.

The door opened as soon as she knocked. The driver was holding the keys and looked ready to head out. He wasn't in his official uniform, so she guessed he was going to the village to pick up some breakfast, before heading to the winery for his police interview.

"Good morning," he greeted her, looking surprised.

"I thought I'd pop in to say hello," Olivia said. "I hope you're feeling better after the terrible day we all had yesterday."

"I am, yes." The driver nodded. "What a day it was! And all caused by the bus breaking down."

Glad that she was able to get to the point, as she was sure the driver was in a hurry to leave, she gestured to the dark, gleaming vehicle.

"Has it had problems before?"

"Up until now, this bus has been totally reliable. It is a beautiful machine, and a joy to drive," he said. "It is the perfect vehicle to seat thirteen guests, as there is room for sixteen, so they can sit comfortably."

Clearly, the driver was misremembering the numbers, as Olivia knew there had only been twelve tour members on the bus. But his comment opened the door for her to ask the question she needed to.

"What exactly was the damage? Do you know how it occurred?"

"Ah, it was very unfortunate!" His eyes lighting up with the prospect of discussing mechanical issues, the driver launched into a detailed explanation. It contained quite a few specialized phrases in Italian, and was accompanied by the expressive waving of arms. Narrowing her eyes in concentration, Olivia tried to understand the gist of it.

She was pleased to realize that she could pick up more of this technical talk than she'd expected, and was able to translate quite a few words. Even though there were some unfamiliar mechanical terms,

Olivia didn't think she'd have understood those in English either. Her Italian was progressing well.

"So, basically, you're saying that a stone caused the damage?" she asked, when he'd concluded with a final energetic sweep of his hands.

"A stone, yes, absolutely!" he agreed enthusiastically.

Olivia's suspicions started prickling. Had it been an accident, or could the perpetrator have used a rock or brick to cause the damage?

"Could someone have done that on purpose?" she asked.

The driver looked alarmed. Clearly, he hadn't considered that possibility until now.

"What a thought!" he exclaimed. "I suppose the problem could have been deliberately caused. It could also have been accidental. It is hard to tell. I hope it was accidental. It is terrible to think someone might have damaged this beautiful bus, to delay the tour for their own reasons." He shivered theatrically.

"If you notice, or remember, anything that might point to it being deliberately caused, can you call me? My cell number is on this card," Olivia said. She handed over one of her business cards. She felt proud of the beautiful cards, designed by herself, with gold lettering etched on an oaken-brown background. As part of her marketing campaign for La Leggenda, Olivia had made business cards for everyone working in the winery, and always kept a few in her purse.

"I will certainly do so." Nodding a friendly goodbye, the driver headed to his gleaming bus and climbed inside. It started smoothly and purred away as if nothing had ever been wrong with it at all.

Olivia headed back to her own car, feeling thoughtful. She wished that the driver had been able to give her a firm yes or no. As it was, though, she couldn't rule out sabotage.

Her next stop was back at the winery to prepare the gift packs for her interviews with the billionaires. She'd have to get them together in a hurry, or risk bumping into Detective Caputi when she arrived.

The winery's main doors were closed, though not locked. Opening them quietly and tiptoeing inside, Olivia heard Marcello speaking on the phone in his office. He sounded stressed.

She headed into the storage room to prepare her wine gifts, making sure to note down the stock numbers and prices of each bottle, so she could include these items in her marketing budget. She and Marcello had discussed the budget together, back in the fall. Now, Olivia felt glad to be using some of it for such a constructive purpose.

117

Working fast, she packaged up the pretty boxes which would provide her excuse for visiting the moguls. She chose duos of the Miracolo red and her rosé, which seemed to have been the most popular with the guests, each elegantly placed in a white-and-gold La Leggenda carrier, with her business card and a raffia bow.

Olivia thought they looked gorgeous. She carried them to the car in two batches and placed them carefully in the trunk.

She was pleased that with the police revisiting La Leggenda, she would have the morning open to question her key suspects within the group. After all, even though Detective Caputi was a skilled multi-tasker, she couldn't be in two places at once!

Her timing was perfect. As she turned left onto the main road, she saw Detective Caputi's gray Fiat appear over the hill from the opposite direction, indicating to turn into the winery.

The closest accommodations on the list was the Platino Toscana, where Drake and Sid were staying. Drake was on the top of Olivia's list of potential murderers, thanks to his angry confrontation with Rupert. He definitely had a motive, and had seemed eager to get physical, she remembered. He could have followed the older man outside to continue the fight.

Pleased that she was going to be able to interview her prime suspect first, Olivia headed eagerly to the luxury five-star hotel.

The Platino Toscana was well frequented by sports lovers. It had one of the most famous golf courses in the area. A keen supporter of local businesses, their excellent restaurant and wine cellar featured many of La Leggenda's wines.

She pulled up outside the hotel, glad that this establishment didn't have any stringent privacy protocols in place. She knew she might not be so lucky with some of the others, which were designed to keep their VIP guests far away from the public eye.

Heading confidently inside, Olivia greeted the receptionist.

"I have gifts for Drake Rafter and Sid Murray," she said. "Could you call them, or tell me where I can find them, as I'm sure they'll want to receive them personally."

The receptionist nodded, smiling. "Of course," she said, picking up a phone.

Olivia waited, her gung-ho evaporating as she listened to it ring unanswered.

Then the woman tried another extension. This, too, rang.

"They didn't leave the hotel, did they?" Olivia asked anxiously. Would the two men have dared to defy Detective Caputi's orders?

The receptionist tapped her fingers on the desk thoughtfully. Then she made a third call and spoke rapidly for a minute. The conversation was in Italian, but Olivia picked up that she was speaking with the clubhouse manager, who then transferred her to the pro shop.

Disconnecting, she gave Olivia a regretful smile.

"They are on the golf course," she said, confirming Olivia's suspicions.

Her heart plummeted. There was no way she could afford to spend hours searching the busy, eighteen-hole course for two men, dressed in golf shirts and golf caps like all the other players. She would end up causing mayhem, ruining drives and spoiling putts as she tried to get close enough to recognize them. Never mind interrupting their play if she actually managed to find them! That would be a cardinal crime.

"I will come back later," she said regretfully. She guessed that if they were out already, they'd be finished by mid-afternoon. Her most important suspect would have to wait, but luckily there were others she could question in the meantime.

Just down the road from the Platino Toscana was Villa Fiora, a tiny and ultra-elite hotel that catered for very small groups. Olivia had never been inside, but had heard it offered twenty-four-hour VIP service and two personal butlers per guest.

This was where Bernie was staying. The talk in the village was that the place was almost fully booked year round, and was a sought-after destination for celebrities and movie stars.

As she turned down the road that led to the villa, Olivia wondered excitedly if Bernie might be sharing with someone famous. She had a bucket list of movie stars she wanted to meet. Bumping into visiting royalty would also be amazing, she thought, turning into the ornate gateway.

The gate was closed and a doorman rushed to her car. From the look on his face, Olivia guessed he knew she was a mere commoner. Her humble Fiat would have clued him from a mile away.

"I've got a package for Bernie Cooper," she said, giving him a winning smile.

The doorman looked stern.

"I am afraid I cannot allow you in," he said. "You may sign the package over to me, and I will hand it to him."

Olivia goggled at him in consternation. "But I need to deliver it personally," she protested. "It's all part of our winery's excellent service. I work for La Leggenda, a couple of miles away. You may have heard of it."

The doorman stared at her impassively.

"Protecting guests from unwanted visitors is part of our excellent service," he retorted calmly.

Olivia rolled her eyes. She felt frustrated by this man's annoying refusal to let her, an innocent sommelier and amateur sleuth, through the gate.

Getting into a fight with this obnoxious and stubborn doorman would get her precisely nowhere, irritated as she was. Her only hope was to grit her teeth and use all her reserves of charm.

"I totally understand." She smiled sweetly. "Privacy is so important. However, I wasn't aware of this rule." She fluttered her eyelashes at him in a pleading way. "My boss told me that I must hand the wine to Bernie myself, and I really don't want to get into trouble or lose my job. I'd hate to be fired! So, what can you suggest to help?"

The doorman tapped his chin thoughtfully. He seemed to have thawed toward her, and Olivia was filled with relief that her friendly approach had worked.

"Call the hotel and speak to the receptionist," he advised. "You may then arrange a time to drop off the gift at the hotel's reception. Request to hand it over yourself, and they will then notify the guest. It will be his choice whether to see you or not."

Olivia nodded in thanks. She hoped Bernie would agree to be there when she made the appointment. If he didn't—well, at least she'd be in the hotel and a step closer to him.

"Thank you. I'll do that."

She drove off, making the call as soon as she was around the corner and he couldn't see her.

"I will inform the guest, *signora*," the receptionist told her in highfalutin tones. "What time will you arrive?"

Olivia was tempted to tell her she'd be there in two minutes. But she sensed she'd be setting herself up for failure. Even though she was a short walk away from the gate, she needed to exercise restraint.

"At eleven-thirty this morning?" she asked.

"I will note the time. Thank you," the receptionist said.

Olivia disconnected with a frustrated sigh. So far, her investigation was proving fruitless. She'd not managed to interview a single billionaire, and was starting to feel nervous that Detective Caputi would catch up with her. The detective was an impatient person, and Olivia had no doubt she'd be hot on her heels as soon as she'd finished up at the winery.

Checking her list, Olivia saw that the next closest lodging was the private villa Hamilton was occupying. Although he had an alibi, thanks to what Paolo had told her, he had been the most friendly and talkative of the group, and had interacted with many of the other guests, including Rupert. There was a good chance he could have seen or heard something important.

She headed up the hill to his lodging, feeling hopeful that this would be a worthwhile interview. The clock was ticking, and the pressure was on!

CHAPTER TWENTY FOUR

Villa Tivoli had no doorman shielding it from the outside world. However, the massive, secluded property had a high wall, a solid gate, and a doorbell with a buzzer to gain entry.

Olivia pressed the buzzer and announced herself over the intercom. She felt a rush of adrenaline when the massive gate slid open.

The winding driveway was lined with close-packed ranks of cypress trees. Olivia followed its paved perfection until the house came into view.

It looked as she'd anticipated, like a Tuscan wedding cake on steroids. It was decorated with turrets and pergolas and so much ocher paint that Olivia was sure worldwide supplies had been exhausted.

She parked outside the quadruple garage and walked up to the front door where Hamilton was waiting. His red hair was spiky and unbrushed. He was wearing tattered camouflage pants of questionable integrity, and an Aberdeen Football Club T-shirt.

"Come in, come in, lassie. You've brought us wine? How very kind. Morag? Morag, we have a visitor," he called, as he strutted ahead of her over the gleaming, sun-washed interior tiles, past ocher walls lined with a multitude of plants.

Morag?

Olivia hadn't considered that some of the tour might have their families with them. Why hadn't Morag been there yesterday? Perhaps the significant others had preferred shopping to wine tasting, she thought, bemused.

Hamilton made a beeline for the kitchen, where the mouthwatering scent of cooking salmon met them.

A tanned brunette with long, wavy hair and a perfect figure was juggling pots and pans at the stove.

"This is Olivia, the wine waitress from yesterday," he told her proudly. "And this is my wife," he told Olivia, sounding equally proud. "Morag loves cooking. You can't tear her away from the kitchen. It's why we don't stay in hotels much."

"So good to meet you," Morag enthused, glancing over her shoulder and giving Olivia a dazzling smile.

She really was gorgeous, Olivia decided, relieved by her friendliness as she smiled back. From a glance at her stylish pants and designer top, her fabulous shoes and expensive but understated jewelry, she guessed Morag enjoyed shopping. In contrast to her husband, who clearly hadn't updated his wardrobe since his college days, Olivia thought with an inward smile.

"Brunch is almost ready. I've made enough for an army. Since you've brought us wine, I do hope you'll stay for a bite?" Morag asked. She turned around, leaving Olivia spellbound by her colorful Dolce & Gabbana apron.

Olivia thought she shouldn't, and that it was pushing the boundaries of accepted protocol too far. But if she declined, she'd have to leave in a hurry to let them get to their food.

Plus, she was starving. She'd missed dinner last night and only had a quick cup of coffee at Luca's chalet this morning.

"That's so kind," she accepted gratefully.

"Sit down, sit down."

Hamilton herded her over to the kitchen table—an expanse of polished oak, with colorful place mats and shiny, expensive-looking cutlery.

"Coffee? Orange juice?"

Before Olivia could acquiesce to either, both were placed in front of her. A moment later, she was presented with a massive plate of food.

Pink, perfectly cooked fresh salmon, dotted with capers and chunks of cream cheese, rested atop a bed of lightly scrambled eggs. The plate was flanked by tasty-looking triangles of fried ciabatta bread.

"Oh, my word!" Olivia exclaimed.

Morag sat opposite her, looking pleased at the praise.

"Eat, eat," she encouraged.

"Our day yesterday didn't go as planned," Hamilton explained, piling his fork high with food. "You see, Morag was supposed to shop with a friend, I was supposed to taste wine, and we were going to meet at the restaurant."

"Then it all went wrong with that awful death!" Morag's flawless features tightened in concern. "Do they know yet how he died?"

Olivia was too busy chewing on a piece of crispy, buttery fried bread to reply immediately.

"The police are investigating," she said, when she'd finished her mouthful.

"Rupert was a nasty piece of work," Hamilton emphasized. "He was fighting with everyone. He tried to pick a fight with me. He baited Drake until he exploded. I even heard him insult one of the Italian brothers. And then there was another incident," Hamilton remembered.

"Really?" Olivia said. She hadn't seen any interaction between Rupert and either of the Bocelli moguls. But then, she'd been busy and had spent a lot of time checking on the progress of the bus repairs.

"I've been wondering if a certain person followed him outside to fight with him," Hamilton said.

"Was he killed in a fight? I thought you said he drowned," Morag said, sounding confused.

"People don't just drown in shallow ponds." Hamilton sounded sure of himself as he speared a piece of salmon.

Had there been a fight? Olivia ran the scenarios through her head again. A fight was the most logical reason for Rupert's demise, but Rupert would have fought back. Or would he? He had seemed drunk, she remembered.

"Who do you think did it?" she asked.

"I don't think, I know!" he said, wagging a finger at her. Olivia nearly choked on a mouthful of scrambled egg.

"Who?" she asked eagerly.

"I'll tell ye." Hamilton lowered his voice to a confidential whisper. "It was that young lad, the wet-behind-the-ears one who was there to do card tricks."

"Him?" Olivia asked incredulously. She felt shocked. That wasn't what she'd expected Hamilton to say at all. He suspected Instagram idol Ferdie Tooley?

"Why Ferdie?" she asked.

"Ah, yes, that's his name. You see, I overheard an interesting conversation between the two of them. Rupert and Ferdie, I mean."

"What did they say?" Olivia leaned forward eagerly, practically putting her chin in her plate as she listened to Hamilton's confidential whisper.

"Rupert was telling Ferdie that he'd found him out, and he would make sure that he was destroyed," he said, sounding triumphant.

"Really?" Olivia was stunned. This was critical information! Such a dire threat could provide a strong motive for murder. Had young Ferdie committed the crime to avoid being destroyed? And what was the background to this troubling exchange?

She scraped up the last of her salmon. She felt fortified and energized, and even more importantly, her suspect list was growing. Drake and Ferdie were at the top, followed by whichever of the Bocelli brothers Rupert had insulted.

There was no time to lose, Olivia decided, pushing her chair back.

"Thank you for the delicious breakfast," she said, and Morag smiled.

"Going already?" Hamilton sounded surprised.

"I have a lot of deliveries to make," Olivia explained. "Technically, this is a workday for me."

"Better get back to work. That's how the money's made." Hamilton nodded in approval.

Olivia climbed into her car and headed down the drive. Her brain was buzzing with what she'd learned. She still believed that Drake had the strongest motive for the murder, but Hamilton had thrown a curveball into the equation with his mention of Ferdie.

Had Rupert threatened others as well? she wondered.

It was almost time for the delivery she'd arranged with the receptionist at Villa Fiora.

This time, Olivia hoped her appointment would get her through the gate and face to face with Bernie.

*

The interior of Villa Fiora was light and bright, with gold detail and enough marble to make the Taj Mahal jealous, Olivia thought, taking in the exquisite space admiringly.

"I'm here to deliver a parcel for Bernie," she said to the receptionist. "I was hoping I might be able to hand it to him personally."

At that moment, Bernie strolled in from the lounge.

"Ah, Signor Cooper. Your parcel is here." The receptionist smiled.

"Yeah. I thought I'd come by and take it myself."

Bernie was wearing a startlingly unattractive pair of moss-green jeans and a sweatshirt so ancient that the logo was no longer readable.

Olivia wasn't surprised. Nothing about these billionaires could shock her anymore. But she was quietly determined to get Bernie alone, and out of the receptionist's earshot.

"Could we sit for a moment?" she asked. "I'd like to explain the wines to you."

"Sure." Bernie gestured to the next-door lounge.

Taking a deep breath, Olivia led the way into the lounge and headed for the farthest corner. There, a luxurious leather couch faced a modern chair that seemed to be constructed from a surfboard and a clothes horse.

Hoping that Bernie would feel at ease on the couch, Olivia took the chair.

Yup, it felt like a surfboard as well, she realized.

"You're not here to talk about the wines, are you?" Bernie asked her in a low voice. Olivia got such a fright she jumped. The chair wobbled and almost fell over. She stuck out her leg at the last possible moment and saved herself from an attention-grabbing crash.

"My boss said that if any of the guests wanted to discuss the— wanted to speak about what happened at the winery, I should give them the opportunity. Everyone deserves closure," Olivia told him.

"Yeah, true," Bernie agreed.

"Perhaps you want to?" she asked encouragingly. "It's helpful to get things off your chest."

"You're right." Bernie sighed heavily as Olivia sat straighter in excitement. "I do need to get this off my chest, because I've been feeling very guilty about it."

CHAPTER TWENTY FIVE

Olivia couldn't believe it. She was about to witness a freely given confession to murder.

"Why do you feel guilty?" she asked Bernie gently, hoping he'd continue to pour out the truth to her.

"Because I should have told the police about what happened earlier," he sighed. "In fact, I should have personally intervened at the time, and not allowed things to take their course."

Now she felt confused. The conversation seemed to be veering in an unexpected direction.

"Can you explain?" she asked.

Bernie sighed. "Well, when Rupert was threatening the Bocelli brother, it was clear to me he was setting himself up as a target for murder. Who was it? Oh, yes, Aldo, of course. I should actually have told him, right there, that his behavior was unacceptable, that he was clearly too drunk, and he should take a cab home. I didn't, and so he died."

"Threatening Aldo?" she echoed, remembering Hamilton had mentioned the same incident. "When did this happen?"

"It was just after Rupert said the bus was broken," Bernie remembered. "I think you and a couple of others rushed out. Anyway, Rupert was ranting on about how we'd all be stuck here for hours now, and Aldo asked Rupert if he was sure it wasn't just a quick fix. I don't think he meant it to be an insult, but Rupert took it that way. He said that if he was insinuating he was a liar, he should think again, because Rupert would go out of his way to make the rest of the tour, and the rest of his life, a misery for him. Aldo looked extremely angry. I could see he'd taken it badly even though he didn't respond or fight back."

Olivia felt aghast.

"Then what happened?" she asked.

"Then Drake stood up and told Rupert to shut it, that there was no need to speak this way to other guests who were just confirming facts. And then Rupert turned on Drake, as if he was ready to start a fist fight."

Remembering the scene she'd witnessed as she walked back in, Olivia nodded.

Bernie's version made sense. Now she knew how Drake and Rupert had ended up about to fight. It had all started with Aldo.

"Did you see Rupert go outside?" Olivia said.

"Nope. I didn't see that. I got a call from my office back home, asking me to troubleshoot a problem. I was on the call for about ten minutes. I found a quiet corner at the back of the restaurant. There's a glass-covered outdoor room. It was cold, but at least I could hear myself think."

"You didn't go outside?" Olivia pressured.

"I tried. The wind was terrible, and it was impossible to hear what my manager in the States was saying, and for her to hear me. So I went back in. I've actually downloaded the call records just this morning, as I am sure the police will want to see them. I guess they provide an alibi of sorts."

"I'm sure that will help them a lot," Olivia agreed.

Bernie checked his phone. "I've got an urgent mail I need to answer, so I'll head back to my room. Thanks for the wine, and for helping me get that off my chest."

"Thank you for your time," Olivia said politely.

She hurried back across the marble expanse of the reception hall. She felt excited, though unnerved, by what Bernie had said. He had a firm alibi which could be confirmed by concrete evidence.

More importantly, Aldo was now jointly at the top of her list, together with Ferdie and Drake. He'd been targeted by Rupert first, and could have decided to take personal revenge later.

Chico and Aldo were booked in the Gardens of Florence. That was closer than where Ferdie was staying, so Olivia decided to go there first.

"Aldo, I'm coming for you!" she announced sternly, swinging onto the road.

*

Twenty minutes later, Olivia marched determinedly into the sumptuously decorated reception hall at the Gardens of Florence.

"I have gifts for Chico and Aldo Bocelli, who are staying here. I would love to hand them over personally." Olivia smiled at the receptionist.

"Ah, our favorite guests!" the woman exclaimed.

Olivia noted a pot of Chi-Aldo Luxury Hand and Nail Cream stationed next to the keyboard. She guessed that the brothers generously distributed gifts wherever they stayed. No wonder they were popular!

Briefly, Olivia struggled with the concept that such kind, generous, well-loved people could be murderers. Then she warned herself not to prejudge. After all, beautiful waters had deadly currents.

The receptionist called out to the butler. "Where are our local heroes? This lovely lady has brought them wine!"

"They were at breakfast. No, then they went outside. I think they were heading to the tennis courts. Can I escort our visitor there?"

"Please." The receptionist smiled.

Feeling rather like a VIP guest herself thanks to this wonderful treatment, Olivia followed the butler outside. He led her through a formal garden with paved paths, lavender plantings, a central fountain, and small statues punctuating the way. From there, they joined a path crossing verdant lawns, with three modern tennis courts at the far end.

Olivia recognized Chico and Aldo immediately. Chico, dressed in whites and dancing from foot to foot on the green-paved court, waited for Aldo to send down a devastating serve.

Aldo leaped into the serve, coiling over his racket, and the ball flashed across the net, clearing it by the merest inch. But Chico was ready, slamming it diagonally back again.

Olivia gasped as Aldo sprinted for the ball, arriving just in time to deliver a curving backhand. It hit the top of the net, and its speed bled away as it bounced softly onto the opposite side.

Racing desperately toward it, Chico arrived after the second bounce, although his desperate stroke still sent it soaring into the air.

Watching it, Aldo laughed. "Too slow," he called.

"You were lucky," Chico grinned. "Next time, I will win the point."

"I have just won the first set! You have some catching up to do."

At that moment, the men noticed Olivia and the butler.

"*Ciao, ciao*," Chico called.

"May we interrupt you?" the butler asked.

"Of course. I am in the lead!" Laughing, Aldo walked over to the small gate set into the wire fence. He picked up a water bottle, and as he untwisted the top, he stared more closely at Olivia.

"You are from the winery. I remember you."

"Yes. I've come to bring you a gift." Olivia handed the packs of wine over.

"Ah, how wonderful! A reminder of our tasting," Chico said.

"And what followed," Aldo added pointedly.

"We wanted you to have good memories of our winery, even though we had such an unfortunate incident," Olivia said.

The butler was walking back across the lawn, clearly deciding Olivia wanted a private chat. She was very glad to have the chance.

"I hope they arrest the perpetrator soon," Chico said.

Aldo nodded. "It was obvious from the first moment who it was," he said.

"Exactly. Obvious to all," Chico agreed.

Olivia goggled at the brothers. This wasn't going the way she'd hoped. Aldo didn't sound in the least guilty, or as if he was trying to deflect suspicion. It was as if they were both making a statement of fact.

"Who was that?" she asked.

The brothers spoke together.

"Carmody," Chico said.

"Tomas," Aldo said.

Everyone looked at each other as a surprised silence descended.

Olivia's mind was whirling. What on earth? Every time she interviewed a suspect, the suspect named someone else. Meanwhile, the brothers turned to stare in puzzlement at each other.

"Why do you think him?" both asked at the same time.

Chico frowned. "It is obvious to me. Carmody was bragging the whole way to the winery about his experience in Tibet, and what he had learned there. I am sure they taught him martial arts, and that is how he managed to overpower Rupert."

Olivia wasn't sure about this version. Firstly, Carmody hadn't looked the right build for a martial arts expert—his shape was more Buddha than ninja. Secondly, she was sure he'd stayed in the restaurant the whole time. But why did Aldo suspect Tomas?

"That strange pianist was so oversensitive, and couldn't take any criticism," Aldo explained. "As we were walking into the winery, Rupert said he hadn't heard of him and didn't think he ever would. I thought that Tomas was going to kill him on the spot. Pianists have strong fingers, don't they? Perhaps he followed him out and strangled him and dropped him in the pond!"

Olivia filed this information away. She agreed Tomas had an ego and was very self-centered. Could his narcissism have pushed him to destroy his critic?

And, more importantly, did the brothers have an alibi?

"I heard that you and Rupert had words during the evening. I'm sure the police will ask you where you were at the time of his death," Olivia said to Aldo, trying to sound worried and sympathetic all at the same time.

Aldo nodded. "He certainly spoke harshly to me and was very rude and threatening. But, as part of Chi-Aldo Luxury Cosmetics corporate culture, we have super-strict rules about how we behave when in public. Of course I was angry, but our motto in such instances is to walk away, forgive, and forget."

"Exactly!" Chico nodded.

"We observed that Rupert was continuing to pick fights, and we even overheard him having a confrontation with you outside. Deciding to step away from trouble, we went next door to the tasting room, where we read up on the interesting facts about the winery."

Olivia's eyes widened. So Chico and Aldo had been witness to Rupert's bullying, and her hissed threats to the billionaire.

"We heard you putting him in his place, very firmly," Aldo explained.

"We stayed in the tasting room until you called us," Chico added.

"Of course, we did what we always do in such a situation," Aldo said.

"What was that?" Olivia asked, hoping it would provide a solid alibi for the brothers, because up until now, they could just be supporting each other's version. Briefly, she thought about how it would have been easier for two people to overpower Rupert, than one.

"We took a selfie together and posted it on our social media," Chico explained. "With some inspiring words for our followers. Doing that is a wonderful way to calm down!"

"The best," Aldo said.

"Within ten minutes, it had already received more than ten thousand likes. We spent a while interacting with our audience," Chico said proudly. "That photo is now at well over fifty thousand likes! You can view it on our Chi-Aldo page. You will be pleased that your winery's logo was in the background. A number of our fans have already said they want to visit your beautiful premises and buy your wines!"

"Of course, if it turns out to have been a murder, that will not have been such a great idea. Then we will have to take down the photo as our presence at the scene will reflect negatively on our company," Aldo said sadly.

"It would damage our brand," Chico agreed.

"Sales would plummet," Aldo added.

"We're all hoping it's solved very soon. And thank you so much for the selfie and the great exposure," Olivia said.

"Thank you for the wine!" Chico smiled.

Olivia felt relieved that she could rule out the brothers as suspects, thanks to the social media interaction at the time of Rupert's death, and their awareness of the negative publicity a murder could bring.

As she headed back across the lawn to the parking lot, she heard Chico's triumphant cry of, "Ace!"

Immersed in thought, Olivia climbed in her car. As she drove away from the Gardens of Florence she realized she was feeling more confused than ever. This was like playing a game of tag. Everyone was tagging one other person, and it wasn't getting her any closer to her end goal of finding the killer.

Perhaps her next stop would reveal something more concrete, Olivia hoped.

She was going to the Terrazzo Moderna, where she hoped that Ferdie, the mysterious magician, would reveal his secrets. Or, preferably, confess them.

As she drove, she realized with a pang that she hadn't yet called Danilo to apologize for her outburst earlier.

Quickly, Olivia dialed his number while she was stopped at a light. She put the phone onto speaker so she could talk safely as she drove. She needed to give the conversation her full attention. It was important that she smooth things over with Danilo.

But to Olivia's alarm, the phone went straight through to voicemail.

She decided not to leave a long, detailed message. That would be a cop-out. Hopefully he would see her missed call and return it, and then she could say what she needed to.

Even so, Olivia couldn't help feeling a pang of worry as she drove. What if she'd already messed things up too badly, and Danilo didn't call back at all?

CHAPTER TWENTY SIX

After spending most of the scenic journey fretting over her own hotheaded actions, Olivia was glad to arrive at the Terrazzo Moderna. This was a hotel in two parts. There was the ultra-luxury and highly exclusive Terrazzo Magnifico further down the road, and then this one—the larger, though still luxurious, main hotel.

As befitted their status as entertainers, rather than high-dollar earners, Tomas and Ferdie had been accommodated in the Moderna.

Olivia remembered that Sashenka and Jose were residing in the ultra-luxury section of this two-part hotel. However, neither of them was high on her suspect list. Jose had been in the restaurant all evening, and Sashenka had seemed to be amused by the other billionaires, rather than offended by them. Plus, she'd looked genuinely curious about what had happened when she and Erba had followed Olivia outside to the scene.

Heading into the Moderna, Olivia was pleased she didn't even have to ask the receptionist to call the guest she needed. She spotted that dazzlingly loud jacket in an instant. Ferdie was sitting in the coffee shop adjacent to the restaurant.

Olivia prowled purposefully toward him. Since his back was turned, this provided a brilliant opportunity for her to observe this suspected criminal.

Ferdie had a glass of orange soda and a half-eaten salami focaccia on the table in front of him. He was frowning down at a pack of cards as he dealt, flipping the cards over on the polished wood. His lips were moving silently as he worked.

He must be rehearsing, she decided.

Hoping that he would be focused on the card play, Olivia shimmied over, managing to perch on the seat opposite before Ferdie even noticed her. Catching sight of her, he jerked his head up. He looked horrified by her appearance.

"What are you doing here?" he gasped.

Olivia gave him a bright, innocent smile.

"I've popped by to bring you a gift of wine." She placed the attractive cardboard container on the table.

Ferdie barely glanced at it.

"No, you haven't," he insisted. "There's no way you would have driven all this way to give me wine. You barely know me! And I'm not important or rich. So that means you've come here for another reason, and I want to know what it is!"

He scowled at her. Perhaps he intended to look threatening, but it just made him appear more vulnerable.

Olivia couldn't help feeling sorry for him. He looked on the edge of his nerves. Plus, he had shown insight about her reasons for visiting him. He didn't expect people to pander to him and shower him with gifts. That, however, raised another burning question.

"So you're not important or rich?" Olivia asked, grasping the main inconsistency of Ferdie's statement.

Realizing his mistake, Ferdie tried to backtrack.

"Not as important, or as rich," he clarified.

"That's not what you said!" Hoping a stern expression would drive her words home, Olivia tried to channel Detective Caputi as she pierced him with an iron-hard glare.

It was remarkably successful. Ferdie flinched visibly. Then, with a heavy sigh, he picked up the other half of his focaccia and took a large bite.

A stress-eater, just like her.

He chewed and swallowed, and only then did he reply.

"You're right," he said, sounding defeated. "I shouldn't be on this tour at all. I'm going to be in terrible trouble. I may even be arrested for fraud, if I don't get wrongfully arrested for murder first."

He put the focaccia down and regarded her with a sad expression.

Olivia stared consideringly back. Dubious though his dress sense might be, she had the feeling that she was finally getting a handle on the real Ferdie. Was he a killer? Hopefully, she could prod him to reveal more.

"You'd better tell me the whole story," she said in gentle tones, feeling a soft approach would work best. She sensed that harsh words would drive him back into his shell.

"Well, you see, I have this amazing cat," Ferdie said, looking happier. "He has a long, rippling coat that's the color of gold, and he weighs more than twenty pounds. He's enormous!"

"Oh, how stunning," Olivia said.

"Anyway, my cat has his own Instagram page. He loves to do cute things. He drapes himself all the way across the couch, and we have a tree in our garden that he climbs like a koala bear, and we put him on a harness and take him for walks. He has a toy mouse that he hides away in his cat castle, and then he hunts the mouse as if he was Superman! He jumps onto the counter and takes treats from a jar and bats them onto the floor so that Chunky, our beagle, can eat them. He knows quite a few words and he even responds to some of them sometimes."

"For a cat, that's incredible." Olivia felt she was speaking with authority in this matter.

"So anyway, Magician—that's his name—has thousands of social media followers. I think we're over a hundred thousand."

"Magician?" The puzzle pieces were starting to fall into place for Olivia. She thought she saw where this sad tale, or perhaps tail, was heading.

"Yes. So, a week ago, I got messaged by this weird lady, Stella. She said that they'd had a last-minute opening for an entertainer on a very famous tour, and that one of her researchers had put my name forward for it."

"What else did she say?" Olivia asked, intrigued.

"Well, she said that there would be an appearance fee, and that I'd stay in top hotels for a week with all expenses paid. The fee was serious money! And my fiancée and I are looking to redecorate our home. So I accepted. I thought it was great that they wanted the owner of a famous cat on the tour. I even prepared a slide show of pictures and a hilarious short video of him doing his tricks. But when I arrived, and I got told I had to do a magic show... well, I started to realize what a hideous misunderstanding it had all been."

"Oh, goodness!" Olivia felt caught up in this story. She could imagine Ferdie's horror. In the circumstances, admitting that he wasn't a magician would not have been a wise move. For a start, she was sure the researcher would have been instantly fired.

"I didn't know what to do. I went out and bought an appropriate jacket. Then I decided to Google a few card tricks, hoping maybe I could learn quickly and get away with it. However, doing magic is much harder that it seems, and I don't think I'm a natural at it. So I am basically heading for disaster."

"Why?" Olivia asked. "You're off the hook now, aren't you?"

That was thanks to the murder. As she spoke, she couldn't help wondering how far Ferdie would have gone in his desperation to stop the tour program. Had he deliberately caused a tragedy, hoping to save himself as a result?

"No! You're wrong. I'm not off the hook at all. I'm still on the hook!" Ferdie picked up the pack of cards and shuffled them disconsolately, dropping a few in the process. Olivia leaned over and grabbed one that had fluttered to the floor.

"Why's that?" she asked, handing it back to him.

He stared at her, looking agonized. "Haven't you heard? The entertainment and dinner have been rescheduled, starting at five p.m. this afternoon! I'm being picked up from here at four."

Olivia's jaw dropped. "They're allowing it?" she squeaked.

Ferdie shrugged. "The organizers spoke to the police. They agreed that the event can go ahead on the condition that the party is bused as a group, and does not leave the venues, and that everyone is signed in again at their lodgings afterwards. I believe there will be a police officer outside the venues throughout."

Olivia was appalled to hear this, because it put a spoke in the wheel of her plans. She'd thought she would have the whole afternoon to question the group, but in another hour, they'd all be getting ready. She didn't have a moment to lose, and needed to drill down to the important facts.

"One of the guests told me that Rupert threatened you," she said.

Ferdie nodded glumly. "He saw me practicing. It was after the bus had broken down. I was standing by the restaurant door, trying to get that three-card trick to work. He marched past me with a wineglass and threw it out. The wine, not the glass. He said it was revolting acidic rubbish and was giving him heartburn and indigestion and he didn't feel well. Then he turned and saw me and called me a fraud and made all sorts of horrible threats."

"Did you think about the damage he could do?" Olivia said carefully.

"The damage he could do?" Ferdie looked up at her, confused. "What more damage could he do to me, than I will do to myself? They'll probably demand my fee back. And we've already spent some of the money on tiles, and splashed out on a new stove, and bought a huge number of bulbs for the garden."

"Oh dear," Olivia said. She felt terrible for Ferdie. He really was in a dire situation. His acceptance of his fate proved to her that he wasn't the killer. Why would he worry what one person thought, when he knew all of them would think the same after his show?

How could she help him? she wondered. Suddenly, she had a workable idea.

"You know what you should do?"

"What?" Ferdie asked her in a hopeless tone.

"Bandage up your right hand. Say you slipped on the stairs and sprained it, that you're in a lot of pain and you unfortunately can't do any magic. And then ask the audience if they would like to see some photos and videos of your cat instead. I'm sure the venue could prearrange a large screen for you."

Ferdie stared at her with hope dawning in his eyes.

"You think it'll work?"

"They're all animal lovers. Look at what a hit my goat was," Olivia said. "If Stella herself is there she might not be too happy. But if it's just the billionaires, I think they'd actually prefer the cat. They seem to be very egotistical and like to be in control all the time. I'm not sure that magic tricks would be their thing."

Ferdie stared at her as if she was the rising sun itself.

"Oh, Olivia, you're amazing! You have given me hope! I feel this can work." He stared down at his hand. "It feels sore already. And I saw a pharmacy in the village when we passed through. I can go there and buy lots of bandages."

"Good luck." Olivia smiled as Ferdie rushed away.

She felt glad she'd managed to solve one mystery, even if it wasn't the main one. And she'd been able to help someone in need. However, she now had a short day because the tour was going ahead.

Her final stop would have to be at this hotel, with a quick chat to Tomas. After all, the pianist had been named as a possible killer, and even if he was innocent, he might have seen something.

She hoped the receptionist would agree to call him to the front desk, and that Tomas would be lured by the gift of wine.

But, as she headed back into the lobby, Olivia realized she might not have to ask at all. Piano notes from the lounge on the far side clued her as to where he might be.

She headed to the lounge, where she was pleased to find her hunch was correct. Tomas was seated at the grand piano, dressed to the nines in a smart tuxedo, his fingers cascading over the keys as crashing notes poured out.

Looking around the room, Olivia saw that this was the venue for afternoon tea. Cakes, finger sandwiches, macarons, tartlets, and scones were artfully arranged on the sideboards, and the tables were filling up with guests who had arrived to enjoy the spread, and the music.

Except, Olivia realized, there was a developing situation here.

A tweed-jacketed man with a sheaf of music in his hand stood near the piano. He was shifting from foot to shiny-shoed foot, glancing uneasily at his watch and then at the piano. There, Olivia saw, Tomas was studiously ignoring him.

With a flicker of amusement, Olivia deduced that Tomas was hogging the piano in order to showcase his talent to the high-tea guests, while the actual booked pianist was waiting anxiously to take his place.

She sidled over to him.

"Hello, Tomas," she said.

He glanced up. Upon seeing her, he startled. An audible discord jangled around the room, and a woman at the nearest table dropped her fork.

Tomas raised his hands, lifting them off the keys. He glared furiously at Olivia.

"What, what, *what* are you doing? Do you realize you interrupted one of the most important, poignant moments of this piece? You have ruined it, for now and evermore, for every person listening!"

Now that the only sound was the chink of cutlery and Tomas's irate voice, more guests were starting to look around. Olivia didn't want to cause a scene.

"Can we talk somewhere more private?" she muttered.

Still fuming, Tomas stood up, scowling down his nose at her.

"Since you have destroyed this impromptu performance given generously by me, the experience of a lifetime for every listener, I have no choice."

Angrily, he strode out of the room, with Olivia hastening at his heels. As she reached the door, she looked back to see the booked pianist taking his seat, looking vastly relieved.

Tomas stalked down the corridor, heading into another, smaller lounge. This was peaceful and quiet. A brazier glowed, and leather armchairs concealed a few guests who were reading or snoozing.

Tomas perched on an ottoman, still smoldering.

"Why did you come here to interrupt me?"

"I'm so sorry." Olivia hoped a heartfelt apology might placate him. "I came to ask you about yesterday. I thought someone as observant as you, so finely tuned to your audience, might possibly remember some details that could be helpful."

Tomas preened at the praise.

"Well, I felt the organizers made a wise decision inviting me on this exclusive tour. Being part of an exclusive group of thirteen, to me, is as important as performing for an audience of thirty thousand. But yet, I knew instantly that they would appreciate me even more, in the intimate environment."

It had been a group of twelve, but she decided not to correct him. Instead, Olivia found herself fidgeting. Had Tomas noticed anything at all? When would he get to the point?

"Did you take special notice of the guest Rupert Curren, who sadly passed away?" she probed.

Tomas nodded. "During the wine tasting, it was very clear that the wine was a mere interlude, and that Rupert and the others were awaiting my later performance."

Olivia frowned in concern. It didn't sound as if Rupert's death had impacted Tomas at all.

"Did you see any of the guests fighting with each other?" she tried.

"It is common for those attending my shows to fight for front places in the hall. I was looking forward to gifting them with my chosen piece of music. What a privilege for this wealthy crowd to be exposed to something so unique—a precious concert by myself."

Olivia glanced at the clock on the wall, trying to stop herself from tapping her foot impatiently. She didn't have time for this, and surely neither did Tomas, although on second thought, he was all ready for his recital. She needed to cut to the chase.

"Where were you at the time of the murder? Were you with anyone?"

"I divided my time equally among my admirers, being everyone in the group," Tomas said. "I had just finished telling Carmody and Jose about the concert I gave in Singapore. My account was so powerful that both men closed their eyes as I spoke. I am sure they were imagining themselves among that privileged audience. Then I went to the men's room and was there when you called everyone to the bus."

Finally, an alibi! All it had taken was every ounce of patience she possessed!

"Do you know who could have killed him?" she asked.

Tomas sighed. "I have no idea, but feel it is a great pity we are now one audience member short. The praise of every person in attendance is valuable to me. Nonetheless, I will keep this smaller group captivated by my talent later."

"I'm sure they'll be enthralled," Olivia said. "Well, the time is—"

"Not many world famous pianists agree to pour their skills into a limited-numbers recital for VIP billionaire guests."

Olivia decided to agree. Anything to stem the flood of self-praise so she could get away.

"Absolutely. You're very generous. Well, thank you so much for explaining. I now have to—"

"I could see they were enthralled by my presence."

Olivia stood up.

"Thank you so much, Tomas. Everyone is going to treasure your concert this afternoon."

"Exactly." Tomas nodded approvingly.

Olivia hotfooted it to the door and hurried out. Tomas had an alibi, and in any case would never have murdered an audience member who would have added to the attendance numbers. Not before his show at any rate, Olivia acknowledged wryly.

She followed the exit signs that led to the hotel's side door.

It had been a frustrating day, she decided, heading across the courtyard and climbing into her car. She'd hoped to solve the crime. Now, everyone was being bused off to their evening entertainment so she would have to go home.

Before she drove out, she tried calling Danilo again.

She dialed the number, planning what she should say, feeling a flicker of guilt as the call connected. It rang, and she listened anxiously, formulating the words in her head.

But Danilo didn't pick up. The call went through to voicemail unanswered, and her guilt turned into a frisson of worry.

She'd messed up, and created a serious problem. Danilo was offended, and wasn't taking her calls. Perhaps he was regretting his decision to date her. Or was this a message that she'd gone too far with her angry outburst, and they weren't dating anymore?

Feeling stressed, Olivia drove out of the hotel. Her relationship issues might already have escalated out of her control, and that was a scary thought.

There was only one thing left to do today that might make a difference, and Olivia decided to tackle it. Instead of going straight back to her farmhouse, she took the side road that led to the winery.

The critical issue of Marcello's mentorship was burning in her mind and she was determined that she was going to get the outcome she needed.

CHAPTER TWENTY SEVEN

Olivia felt resolute as she strode into La Leggenda. Even though the winery was closed to the public, she was sure Marcello would still be in his office, juggling a multitude of urgent tasks.

She picked up the sound of rapid tapping on the computer keyboard before she walked in the door. Marcello looked up as she entered, and she was pleased to see that his face warmed, the stressed expression softening slightly.

"Olivia. Can I help?"

"I was asking a few questions today," Olivia said carefully. She hoped she wouldn't attract more criticism for her efforts. She was glad to see Marcello looked relieved and intrigued.

"Did you find anything out?" he asked.

"Not as much as I hoped, but I did a lot of groundwork," Olivia confessed. "Everyone is blaming everyone else. And the detectives haven't determined the cause of death yet."

"How do you know?" Marcello sounded curious.

"They are allowing the group to attend the concert and Michelin-starred dinner this evening, with police supervision. They'll be getting ready for the concert now," Olivia said. "I'm sure that if they had concrete evidence of a crime, they would be re-interviewing or arresting people instead."

Marcello nodded thoughtfully. "Perhaps a verdict of accidental death will be our salvation."

"Oh, I hope so!" Staring at him earnestly, Olivia continued, "Marcello, I know you're still unsure about the mentorship. Please promise me something."

"Promise you what?" He stared at her intensely, his eyes deep blue.

"That you'll take it. Don't allow this mess-up to distract you from your goal. You can't allow anything to stop you from it. Not even a death—whether it turns out to be natural causes or not."

"Olivia." Marcello's voice was soft. "Sometimes, when I am feeling discouraged, it is your passion that rekindles my own fire. You are so focused, so determined. I believe, when I am with you, that nothing can hold our winery back, and that all problems are trivial."

Olivia could barely breathe. This was an unexpectedly intimate moment, even though they were talking only about work.

"That's not always how I feel inside," she admitted, with a smile. "You always see the best in me, and bring out the best. Please, think about your passion, and what this would mean. Put aside your worries, even though I know they seem huge. I will try my best to solve this case. I'm almost there, I know it! Tomorrow I'll have answers for you."

Marcello reached out his hand and covered hers with his broad, warm palm.

Olivia couldn't breathe. She hadn't expected such a tender gesture. It felt for a moment as if Marcello were testing the boundaries of the no-romance-at-work agreement they'd made.

He didn't know she had a boyfriend. Now was not the right time to mention it. It would sidetrack the purpose of her visit, and in any case, this was simply a gesture of support and friendship.

Wasn't it?

Olivia felt uncertain. She'd thought the door between Marcello and herself was firmly closed, only to find that it was not even on the latch, and might swing open in the slightest breeze.

"I promise I will take the mentorship," he said, and she knew from the tone of his voice that this was a guarantee. He was not just saying it to placate her, but because he meant it and would abide by it.

"Thank you," Olivia said. Her voice came out rather croaky, and she cleared her throat hurriedly.

Marcello moved his hand away, and slowly, the weird tension between them dissolved.

"I'm going to go home now, seeing I can't do any more investigation today. But I promise you, Marcello, by this time tomorrow, the winery will be cleared."

Olivia stood up. Whatever it took, she was going to make good on her word, just the same as Marcello was.

His blue gaze warmed her. She turned and walked out of the office, uneasily aware that the touch of his hand was still tingling on her skin.

As she headed out to her car, where Erba was waiting loyally by the back door, she let out a frustrated sigh. Why couldn't life be simpler? Why did emotions, and people's reactions to them, make everything more complicated than it should be?

Olivia used the short drive home to calm herself, trying to quiet her thoughts, which were flitting in all directions. She felt so confused, and as if nothing made sense anymore.

By the time she drove through the farmhouse gate, she was feeling more settled, if lightheaded from all the deep breathing she'd done. Climbing out of the car, she decided to take a walk to her barn to check on her wine.

Then she was going to head into the hills to try the key in the lock of her secret storeroom door. After all, Danilo was too busy to call her back or was deliberately avoiding her. They might not even be in a relationship anymore. And she had to proceed with her own life, regardless.

She changed into comfortable sweatpants and trainers before pocketing the key and heading outdoors.

As the wind tugged at her hair, her spirits felt lifted by this overcast, atmospheric evening. The air was fresh and the darkening view was green, mysterious, and lovely.

Romantic problems must not overtake her world, Olivia thought firmly, as she headed along the well-trodden pathway that led to her barn. There was more to life, after all! Such as being the very first person in Tuscany to produce a small commercial batch of ice wine which was almost ready for bottling.

Olivia unfastened the latch and pushed the large barn doors open, breathing in the smell inside. When she'd first started cleaning out the barn, it had been musty and decrepit. Then, when Erba had been stationed in here for a while, the space had acquired a flavor of fresh straw, lush alfalfa, and an undertone of clean, furry goat. Now that Erba had her own cozy Wendy house to sleep in, the barn's interior held a magical hint of the sweet, sumptuous processing of wine.

Heading over to her oaken barrel and steel fermentation vat, Olivia stared down hopefully, wishing her gaze could pierce through the containers and enhance the wine inside. The fermentation was so nearly complete! Any day now she could transfer the contents of the vat to the other barrel for a few days. There, her wine would complete its journey of maturation in brief contact with oak.

Of course, thanks to one of the steel vats malfunctioning, half of the batch had already entered this journey too early. Olivia hoped that having to transfer the wine to the barrel prematurely hadn't ruined it. What did she know?

Tomorrow she would test her wine, Olivia decided. Then she would know if the long weeks of patient waiting had resulted in success, or been a huge waste of time and grapes.

Stepping outside, she closed the door, her breath misting in the chilly early evening. She headed into the hills, stumbling over the stony terrain. As she traversed the rolling landscape, she wondered again why the previous owners of this farm had chosen to construct this small storage room in such a remote area.

"What were they thinking?" Olivia wondered aloud, tripping over a boulder hidden behind a tussock of grass. Clamping her hand over her pocket, she checked the key was still there. If it fell out now, it would take her another year to find it again.

The journey up the hill always left her breathless. She got her bearings by focusing on the cluster of trees a few hundred yards away. Determinedly she headed there, knowing it would be getting dark in a short while.

There it was ahead, shrouded by the trees that concealed it. She felt a shiver of tension and excitement as she neared the lonely building. What secrets did it hold?

She glanced back, glad to see that in the cloudy dusk, the glow of light from her farmhouse was visible over the hill. She'd never have thought that she'd own a piece of land that was large enough to get lost, or at any rate disoriented, in the darkness!

What a strange turn her life had taken.

As she placed her hand on the cold, rough stone wall, a sense of wonderment overtook her at being the new caretaker of this mysterious room. Who had constructed it, what had their purpose been? So many decades had passed that she would never know. The original motivation was lost in the mists of time.

"Please, let me find out what's in here," she said, hoping that her words would come true.

At that moment, there was a creepy rustling noise from the nearby bushes, and Olivia jumped, feeling vulnerable and alone.

She let out a relieved sigh when an orange and white face peeked out from behind a wild rosemary shrub.

"Erba!" Olivia chastised. "Why are you sneaking up on me? It's spooky out here!"

She wished Danilo was with her, and the fact he wasn't reminded Olivia of her predicament with a surge of regret.

At least she had her loyal goat, she thought, as she inserted the key carefully into the lock. Her stomach felt tight with anticipation as she eased it inside.

It felt rusty, as if the long years of disuse had clogged up the aperture. For a moment she worried that it would break, and she would never know the secrets that lay behind it—not without breaking the whole door down, at any rate!

Then, after some hopeful pushing and jiggling, the key was in.

Would it work? She felt breathless with anticipation and her heart was hammering. This was the moment—finally—where this room's hidden secrets might be discovered!

Olivia turned the key carefully. Her hands were trembling, making the key wiggle. With an effort she steadied them, clenching her teeth as she felt the disused mechanism grind sullenly against itself.

Deep inside the workings of the lock, she felt it open. It didn't spring apart. Rather, it reluctantly loosened.

Olivia caught her breath in amazement. The key had worked, and the lock had opened. She felt dizzy at the thought that this was one of the biggest mysteries on her farm, and now it was solved! Finally, she could see what was inside.

Olivia grabbed the rusty door handle, feeling a reluctant grinding as it turned, breathless with anticipation about what she would discover.

CHAPTER TWENTY EIGHT

The door hinges screamed, as if they were trying their best to resist her efforts. But with Olivia pulling, applying steady, consistent pressure, the door eased open, giving an inch, then two.

Breathing hard, Olivia stopped. She rested her hand on the cold, rusty handle of the secret storeroom door as thoughts whirled through her mind. She felt torn. Although her brain was begging her to pull it wide, her heart was pleading with her to reconsider.

Firmly, she drilled down into her own thoughts, searching for the reason behind her hesitation.

It wouldn't be right to open this now, she decided. Alone, in the gloom, with only her curious goat for company, she was letting her impatience consume her. And perhaps she was also assuming the worst had happened in her relationship.

Doing this without Danilo felt as if she were taking preemptive action to cut him out of her life and avoid the risk of further hurt. She was allowing her own fears to get the better of her.

Olivia sighed, feeling ashamed now that she'd uncovered her hidden reasons.

Testing the key was one thing. That was a sensible move, and she now knew it worked. But opening the door alone—well, that was something different. She couldn't go through with it. Not until she'd spoken to Danilo and she knew if things were really over between them. After all, she might be wrong.

Olivia let go of the handle.

Then she pushed her shoulder to the door and firmly pressed it closed, letting out an unexpected giggle as she wondered what the poor door must think of her strange behavior.

"I'll be back," she explained to the door. "It's not the right time yet."

She turned away feeling a massive sense of relief, as if she'd almost made a terrible mistake, but at the last minute, sanity had prevailed.

As she turned away, her phone rang.

Her heart leaped. At this pivotal moment, she was certain it was Danilo calling back.

She grabbed it, smiling in delight, but her smile vanished as she saw her mother on the line.

This, now? Dealing with her mother was the last thing she needed. Grimacing, Olivia struggled yet again with her conscience, this time over whether to simply send it to voicemail and call her mother back later.

Of course, she couldn't do that! With a sigh, she answered.

"Hello, honey," Mrs. Glass announced. "Have I got the time difference right? It's not midnight there yet?"

"No. It's early evening."

"Ah. It's mid-morning here, and snowing! I hope your weather is milder. It's at times like this your father and I start browsing real estate in Florida."

"We haven't had any snow here this winter," Olivia said, a comment that proved to be misguided.

"No snow? That makes me want to book a flight immediately and come to Tuscany for a vacation! Is your spare room livable yet?"

"The weather has been very cold," Olivia said hurriedly. "And raining nonstop. And the spare room has a bed, but still needs a lot of renovation."

"Andrew, Olivia's only been getting light rain, and the room's ready!" her mother called.

Rolling her eyes, Olivia began the trek back to her farmhouse.

"I think we must come for a vacation sooner than later. After all, you may not be there much longer."

Olivia spluttered, unable to get out a coherent reply as her mother steamrollered smoothly onward.

"We definitely want to have the Tuscan experience, after all!"

"Rather plan for summer," Olivia begged.

"I believe flights are also quite inexpensive for the next month or two," her mother added. "By the way, sweetheart, I think you mentioned you were seeing a local man? Is it serious with him?"

Olivia made a face. She hadn't thought this conversation could get any worse, but by veering roughshod into the sensitive topic of Danilo, new lows had been achieved.

"We're good friends and taking it slow," she began, but this comment, too, seemed to trigger her mother's selective hearing.

"I'm asking because I heard yesterday that the Italian deli down the road from us is in need of a good manager. They told me they're not in a rush to fill the position, but do prefer an Italian speaker who can pronounce the names of the meats and pastas. Perhaps your young man would be keen to apply for this job, if you're still together when you come back?"

Trudging over the tussocks of grass on the hilltop, Olivia found herself spluttering yet again. Her mother was being downright impossible! As if Danilo would be happy managing a small suburban deli, when he was the local craftsman here in Tuscany and master of his woodworking art. Worse still, her mother was assuming he would be happy doing this job *just because he was Italian*!

Olivia rolled her eyes so wildly they hurt.

Why, oh why, did her mother persist with this notion that she would come back home one day?

"I have some other interesting news for you," her mother continued, as Olivia opened the farmhouse door and let herself in, grateful to be back in the warmth and light, and to see Pirate meowing hungrily for her food.

"What's that?" Olivia asked, heading straight for the kitchen. After giving Pirate her kibble, she opened the fridge and took out a bottle of chenin blanc, pouring a large glass. It was early to start drinking, but under these circumstances, she felt her decision was justified.

"I have a friend, Iris, who knows someone who's involved with tourism in Italy. Iris mentioned this morning, when we got together for coffee, that a very wealthy businessman on a local tour in your area was found dead under suspicious circumstances. It is breaking news, apparently, and was at a winery called A La Loggio, if I remember correctly. Do you know of it, angel? Were you aware that working in that area is so risky?"

Olivia choked on her wine. Eyes streaming, she put down the glass before it spilled and did her best to cough quietly.

"I—I'll look into it," she said in a squeaky voice as soon as speech had returned.

"I'm seeing Iris again on the weekend and will find out more from her. I think your father and I need to get to you as soon as possible. But for now, I have to go. I put a pie in the oven and must check on it."

Olivia disconnected with a sigh of relief.

"Please don't visit," she begged, knowing that her mother would be picking up subliminally on Olivia's desperate request and most probably booking the flight at that very moment.

It was a terrifying thought.

Plus, she didn't want to imagine the conversation she would end up having if she hadn't solved the crime by the weekend, and her mother remembered the *right* winery name!

Olivia collapsed onto a kitchen chair, feeling wrung out by her day. Having finished her kibble, Pirate stalked past with her sensitive feminine nose in the air and clearly still out of joint after Olivia's callous treatment of her.

"Pirate!" Olivia called.

The cat didn't glance in her direction, but at least her tail lifted up like a pretty, black antenna before she jumped onto the counter and wove her way elegantly out the window. So Olivia knew, deep down, her cat still loved her.

About Danilo, she was far less sure. Why hadn't he called her back? Had her sharp words this morning put him off completely? She felt agonized about it. Trying to call him yet again would be wrong. She didn't want him to feel as if she was chasing him—especially not if he'd decided to call it quits.

At the thought, her stomach twisted uncomfortably.

"Why do I feel my life has reached a nadir?" Olivia said aloud. Nothing seemed to be going right. Not her investigation, not her relationship. Her cat was holding a tangible grudge against her, she'd chickened out of opening her secret storeroom, and her mother was still not taking her new life seriously.

Thinking about all these irritations made Olivia feel as if she were holding a fistful of thorny branches, all prickling at her skin.

"By tomorrow, this is going to change!" Olivia promised. "Firstly, I'm going to find the killer. Secondly, I'm going to make things right with Danilo. Thirdly, I'm going to clear the winery's name, and fourthly, I'm going to tell my mother, once and for all, to back off and stop being annoying!"

Even though she had a sneaky feeling that only three out of those four points might be possible, Olivia was determined that tomorrow would bring some serious changes for the better in her life.

CHAPTER TWENTY NINE

Pirate's warm weight on her feet woke her in the morning, but as soon as Olivia sat up, the cat leaped off the bed and stalked out of the room, looking offended.

Olivia grimaced. Would Pirate hold a grudge against her forever?

Trying to put her feline's problematic cattitude aside, she climbed out of bed, thinking of the day ahead. The billionaires would be safely in their lodgings, probably sleeping in after their dinner yesterday.

If she moved fast, she could get the jump on them, and question them while they were still hazy and hungover from their outing.

Drake would be her first stop, she decided. She'd thought from the start that he had the strongest motive, because Rupert had insulted him nonstop, and they'd almost ended up having a physical fight. If he hadn't been on the golf course yesterday, she might already have solved this crime.

Swiftly, she raided her wardrobe for smart yet workmanlike clothing. She brushed her hair into a neat ponytail and headed downstairs.

Erba was already looking expectantly through the kitchen window, waiting for her carrots.

"Only four," Olivia told her goat.

She bought the carrots in bags of twelve, and doled them out at the rate of four a day, which seemed like a fair morning snack for an energetic, growing goat.

But this morning, when Olivia reached into the bag, she found there were five carrots left.

"Well, who's a lucky goat?" she told Erba laughingly. "You got an extra one. They must have made a mistake up at the grocery store, and put thirteen into the bag."

As she placed the carrots into the pink bowl, Olivia found herself mulling over those numbers.

Two people had used that word "thirteen" yesterday. The bus driver had mentioned it, and Tomas had also referred to the number of guests. In her ignorance, Olivia had thought they'd both made a mistake. But what if she'd been the one who wasn't picking up on the correct information?

"What if there originally were thirteen people and someone canceled at the last minute—and that person has crucial information on one of the other tour guests?" she said aloud, feeling perplexed by this new possibility.

Since La Leggenda was on the way to the Platino Toscana, Olivia decided she'd make a quick stop at the chalets and check this discrepancy with the bus driver.

Grabbing her jacket, she powered out of the front door, surprised to see that Erba had abandoned her carrots and was trotting in the same direction, looking equally decisive.

"I need you to stay home today," Olivia told her goat. "I don't know where I'll end up, or whether I'll be able to fetch you later."

Stern as her words were, she could see they were being ignored. The gleam in Erba's eyes told her that her goat was standing firm on this matter. Erba wanted to come for a car ride and could sense Olivia was going to the winery. From the way she was already shoving past her adopted owner and pushing her nose against the car, Olivia didn't rate her chances of stopping her.

With a sigh, she opened the back door, and Erba sprang victoriously inside.

Getting in the front, Olivia set off, glancing at the gathering clouds that were making for a dramatically red sunrise and hoping it wouldn't start to rain.

On the short drive to the winery, Olivia thought carefully about the questions she would need to ask Drake, and how she could get the results she needed.

Heading through the gates, she detoured to the chalets. Glad to see the gleaming bus in its place under the carport, she parked next to it and hurried up the path to the chalet's front door.

The driver opened it looking bleary-eyed, and less pleased to see her than he had yesterday.

Olivia realized that she'd have to come up with a good excuse for waking him up. She only had one reason currently available in her artillery, so she used it.

"Sorry to bother you again," she apologized. "I forgot to give you your gift yesterday. I brought a pack of wine for you, and one for Luca, to say thanks for all your help."

"Oh." The driver's face warmed. "That is kind of you."

"I've got them in the car. How did everything go last night?" Olivia chattered as she led the way back to her Fiat.

"It was a pleasant outing. Everyone seemed to enjoy it. On the way there, they were discussing business, the weather, and of course how the police had inconvenienced them," the driver explained.

"What about on the way back?" she asked, choosing one of the wine packs and handing it to the driver.

"On the way back, the topic was mainly food, of course. Although I do remember several of the party said how much they had enjoyed the cat video."

Olivia couldn't conceal a smile. She felt thrilled that her good advice to Ferdie had worked.

"About the wine gifts." Olivia paused, looking thoughtfully at her parcels. "I'm wondering if I counted one short? We would like to give everyone—er, every surviving person on the tour—a gift. But while twelve arrived at the winery, you mentioned that there were thirteen places booked. I wanted to check that with you."

The driver nodded. "Yes. There was a thirteenth guest. She canceled just before the tour began. I understand that she felt ill, and checked into a spa near Florence."

"What's her name? And where is she staying?"

The driver scrolled through his phone.

"Marilyn Watkyns. She's staying at the Aqua Millionaire."

Olivia recognized this as being one of the most exclusive spa hotels in the wider area.

"Why didn't she come to dinner yesterday? Is she still ill?" Olivia asked.

"She canceled the rest of the tour and told us she would remain at the spa," the driver explained.

"Oh," Olivia said. That didn't sound as if she was ill, just that she preferred not to be on the tour.

"Thank you," she said to the driver. "Enjoy the wine."

The weather hadn't held, and it was starting to rain lightly as she climbed back into her car. She checked the time, remembering how grumpy and bleary-eyed the driver had been. If she arrived at Platino Toscana too early, Drake might lose his temper and refuse to see her.

Instead, she decided to spend a few minutes researching the new guest.

She scrolled through her phone, typing Marilyn Watkyns into the search field.

Movement at her car window distracted her. Erba was standing outside, looking at her pleadingly through the glass.

Olivia buzzed down the window an inch.

"Erba, no!" she said firmly. "What's wrong with the dairy today? Go and play with your friends. It's starting to rain. I don't want a car smelling of wet goat."

Erba pushed her nose determinedly against the tiny gap. With a sigh, Olivia relented.

"I think you're just enjoying car rides," she told the goat, opening the back door. Erba leaped eagerly inside.

Breathing in the strong smell of rain-soaked goat, Olivia returned to her research. Here were some links, she saw excitedly.

"Marilyn Watkyns, owner of Watkyns Enterprises, stands in front of the brand new bottling plant, opened after a long legal battle over the environmental sensitivity of the site, which she insisted on as being the most cost-effective location."

"Marilyn Watkyns, owner of Watkyns Enterprises, is in court today over the perceived copying of a trademarked label. The billionaire businesswoman, who manufactures the recently launched soda Zingy Lemonade, argues that in fact the smaller supplier copied her label, and not the other way around, and is suing them for trademark infringement."

"Marilyn Watkyns has stated she will take legal action over a 'slanderous' comment by competitor Bondi Beans, who made a joke during a public interview that the popular baked bean brand she owns, Fargo Beans, should be renamed Fart-Go as it uses inferior beans that cause consumers to suffer from excessive wind."

Olivia's eyes widened as she read through the reports. For a businesswoman who seemed to deal in consumer goods, Ms. Watkyns sure seemed to spend a lot of her time in court, and Olivia suspected that she wasn't always in the right. She felt nervous at approaching such a person. One wrong word from her was likely to end up with Olivia herself being slapped with a lawsuit.

Hopefully, Drake would be her last stop, and there would be no need to interview this scary woman.

"Erba, here's a picture of her," Olivia told her goat, who was peering intelligently over her shoulder at the phone screen.

Ms. Watkyns looked to be in her thirties or forties, an attractive woman with smooth skin and expensive-looking, ash-blond hair. Since another report had mentioned she'd recently celebrated her fifty-fifth birthday, Olivia guessed her looks were either due to good genes and healthy living, or an excellent surgeon.

Staring at her strong, uncompromising face, Olivia found herself feeling glad she hadn't been on the tour. There was no doubt that she would have been a difficult customer!

Erba nibbled at Olivia's hair in a questioning way, making her laugh.

"Let's read one final article before we go get Drake," Olivia told her goat.

But, as the screen refreshed, Olivia gasped. Her eyes took in the words as her brain reeled in shock. How was this possible? How?

This unexpected revelation had changed everything. Drake would have to wait, because she needed to speak to this terrifying woman immediately.

Marilyn Watkyns was the wife of the deceased, Rupert Curren.

CHAPTER THIRTY

Heading determinedly out of the winery, with her windshield wipers flicking at the worsening rain, Olivia felt numb with shock.

Ms. Watkyns must have a wealth of information about her husband. This would be a critical and urgent interview. But at the same time, Olivia felt intimidated by the task.

Though obnoxious, Rupert had been Marilyn's life partner. As a grieving widow, she was likely to be devastated. A mere gift of wine would seem shallow, like a sham.

Olivia took a deep breath. Her only hope was to go there and admit honestly to the bereaved woman that she'd only just heard about her existence, and had come to offer her personal condolences.

Skirting the compact, historic city of Florence, she headed out into the countryside beyond, feeling her stomach churn as she thought of the challenging ordeal ahead.

She parked outside the spa's marble-clad buildings. The grounds were green and rolling, and she could see Erba peering longingly at the lush grass.

"No!" Olivia told her goat firmly. "Absolutely not!"

Leaving the window open a crack so that Erba could enjoy fresh air, Olivia climbed out into the cold, rainy morning and rushed through the downpour to the hotel.

The interior was cream and blue, lemon scented, spacious and peaceful. Soft classical music played in the background.

"*Buon giorno*," she greeted the receptionist. She approached the desk, which looked like a pastel-hued spaceship console, and leaned over it, getting close to the white-uniformed receptionist.

"This is a difficult question," Olivia confided in a low voice. "I'm hoping for a word with Marilyn Watkyns. I know she must be overwhelmed and probably has a whole lot on her plate, but I would like to offer my personal condolences."

"We do not allow visitors into the hotel," the receptionist said regretfully.

Olivia's face fell and she stared at the other woman in consternation. She'd come all this way! In a goat-scent-infused Fiat!

"Is there no possibility?" she pleaded. When the receptionist's face remained stern, she added, "I feel so terrible about all of this! Plus, I'm likely to be fired if I go back and tell my boss I couldn't do it!"

Even though she felt bad blaming Marcello, she remembered how well the "my boss will fire me" story had worked with the doorman at Villa Fiora.

To her surprise, it worked equally well here, and the receptionist relented.

"We do not allow visitors into the hotel. However, at present, Ms. Watkyns is in the spa, awaiting a treatment program which starts shortly. So yes, you may go through to the spa reception quickly, as long as you do not delay her."

Having a spa treatment? That surprised Olivia, but she guessed everyone had a different way of coping with grief. At any rate, this was a stroke of luck for her.

"Thank you so much," she said gratefully, hurrying in the direction of the spa.

She recognized Marilyn from her online research as soon as she walked in. Clad in a toweling robe, the new widow was relaxing on a chaise-lounge with a cup of herbal tea by her side. She glanced up inquiringly when Olivia entered.

"Ms. Watkyns," she said in a low voice. She was quivering all over. This wasn't a situation she'd ever wanted to be in. Terrified that she might say or do the wrong thing, offend Marilyn or even worse, upset her, she took a seat opposite.

"I hope you don't mind me coming here. I work at the winery, La Leggenda, where Rupert—er—"

She stared at Marilyn wordlessly. Luckily the other woman picked up the conversational reins.

"Where he passed away," she said sadly. "I hope you understand it's not a place I ever want to visit. Or hear about again." Her voice sharpened.

"Absolutely," Olivia sympathized. "I came to offer my condolences. This is such a tragedy. I can't begin to think how you must be feeling."

"Devastated," Marilyn said, sipping at her tea. "This is not what I expected to happen on a luxury vacation."

Again, her words were barbed.

"I hope that the police can provide answers," Olivia said softly.

"The police? Italian police are all corrupt, incompetent, or both. I have no faith in them. They have already been here to interview me. I am sure that is the last I will ever see or hear of them," Marilyn said dismissively.

Olivia stared at her, horrified. She couldn't believe anyone would dare to say such a thing about the formidable Detective Caputi.

"Do you know how it might have happened?" she asked carefully.

Marilyn stared at her with a strange expression, as if she hadn't taken in the extent of Olivia's stupidity until that exact moment.

"I have no idea," she said slowly. "You said you work for the winery. Did you not notice I wasn't there?"

"Of course," Olivia said soothingly, worried that Marilyn was on the attack. Luckily the other woman continued to provide more detail.

"We spent the previous day here, both enjoying spa treatments. Then we were supposed to leave for the tour, but I had a migraine in the morning. I decided to cancel the tour, and instead booked in for a sauna session, a head massage, a manicure, pedicure, bikini wax, hot stone massage, reflexology treatment, and an ozone session to help me feel better, with a light lunch and French champagne included. That kept me occupied the whole day. My last treatment ended at six-thirty p.m., and I planned to join Rupert for dinner. Of course, that never happened. At seven-thirty p.m. as I was about to leave for the restaurant, the police arrived here and broke the news."

She took another slow sip of tea.

"Do you know any of the other people on the tour?" Olivia asked.

Marilyn sighed impatiently.

"The police mentioned some names. I have had dealings with a couple of them in the course of business. I have no idea who the others were, since that was only the first day of the tour."

Olivia nodded sympathetically.

"Did you or your late husband have any dealings with Drake Rafter? They seemed to clash on the tour and I wondered if there was any history between them," she asked.

"Oh, yes. Drake and Rupert played golf together a number of times, usually at charity events and the like. I know that Drake was very jealous of Rupert's lower handicap. Rupert often shared with me how he thought Drake hated him as a result. Perhaps he killed him," Marilyn wondered aloud.

Olivia's eyebrows shot up. This added yet more weight to Drake's motive. She needed to hustle over to Platino Toscana, and not spend any more time keeping the grieving widow from her spa treatment.

Even though she was in a hurry to leave and focused on Drake's guilt, she thought of a kind gesture as she stood up.

"I know it's only a small thing, but would you like me to drop off a pack of wine for you later? A selection of local bottles from the area as a gift, something to help ease your sorrow?"

"You may," Marilyn said. "I am staying in suite twelve. You can leave the gift at reception for me, or else bring it to my rooms. I prefer dry white wine. Don't bother with any of the reds."

Pleased that she'd agreed to take receipt of some free stuff, Olivia got up and tiptoed out of the spa. What an ordeal that had been! Stressful as she'd found the visit, it had been worthwhile, Olivia mused, as she headed back to her car and goat.

Marilyn herself had a watertight alibi. She'd been having treatments the whole day, and could not possibly have slipped out in the late afternoon to embark on an eighty-minute round trip to murder her husband.

More importantly, she'd implicated Olivia's main suspect!

Olivia drove out of the spa deep in thought. She was so focused on what she would say to Drake that she didn't stop to admire the passing scenery, or even gaze at the pretty village on the way to Platino Toscana, which was slightly bigger than her local village, and with a wider selection of shops.

Then, suddenly, a familiar face grabbed her attention.

She hit the brakes so hard that Erba lurched forward, frolicking into the front seat to keep her balance and perching expectantly on its edge.

There was Danilo, walking in town.

He was out and about, and, worse still, he was with another woman!

Olivia couldn't believe her eyes. She felt devastated as she watched him talking and laughing with the young, pretty, dark-haired woman who was trendily dressed in low-slung jeans and a fluffy, cropped jacket that showed off an inch of toned belly.

They were huddled together under a white umbrella. Sharing it, Olivia noted, feeling sick. This was disastrous. Already, at this early stage, her new romance had gone the way of her last one. She was being cheated on! Were they meeting in this nearby village so as to avoid the watching eyes of the locals?

Olivia felt dark suspicion uncoil inside her as she thought about that.

Spotting an empty bay, she pulled in and climbed out of the car, marching along behind them with all the energy of righteous fury.

This was unacceptable! How wrong she had been to ever trust Danilo. Shouldering her way past the shoppers, Olivia realized she was walking bare headed in the pouring rain. She didn't care. Being cheated on was much worse than getting wet.

To her horror, she watched them stroll into a small jewelry store.

This was why they'd come to this village. Because it contained a destination store.

Olivia whimpered softly as she watched them lean over the gleaming glass cases, clearly discussing the contents. Both looked smiling and happy—contented and comfortable in each other's company.

Danilo turned to his pretty friend, his hands spread, in the way he did when he was asking Olivia to choose something.

Then the younger woman pointed to an item of jewelry decisively.

Even though she was too far away to hear Danilo speak, Olivia could see from his body language exactly what he was saying.

"That's the one? You are sure?"

The woman nodded, clearly sure.

Danilo looked again at the price tag, and glanced once more at his pretty companion.

"You are very sure? This is an expensive piece!"

She wasn't budging. She placed her hands on her slender hips and nodded decisively.

Olivia felt nauseous as Danilo laughed in agreement, pointing out the piece—whatever it was, she couldn't see, but it seemed to be in the bracelet section. Clearly it was a feminine and pricey piece of jewelry.

She was being two-timed by her new boyfriend!

Hurt and anger curdled in her stomach. Olivia was tempted to march into the store then and there, confront them, and have it out in public. But she couldn't bring herself to do it. She felt too shocked and raw. Instead, she turned away and trudged back to her car, wishing that she'd never been stupid enough to start dating someone who even though he seemed different from her previous boyfriends, was clearly exactly the same type.

What an idiot she was!

She climbed into the car, soaked and upset and thoroughly discombobulated. She wanted to go home with a large to-go pizza, eat it, and then bury herself under the duvet and never come out again.

That wouldn't work, of course.

She still had a murder to solve. Despite her emotional trauma, a killer was walking free. Until she found who it was, her job, and the winery, were at risk.

Erba nuzzled her in a friendly way and Olivia stroked her fur, glad of her goat's comforting presence. She took in a huge, shaky breath and let it out again. Finally, she felt more on an even keel, at any rate, enough to be able to go and interview the last two suspects on her list.

"Well, Erba, my whole life's falling apart. My mother is refusing to listen to me. My boyfriend is buying gifts for another woman. My cat is ignoring me. It's all gotten worse since yesterday! But I am going to do this one thing. I am going to find out who the killer is."

Gripping the wheel, Olivia drove out of the village and took the turning for the hotel, knowing that this was her very last chance.

CHAPTER THIRTY ONE

Arriving at the Platino Toscana, Olivia was glad to see a Maserati reversing out of the bay closest to the door. Nipping into it, she warned Erba to stay, grabbed her wine packs, and dashed through the rain into the warm, plush hotel.

Luckily, the receptionist and butler were both involved in emergency leak control. One of the ceiling spotlights was fizzing and flickering, and a stream of water was dripping down to the floral-etched tiles below where a bucket had been placed. This was clearly a catastrophe. They were both pointing at it in distress and as she watched, the manager came and joined them, pointing even more vigorously at the offending trickle.

With all eyes fixed on the ceiling above, it meant she could get into the hotel without any questions. Quickly, Olivia slunk into the bar.

There, to her astonishment, were her two final suspects. Drake and Sid were sitting at the bar, drinking large Negronis. The sunset-colored cocktails had been served in tall glasses, with ice and a twist of orange.

Well, Olivia supposed, it was nearly lunch time—if you liked to eat before noon. Why shouldn't they indulge in some liquid refreshment? More than likely, it was the hair of the dog after the heavy dinner they'd had.

"Hello. Look who's here. And she's carrying wine!" Drake welcomed her, in tones so festive that Olivia began to suspect it wasn't his first Negroni of the day. She hoped the alcohol would make him more talkative.

"Yes, I came to bring you these gifts, and to ask you a few questions," Olivia began.

Sid looked less pleased to see her, frowning suspiciously as Olivia placed a pack of wine on the shiny wooden bar in front of each man.

"Have you been crying?" Drake asked.

Too late, Olivia realized that her mascara must be irreparably smeared, and relocated mostly under her eyes.

"She's been in the rain," Sid noted irritably. "Her hair's soaked as well. Looks like it's pouring outside. I guess golf is a write-off today."

"Yeah, maybe darts?" Drake glanced toward the corner of the bar.

With the conversation on sporting activities, Olivia decided to pursue this angle.

"You're a big fan of golf, I can see. Did you and Rupert ever play together?" she asked Drake as she carefully wiped her fingers under her eyes, hoping she was removing all the mascara tracks.

"Yeah, a few times." Drake cackled with laughter. "Rupert was a hopeless golfer and always used to lose his temper during the game. It was worth playing with him for the entertainment value, but it could be embarrassing when he caused a scene and threw his clubs around."

Olivia frowned. This wasn't the same version Marilyn had told her. She'd insisted Rupert was a better golfer and Drake had been murderously jealous. Who was telling the truth?

As she was thinking what her next question should be, Drake asked one in turn.

"What's the wine for?"

"It's to apologize for the inconvenience during your tour." She smiled at both men.

"Well, it wasn't your fault," Drake said generously, taking another large gulp of his Negroni. "Actually, I think we had the best time there. I've been on a few tours before and to me, they've been becoming stuck up and pretentious. I enjoyed the grilled cheese. That's proper food."

"I agree," Sid enthused.

"All the same, it was traumatic for everyone. And as yet, the crime is unsolved," Olivia said sadly. "I was hoping that someone might have seen Rupert, and perhaps noticed if he was being followed. Did you see him go out at all?" she asked Drake.

"Nope, not me." Drake shook his head. "I was outside, round the back of the restaurant, getting some air. There's a stone bench there where I sat, and only came in when I heard you calling everyone."

Olivia saw Sid was looking at Drake curiously.

"Must be a big bench," he said.

"Why?" Drake frowned.

"Because I was sitting there myself, right up until this young lady here with the mascara malfunction called us in. And I don't recall you being there!"

Olivia drew in a sharp breath. Finally, she had picked up an inconsistency in the versions. One of these men was lying, and she was sure it was Drake. Perhaps he was a compulsive liar, she thought.

Then, from behind her, she heard a sound that sent a bolt of electricity though her.

It was the sharp, unmistakable noise made by an angry police detective clearing her throat.

Olivia whirled round.

There stood Detective Caputi, flanked by two officers.

"I—hello! I was just giving some gifts of wine. As consolation prizes," Olivia babbled, needing to deflect that laser glare before it drilled an actual hole in her.

Luckily, the detective's gaze shifted, and she directed it to the two men, who both started looking deeply uncomfortable.

"We have made progress on this case. A forensic specialist has examined the partial footprint by the pond. Given the inconsistencies in your accounts when we interviewed you after the crime, we drove straight here. Show me your shoe," she commanded Drake, pointing at his left foot.

"My shoe?" A myriad of emotions flitted across Drake's face. He looked puzzled, furtive, worried—and guilty. He raised his leg high into the air, nearly toppling off his bar stool. Olivia grabbed his arm.

"Not like that," she advised, glad to be able to share the wisdom of her own past experience. "When she asks you to do that, she wants you to take the shoe right off."

That took some more unbalanced fumbling, but in another minute, Drake was handing his scuffed leather moccasin to the detective.

Detective Caputi inspected the aging footwear carefully. Olivia felt the atmosphere in the bar grow suddenly colder, and there seemed to be less air in the room than there had been. This was scary!

The detective snapped her fingers, and an officer passed her a cardboard folder and an iPad. They opened both and put their heads together, looking at the shoe, and the page, and the device, and the shoe again.

Drake picked up his Negroni glass. Ice clinked as he knocked the contents back in one large gulp.

"Undoubtedly, this is the same sole pattern!" Detective Caputi announced triumphantly, placing the moccasin in an evidence bag.

Olivia gasped. She exchanged a horrified glance with Sid.

Drake *had* been lying. He hadn't been sitting on the bench where Sid had in fact been innocently resting. Instead, he'd been prowling around, waiting for a moment to dispose of the unlikable Rupert.

"Look, okay, so I left out a few details," Drake protested, his eyes widening in alarm as the closest police officer stepped toward him. With his voice now higher in pitch, he continued hurriedly. "I stayed on the bench for a moment. And then I saw that opinionated idiot lurching away from the restaurant. I mean, he looked like he was auditioning for a zombie movie. He could hardly walk! So I reckoned it would be a good time to follow him and tell him what I thought of him, and that he'd better shape up or ship out for the rest of the tour."

"Indeed?" Detective Caputi asked. From her emphasis, Olivia could tell she didn't believe one word of this version. Not one syllable, in fact.

"So I headed after him. I caught up quickly seeing I took a much more direct route. He was weaving all over the place," Drake elaborated. "He arrived at the pond and peered into it like it was a wishing well. So then I clapped him on the back and said, 'Look, you need to change your behavior. You're ruining this for everyone. Stop acting in such a dislikeable and aggressive way. And while you're about it, you should change your behavior on the golf course too. Either practice more, or be a better loser when you end up in all the bunkers.'"

"Rupert was a terrible golfer," Sid added helpfully. "I was in a four-ball with him once. He got angry and threw his putter so far away he lost it in the rough."

If that was so, then Marilyn's version had been wrong, Olivia thought, feeling confused. But there wasn't time to explore that idea further, and maybe, given the other evidence, there was no need. In any case, Detective Caputi wasn't listening to Sid. Her gaze skewered Drake, who blushed slightly.

"Okay, I might have used stronger words when I spoke to him. But I'm telling the truth, I promise," he insisted.

"Stronger actions is what I am more concerned about," the detective retorted acidly.

"I didn't push him in!" Drake protested, but the detective ignored him. She stepped forward and grasped him firmly by the wrist.

"This sole print match has provided sufficient evidence for us to take you to the police station for further questioning. If you cannot prove your version, we will be arresting you on suspicion of the murder of Rupert Curren," she announced in ringing tones.

Drake looked astonished. "Hey! Dammit! I was going to order a third Negroni and then have lunch. Wait, don't take me in! I need a pizza. I have a headache. I need an Advil. Are you guys crazy? Give me back my shoe, I can't hop out of here!"

His protests cut no ice with the determined detective. In another moment, Drake was escorted out, hopping along, firmly bracketed between the two sturdy male officers, with Caputi leading the way.

Olivia let out a huge sigh of relief. Finally, this mystery had been solved and a suspect with a strong motive had been arrested. She was sure that Drake would soon offer up a full confession, given the sole print evidence and Detective Caputi's relentless interrogation technique. Once that had happened, she hoped the winery, and Marcello's name, would be cleared.

Since her morning had turned out so well, Olivia decided she wouldn't go straight to work, but would detour back to the farm and taste her ice wine. With the murder investigation concluded, she hoped that this day, which had seemed so bleak at the start, might end up bringing two successes.

CHAPTER THIRTY TWO

Back home, Olivia found herself wishing that Danilo could be with her for this important moment. Now that she'd seen him out and about, selecting a bracelet for another woman, that idea was a non-starter of course.

She was tempted to pick up the phone then and there, call him, and vent her anger, but she couldn't do it. The whole jewelry store episode still felt too raw and upsetting.

Instead, she headed outside, following the path to the barn.

What if the wine was awful and she ended up throwing it away? she worried, as she unlocked the tall wooden door.

That summoned up a vivid image of Rupert. Ferdie had described him staggering outside and tossing his wine angrily away.

If he'd thrown most of his wine out, how had he managed to get so incredibly drunk? she wondered. He hadn't shared Carmody's whiskey. He hadn't consumed much alcohol at all. Apart from insulting people, it seemed like he hadn't had any real purpose for being there!

Olivia felt a weird shift in her head, as if puzzle pieces she hadn't even known about were slotting suddenly into place.

And then, as she was about to reach an epiphany, her phone rang.

It was Marcello, and seeing his name on the screen made mixed emotions surge inside her all over again.

"*Ciao*," she answered quickly.

"Olivia. I thought I would warn you." Marcello sounded stressed. He spoke fast and in a low, furtive voice.

"What?" Olivia's heart sped up. What was Marcello going to say? Had he given up on the mentorship? Was he closing the winery permanently? She waited, feeling nervous, for him to explain.

"Detective Caputi has just been here. She was looking for you, expecting you would have returned to work."

"What?" Olivia squeaked. The case was closed. Or was it? Had Drake managed to wiggle out of the charges, and accused her instead?

"What did she want?" she asked, swallowing hard.

"She refused to disclose much." Marcello paused. "But I was able to ask a few questions that she was willing to answer."

This was a massive understatement, Olivia realized, with a rush of gratitude toward her boss. The charm offensive that Marcello must have launched in order to tease snippets of information from the reluctant and grumpy detective had clearly been on an unprecedented scale.

"What did she say?" Olivia asked anxiously.

"She said the toxicology tests had just come back, and they showed evidence of highly irregular blood work. Apparently, an hour or so before his death, Rupert must have consumed something that proved to be fast-acting and highly toxic. She explained they are looking for a prior cause. And they want to speak to you!" Marcello's voice rose in panic.

Olivia could see exactly where this was heading. The detective now suspected that she had slipped something into Rupert's wine—perhaps deliberately poisoned him as punishment for his obnoxious behavior. This was a disaster for her, and the winery! The blame was firmly back on La Leggenda's doorstep again.

And then, as she thought frantically back to how the afternoon had played out, the final puzzle piece slotted into place.

At last, she knew for sure how Rupert had died, and who had committed the crime.

"Marcello, she can come and look for me. I won't be here. I've just worked out what happened, and I'm heading out now, to prove it."

Disconnecting hurriedly, Olivia locked the barn door again and rushed to her car.

She arrived at the same time as Erba.

"Not now," Olivia said firmly. "I'm on my way to apprehend a murder suspect! You must stay home!"

The goat stared her down.

Olivia sighed. It had been a short workday for Erba, and she loved car rides. More worryingly, she remembered that Erba's hoof prints had also been beside the pond. What if the detective arrived and arrested her goat on suspicion while she was gone? Erba would be traumatized! Olivia couldn't risk it.

"Get in," she snapped, deciding to relent for safety's sake.

With both of them safely in the car, Olivia headed out, burning rubber as she sped down the road.

*

167

The luxury spa looked exactly the same as it had the last time Olivia arrived there—calm, serene, and tranquil. She was the one who felt different, filled with surging emotions. Hope, anxiety, and determination churned inside her as she told Erba to wait and cranked the window down a half-inch before rushing in.

She'd put some sketchy plans into place on the way and left important voice messages. Olivia hoped those plans would hold up! Otherwise, she would be the one getting arrested.

Her hands felt damp at that possibility and her knees were quivering.

Thank goodness Marilyn Watkyns had told her what room she was staying in, she thought. Trying to seem purposeful, she marched down the corridor, glancing discreetly at the numbers as she passed.

Here was suite twelve. She tapped lightly on the door, trying to sound like someone checking on the minibar or arriving with refresher towelettes. Her hands felt cold. So much hinged on what would play out in the next few minutes.

Marilyn opened the door and smiled regally as she recognized Olivia.

"Ah. My wine," she said in pleased tones.

Her smile disappeared as she saw Olivia was empty-handed, but by then she'd pushed her way inside the sumptuously furnished suite.

"I didn't bring the wine," she said. Her voice came out in a nervous squeak. She was sure her suspicions were correct, they surely had to be, but if she was wrong, Olivia knew she'd just set herself up for the biggest lawsuit in legal history. No wonder she was nervous!

"Why no wine for me?" Marilyn stared at her with an expression that caused Olivia's stomach to churn.

"I came here because I needed to ask you a few questions," Olivia began, hoping to ease into this difficult interview.

"What right do you have to ask me, a grieving widow, anything at all? Get out!" Marilyn replied in a voice that sounded like a steel blade.

Olivia swallowed. She felt as if she were treading on thin ice that could shatter at any moment and plunge her into a world of trouble. But, as she considered Marilyn's words, she realized that her response was strangely defensive. After all, she could just have come to ask exactly what dry white wine she preferred!

"I need to clarify more details about the crime," she said, forcing herself to stay strong.

"There is no reason for me to tell you anything. And I will not. You are a nobody, acting way beyond your limited scope, and in fact probably deranged. You could even become violent and dangerous! I'm going to call hotel security and ask them to remove you."

She wasn't joking! Olivia watched in horror as Marilyn headed purposefully toward the telephone on the desk. In a moment she would make the call and it would all be over. Of course the hotel would believe the guest's version. Olivia felt her knees start to quiver. The only way to stop this would be to come straight out with the accusation, she decided.

"I'm not the dangerous one. You are, and you know it, since you murdered your husband. I know exactly how you did it, too." Jutting her chin to conceal her fear, Olivia delivered her bombshell.

She was relieved that Marilyn turned away from the phone, clearly distracted from her mission to evict Olivia.

For a nasty moment, Olivia thought that Marilyn was going to physically attack her. She looked furious! But instead, the billionaire folded her arms and gave a callous laugh.

"I hope you have a very good lawyer," she said, looking Olivia up and down in a critical way. "This is defamation, at a level where it will require significant compensation on your part to make good on this horrific character slur, which you have had the gall to accuse me of at such a vulnerable time. Actually, it doesn't matter what kind of lawyer you have. Looking at your cheap clothing, your outgrown roots, and those aspirational shoes which clearly stretched your budget to its limit and meant you ate toast for a week, it's quite clear you couldn't afford anywhere near the amount of compensation that I will require. But it's all right. We can look at other parties who may be jointly liable due to a personal or business connection. Perhaps your employer. That would be the winery, right?"

She sounded brisk. Olivia clutched at an antique bookshelf for support. Not only was she stung to the quick by Marilyn's devastatingly personal insults, but she was seriously worried that the other woman would manage to destroy the winery, using her highly paid legal team as a weapon.

At that moment, the door burst open. Olivia spun round.

There stood Detective Caputi, her steel gray hair gleaming like a shield, flanked by two police officers—one tall, the other very tall.

Just in time, her cavalry had arrived! But as Olivia gasped in relief, the next devastating blow occurred.

169

"Olivia Glass, you are under arrest on suspicion of murder," the detective announced in crisp, yet satisfied, tones.

CHAPTER THIRTY THREE

"No!" Olivia pleaded, her voice quivering. Yet again, Marilyn uttered that callously unpleasant laugh that she was starting to loathe.

"Take her away. I'll be in touch later. We'll press the civil suit when she comes out of jail after the criminal one," Marilyn said in derogatory tones.

Olivia stared at the policewoman in horror.

"Wait, please! Did you listen to both my voice messages?"

Now it was the detective's turn to look taken aback.

"Both?" she asked carefully. She stuck out a hand to stop the very tall officer with the handcuffs from actually stepping toward Olivia. At such a tense time, Olivia was grateful for this small gesture.

"I left two messages," Olivia gabbled. "The first was to tell you where I was. Then my signal cut out and I had to send a second one, to tell you why I was here. This is the murderer!" She pointed determinedly at Marilyn. "And if you give me just two minutes, I'll tell you why!"

"Why?" Detective Caputi asked, folding her arms.

"Because of the toxicology. You see, I noticed that Rupert wasn't drinking heavily. Although he consumed some wine, he spent more time insulting it. In fact, Ferdie said he saw him pouring wine away. But yet, by the end of the evening, he was staggering, slurring, and uncoordinated. I started wondering how that had happened, and I remembered a small detail I'd forgotten about."

"What was that?" the detective asked.

"He took a tablet. It wasn't directly from a blister pack. It was from a gold pill box he had in his pocket. He said the tablet was for his health. But I think that his wife substituted the medication for something that would fatally poison him. Perhaps it was something that would react badly with alcohol. At any rate, I believe it was that medication that killed him, and that was why Marilyn canceled her place on the tour. She wanted to be far away from him and out of suspicion when it took effect."

Olivia felt breathless after this detailed explanation. Of course, Marilyn was ready with an instant denial.

"What a flimsy little story, rooted entirely in this woman's deluded imagination," she said to Caputi. "Of course I'm innocent. This is a weak attempt to frame me. I assume you'll see through it immediately."

Detective Caputi looked thoughtful. Olivia guessed she was remembering what the toxicology report had said.

"Seeing you are so sure, I take it you will not mind if we conduct a brief search of your rooms?" Caputi asked, fixing Marilyn with her scary glare.

"Please. Go ahead. I've nothing to hide!"

Although she wasn't off the hook yet, Olivia didn't think her own arrest was imminent. Her version had been accepted—in part, at least. She watched, fascinated, as the officers pulled on latex gloves before walking into the room. It was a large room with many different pieces of furniture. There was a giant ottoman painted in immaculate cream, exquisitely carved bedside tables, a large and roomy wardrobe, a writing desk with several drawers, and Marilyn had several pieces of luggage stowed in a corner. Olivia thought the search could take a long while. She'd noticed Marilyn's leather purse, also, slung over a hook on the back of the door—quite a fine accessory given the general poor taste of the billionaires.

Olivia glanced again at the purse. That would have been her hiding place for poisonous medication, for sure.

But, to her astonishment, the hook was empty.

Not only that. Apart from the police, the room was empty, too!

Marilyn had disappeared. Olivia felt shocked as she realized that the mogul must have done a runner.

"She's gone! Quick, stop her!" Olivia shouted. This was a desperate moment for the investigation, the winery, and herself. If Marilyn managed to get away, suspicion would rebound onto Olivia.

The police spun around. For a moment, they froze. And then everyone charged out of the half-open door—the very tall policeman first, then the tall one, and then Olivia. Detective Caputi brought up the rear at a brisk walk, snapping out instructions on her walkie-talkie.

They flew down the corridor and, as she turned the corner to pound down the longest stretch, Olivia caught a hint of bright blue. Marilyn had been wearing a bright blue jacket. She was far ahead, and seemed to be gaining. This was a dire situation.

Olivia remembered there were several cabs and buses parked outside. Marilyn could commandeer one of them and be gone in the blink of an eye. No doubt, her passport was in her purse, and she could be out of Italy and over the border in no time at all.

They burst out of the passage. Marilyn was already nearing the exit door.

"Stop, stop!" Olivia cried breathlessly.

Ignoring her, Marilyn powered toward the doorway.

But, as she reached it, she recoiled with a shriek. Her heel caught in the red carpet, and she tumbled to the ground, sliding on her backside along the plush woolen rug.

Olivia gasped. There stood Erba, foursquare in the doorway, peering curiously at the billionaire as if she wasn't used to humans acting that way when they saw her.

How had Erba even gotten out? Olivia wondered, hurtling toward the scene in total confusion.

The policemen reached Marilyn in a flash. They surrounded her and hauled her to her feet briskly, yet professionally.

But before they could proceed any further, an irate, crimson-faced woman wearing a red padded coat and Union Jack scarf marched up to Marilyn and tapped her angrily on her chest.

"Is this your goat?" she asked furiously, gesturing at Erba, who looked pleased to be included in the conversation.

Without waiting for an answer from the clearly winded Marilyn, she continued.

"I freed her from the vehicle a moment ago, and was coming in to confront the owner. Do you have any idea how cruel it is to leave animals in cars? They can die of heatstroke within minutes!" She glanced up at the cold drizzle before resuming her attack. "Heatstroke or—or other causes. She didn't even have hay or water available. This would be a criminal offense back in England! The RSPCA would take you to the cleaners, madam. I see the carabinieri here feel the same way, and a good thing too. I hope you spend many months in prison for your unthinking, uncaring ways. Animal rights must prevail!" she concluded.

Olivia sidled closer to one of the doorway pillars and slunk behind it. She didn't want to get into this eccentric woman's firing line, or be outed as Erba's rightful owner at this tense moment!

Luckily, the red-faced woman seemed to have had her say. She turned and marched over to a waiting Land Rover, climbing in on the passenger side.

The car puttered away.

"Come here, Erba!" Olivia commanded, quickly emerging from the refuge of the pillar, frantic with worry that her goat might caper off into the spa grounds and take weeks to be recaptured.

Thankfully, Erba was pleased to see her and trotted over, pushing her head against Olivia's leg in a loving way.

Olivia unbuckled her pants belt. Having sagging pants was an insignificant problem in the greater scheme of things. She looped the belt around Erba's midriff and hung onto it firmly.

"Why did you attempt to flee the scene, Signora Watkyns?" Detective Caputi asked in harsh tones. "Pass me your purse."

Reluctantly, Marilyn handed over the smart leather bag, looking daggers at the detective.

"Why should I stay and listen to your trumped-up charges?" she shot back. "You'll be hearing from my lawyers. Release me this instant! Everyone knows that the Italian police are useless and corrupt."

Olivia narrowed her eyes, expecting an explosion. Instead, Detective Caputi remained remarkably calm.

"So that is your perception? Interesting. It certainly adds to your motive for committing this crime while in Italy."

Marilyn looked aghast as Detective Caputi neatly used her own words against her.

"You have no grounds on which to arrest me. What reason could I possibly have had to commit such a terrible act?"

"Actually, I can think of one," Olivia volunteered. She hoped she wasn't talking out of turn, but as well as the internet research she'd done earlier, she had just remembered something Sashenka had said at the start of the tour.

The blond vodka mogul had been pointing out the various guests to Olivia, who'd had her back to the crowd and hadn't been able to look. But one of her comments had stuck in her mind.

"He married into the business and his wife runs it."

Olivia took a deep breath. Now Marilyn was glaring at her. For a change, though, Detective Caputi was regarding her without her customary incredulous sneer.

"I did some online research before coming here. It seems that all the businesses you own are yours. It's all Watkyns, not Curren. You built them up before your marriage. Also, there's nothing online showing you and Rupert together or even mentioning you as a couple. I think your marriage had fizzled out and you wanted a divorce. Maybe you didn't want to pay the settlement and give your money away when he'd

174

done nothing to deserve it. Or else, you didn't want him running around saying bad things about you, because you don't seem to like it when people do that. So you decided there was an easier way."

Erba spied a young woman carrying a colorful bowl of fruit into the hotel. She lunged forward, making a bid for freedom, but luckily Olivia was ready for her and hung on.

"You waited until you traveled to a country where you believed the police force was inefficient, and you obtained some sort of drug, or poison, in tablet form. Then all you had to do was substitute it when he set off on the tour, and make sure you were nowhere nearby when he took it. You knew how obnoxious he was in public, and how easily other people could be blamed for killing him," Olivia concluded.

Marilyn stared at her and Olivia saw disbelief and horror chasing each other across the woman's satin smooth features.

Then she gave a small shrug and turned back to Detective Caputi.

"All right," she admitted. "It's all true. So, how much?"

"How much?" the detective repeated, perplexed.

"How much to let me go?" Marilyn sounded as if she were concluding an ordinary business transaction. "A hundred thousand euros? More? Can I throw in a decent car, too, as that gray jalopy you arrived in yesterday is simply embarrassing?" She lowered her voice confidentially. "Perhaps we should go inside and discuss it in one of the lounges, while sitting down. Don't worry about this blonde. My lawyers will take care of her, and she won't talk."

She glanced disparagingly at Olivia.

Olivia caught sight of Detective Caputi's expression. For a moment, it was so shocked that the detective looked almost human, she thought in amazement.

Then her usual stern facade resumed, but with a flicker of satisfaction in her eyes.

"You are formally under arrest, Signora Watkyns," she announced. "You are facing two very serious charges—the premeditated murder of your husband, and the attempted bribery of a police detective in front of witnesses. Now, accompany my officers to the car. We will resume this conversation in the interview room at the police station, while my team completes a full search of your rooms, and your purse."

Upon hearing that, Marilyn uttered a shriek of rage.

Turning to Olivia, Detective Caputi nodded in an approving way before climbing into the driver's seat.

The very tall officer helped Marilyn into the car—with the aid of handcuffs since she'd begun to struggle and shout. The tall one got onto his walkie-talkie, calling for backup before heading purposefully into the hotel again.

Olivia watched the car until it was out of sight. She felt stunned by how events had played out. Thanks to her efforts, the right perpetrator had been arrested. But would this be enough to save the winery?

It was time to head back to La Leggenda and find out.

CHAPTER THIRTY FOUR

When Olivia and Erba arrived back at La Leggenda, she was thrilled to see Marcello outside the winery, with the tasting room doors wide open. They must have been cleared by the police, and were back in business again.

He hurried to her car as soon as she'd stopped.

"Olivia! Your efforts were successful! What an incredible result."

He embraced her and Olivia hugged him back hard.

"We were at risk of losing everything. Now we are regarded as heroes, together with Detective Caputi and her team," Marcello explained. People are saying we played a crucial role, along with the police, in solving a dastardly spousal murder that could otherwise have damaged Italy's reputation as a tourist destination! This could not have been a better outcome for us!" He grinned at her, his teeth white in his tanned face.

Relief washed over her as she took in Marcello's words.

A spousal murder absolved the winery entirely. It had simply been coincidence that Rupert had taken his medication while at La Leggenda.

"That's absolutely amazing," she said, feeling elated by how things had played out.

"We have several media interviews lined up, and there are two international news channels arriving tomorrow to film the winery. We have also received messages of thanks from four of the billionaires for solving the crime before the adverse publicity could affect their businesses, too."

Olivia was sure that Chico and Aldo had been among them. Now their social media post could stay up, enticing their followers to La Leggenda.

"That's wonderful." She smiled. Never had she dreamed that this terrible situation could have such a positive outcome. Best of all, Marcello could go forward to his mentorship with a clear mind, and be welcomed as a hero at Castello di Verrazzano.

"Come inside. I want to speak to you in my office," Marcello said.

Now, Olivia's smile felt suddenly forced.

There could be only one topic that required a private meeting, and that was the timely matter of who would run the winery in his absence. She felt her stomach churn with nerves as she followed him in, stopping in astonishment as she entered the lobby.

There, Antonio was pulling the cloth cover off a giant stone sculpture that looked to have just been delivered.

The statue was of a very large, very muscular, very naked man holding an enormous, strategically placed bunch of grapes. Olivia blinked when she saw it. She hadn't thought that statue would be to Marcello's taste. To anyone's taste, in fact, she revised. Why had he chosen it?

With a twist of her stomach she wondered if Gabriella had been given control of the winery and had already started redecorating.

"That is a gift to us from Drake," Marcello said. "He phoned me to say he had ordered *The Love of Wine*, as it is called—a very costly sculpture by a famous classical stonemason, to show gratitude to us for clearing his name. He said to tell you he was able to return to the hotel in time for a late lunch and a third Negroni."

"How kind of him." Olivia stared at the stone edifice, trying to think of something nice to say about it.

"It's…" she began.

"Exactly," Marcello agreed with a sigh. "Perhaps in time we can find a more suitable location for it. Now, please come to my office."

Olivia followed him, feeling cold with nerves. She sat down and waited for Marcello to close the door, walk around his desk, sit down on his leather armchair, and finally speak.

"Stella Markham was here earlier and gave us some feedback on the Platinum Tour," he said conversationally, as if trying to put Olivia at ease.

"Really? What did she say?" And had it made a difference to Marcello's decision? she wondered.

"She said that the guests rated us extremely highly. In fact, we received the highest ratings ever, and will be included on the tour again. Common key words mentioned during the feedback included friendliness, ambience, wine, whiskey, snacks, Wagyu beef, cheese paninis, chocolate truffles, and goats."

Olivia felt a surge of excitement that they'd achieved the impossible and satisfied the hard-to-please billionaires! But hot on its heels, anxiety flooded in. It seemed from the key words that the guests had loved the food more than the wine, and that meant Gabriella had made the more important contribution.

"That's great news," she said in a wobbly voice.

"I have made my decision about who will run the winery in my absence," Marcello continued.

Swallowing hard, Olivia waited for him to tell her.

"I took three factors into account when choosing," Marcello explained, counting on his fingers as he explained. "The first, passion. The second, a hunger for learning. Both you and Gabriella share those qualities in abundance, but there is a third important attribute that the person who takes my place will need."

He was going to say leadership, Olivia predicted with a feeling of dread, and that would mean that the strong-willed Gabriella would take the role.

But to her surprise, Marcello said something completely different.

"Responsibility," he told her. "There is no place for egos or self-interest in running the winery, when dealing with so many different people. And, as such, I had made my decision before the Platinum Tour even began. Your reaction, when I told you that it was a choice between you or Gabriella, convinced me that you were the right person to be put in charge. You remained calm, you spoke well of your rival, and you even volunteered to work together with her. That is what true leadership is about, and you showed it, Olivia—at that moment, and every day as you go about your work. I am totally confident that you will make a success of your new role in my absence, and I could not ask for the winery to be in better hands."

Olivia felt stunned. She couldn't believe what she was hearing. Although she'd hoped and dreamed that Marcello might have enough faith in her to put her in charge, she'd never really thought it would happen. Deep down, she'd assumed that Gabriella would be given the job.

"Marcello, thank you! I'm going to try my best to be the person you believe in, at all times. And to exceed your expectations!"

"I know you will," Marcello said in a soft voice, smiling into her eyes.

Then his phone rang, and with a final nod of thanks, Olivia walked out of the office, still feeling a sense of unreality that she would have the care of this magnificent winery. How much it meant that Marcello had placed his trust in her, and what a learning experience it would be.

It would grow her knowledge about the industry she loved, and give her career a valuable boost.

Olivia headed down the corridor, and as she entered the tasting room, she heard an enraged hiss from the restaurant doorway.

Gabriella stood there, glaring at her through narrowed eyes.

"Did you tell Marcello that I switched the wine?" she spat out.

Olivia gaped at her.

"Of course not. I didn't say a word."

"You must have done. I don't believe you!"

Confused, Olivia shook her head. "Why would I tell him that? He didn't know about it at all."

"You are lying! You went behind my back and squealed to him. There can be no other reason for him to choose you over me. Not after the guests praised my food so highly."

"They loved your food, but I think Marcello looked at a few other angles also—" Olivia began. She hoped she could placate Gabriella. Imagine if this escalated into a shouting match and brought Marcello running out of his office to control it.

But it seemed Gabriella didn't want that either, because she kept her voice low.

"I am going to make sure Marcello regrets his actions. Most likely, he will change his mind quite soon, and put me in charge instead!"

Having delivered her muttered threat, Gabriella didn't wait for a reply. She whirled away, leaving Olivia staring after her in consternation.

CHAPTER THIRTY FIVE

What a rollercoaster ride her day had been! Olivia felt shattered by the time she climbed into her car. Thank goodness there was food in her fridge and wine in her cupboard, she thought gratefully. She needed hydration, nutrition, and rest, in that order.

"We're going to have a quiet evening, Erba," she told her loyal goat. "By tomorrow, we'll be refreshed and ready for all the tourists, and the press interviews, and having to face Gabriella again!"

Thinking of world news, Olivia guessed that her mother would hear of this story soon. She would be shocked that it had occurred at Olivia's workplace. Most probably, she would insist on booking a trip to Italy immediately to support her daughter during this difficult time.

The fact that the difficult time would start the moment her mother's plane touched down was something that Mrs. Glass would never understand, she acknowledged with a sigh.

Even though she had her evening well mapped out, Olivia's plans crumbled when she arrived back home to see Danilo's pickup pulling into the gateway ahead of her.

She felt herself bristle into actual spikes. How dare he!

Well, if she was bold enough to read a billionaire the riot act, she was going to do the same now. Before she kicked him off her property permanently, she was going to make sure that Danilo regretted his underhanded actions and cheating ways.

Even so, when he climbed out of the car and strode over to her, she found herself reconsidering. He looked so handsome, and his smile was so warm. His dark eyes lit up when he saw her, and the way his strong arms flexed under the cotton shirt he wore made her feel suddenly distracted.

"Dammit," Olivia muttered, trying to gather her flustered thoughts. She wasn't nearly as over him as she'd hoped. And, from the way he wrapped his arms tightly around her, Olivia guessed, with a shock, that he wasn't either.

"How good to see you," Danilo murmured, his head buried in her shoulder. "I have just heard you solved the crime. You are amazing, Olivia. I am so proud."

"Proud?" Olivia's resolve to kick him straight off the farm faltered. "I thought you disapproved of me investigating."

Danilo stared at her, confused. "Of course not. I was very worried you did not understand the risks, and hoped we could talk about how to do it safely and avoid the police, but you seemed in a hurry. Were you angry with me after we spoke?"

"I was furious, for about a minute. I thought you were trying to tell me what to do! Then I felt bad, and wanted to apologize for shouting at you, and not hearing you out. It was wrong of me to put the phone down on you."

Danilo broke out into the biggest, merriest laugh she'd ever heard.

"Olivia! One of the very first things I realized about you is that you cannot be told what to do! You are fierce, strong, independent. That is what I—" Danilo stopped himself, looking confused for a moment as if a word he was nervous to say was about to slip out. "What I admire so much about you. You are a warrior princess. You are like Pirate! I am sorry that my words seemed too negative. I should have shown you more support. I know you said we should not speak yesterday or today, but I could not stay away."

To her annoyance, Olivia saw that her discerning, sensitive girl cat was already twining around Danilo's legs, purring thunderously.

Well, that was the small issue of the unanswered calls solved, which had been due to a misunderstanding on his part. The huge, burning, and seemingly unsolvable problem of the other woman still existed though, and she wasn't sure how a few smooth words were going to make that right again.

"Come inside. I have brought you something," Danilo said.

Curious despite herself, Olivia walked with him to the farmhouse.

In the hallway, Danilo handed her a small carrier bag. Intrigued, Olivia opened it.

Inside was a deep blue velvet box. And, when she eased it open, she caught her breath.

This was one of the most gorgeous bracelets she'd ever seen! Made of twined pink and white gold, the centerpiece was a sparkling, deep blue flower.

"The flower is sapphire," Danilo said softly. "I hope you like it."

Sudden tears prickled Olivia's eyes and she blinked them away.

"I love it! It's so beautiful. This is the most special gift I've ever received," she said, touching the delicate, laced gold with a sense of wonderment.

"I did not choose it on my own," Danilo admitted. "I was not sure what you would like. But luckily, my niece, Francesca, came with me, and she said that was the one, and nothing else would do."

Now Olivia thought her face might burst into actual flames. She'd gotten it completely wrong. Her own insecurities had made her assume the worst. Meanwhile, Danilo's companion hadn't been a new girlfriend. It had been his niece, and she guessed that Francesca would be the person he had mentioned before.

"Is she the one who does your hair?" Olivia asked, and Danilo grinned.

"Yes, she is to blame for all the weird looks! But she is very talented, and artistic, and I adore her. I would love for you to meet her soon."

"I'm looking forward to it," Olivia said, understanding how much this introduction would mean to Danilo, and that meeting his beloved family was the next step in their relationship.

He clasped the bracelet around her wrist, and Olivia held her arm out to admire it. The filigree gold shone, the flower petals glowed deep blue, but it was the meaning behind this special gift that was the most precious thing of all. Spellbound by the gorgeous piece, Olivia realized it served as a reminder to her to put her baggage down, have trust again, and allow herself to be happy in her new romance.

"So, we have a program now," Olivia said, determined to get things back on track from her side. "First, we have to go and try my ice wine. It's almost ready to be transferred into the oak—all of it—for a short time, and I would love your opinion on it. Then we have to go up into the hills and open the storeroom. The key works, I tested it, but I've no idea what's behind the door!"

"That sounds like a good program," Danilo enthused. "Let us go."

They walked out of the farmhouse into the breezy, dusky evening.

"After that, I thought we could make dinner together," Olivia said. "My fridge is full of food and bursting at the seams with wine."

"I am enjoying this program more and more!"

Their hands touched and clasped as they headed up to the barn.

Olivia felt a tingle of nerves as she swung open the big, heavy doors.

"I guess we should taste some from the barrel, and some from the metal vat. They'll be different, with and without the oak," she said, butterflies fluttering in her stomach.

A while ago, in preparation for this auspicious moment, she'd brought up glasses, packed carefully in a cardboard box. Now, Olivia opened the box and took out two glasses.

She filled one carefully from the fermentation vat, and then used the tap on her barrel for the very first time, to pour the next tasting portion.

She handed the wooded wine to Danilo, and took the other for herself.

Breathing in the aroma, Olivia tried to assess it as critically as she could, even though she felt so nervous, she couldn't think clearly. It looked enticing, with a lighter, brighter color than a traditional red wine. Its bouquet was full and appealing, with a hint of fruity sweetness—to her, at any rate.

She sipped, and wanted to smile as the delightful flavors danced on her tongue. It tasted slightly sweet, intensely fruity, and seemed extremely drinkable.

But that was just her impression. Without saying anything, she switched glasses with Danilo.

They each drank from the other glass and Olivia felt like laughing in relief. The prolonged contact with wood hadn't spoiled this half of the wine at all. It had simply given it a richness and tantalizing complexity that she knew would be enhanced when the other half was lightly wooded.

But she could be wrong, because this was her own creation, after all. It was Danilo's impartial opinion that counted.

"So," Olivia said, unable to stand the suspense another moment. "What do you think? Is it okay?"

She looked anxiously at Danilo.

He shook his head and she felt her stomach twist with disappointment. At least he was being honest.

"Olivia, it's more than drinkable. I know my English is not nearly perfect, but for me, that is a very wrong word. Words I would use instead?" Danilo pursed his lips as he thought. "Unique. Incredible. Unusual! It is different, delicious, sweet without being overpowering. And to me, it tastes slightly of strawberries."

That was exactly the flavor she'd hoped for! The praise was making her head spin, but Danilo had more surprises up his sleeve.

"You know that there is an important wine festival coming up soon, near Siena? It's a huge event, which attracts visitors from all over Italy and many internationally. They have stalls where winemakers can sell their produce, and they also hold a competition for the best made wine. You need to be there. This will launch you to the public, and will allow you to sell many bottles. Once people have tasted this, they will undoubtedly buy."

"You think?" Olivia felt unsure about the idea. Being part of a festival felt like a huge step she was nowhere near ready for, and she didn't think her wine was, either. But Danilo seemed so enthusiastic, and after all, from the time she'd first opened the farm's rusty gate and allowed herself to dream, Olivia realized that she'd been pushing herself far out of her comfort zone.

"It's a deal," she told him, smiling in the hope it would banish her fears. "Let's book a stall tomorrow and get Project Wine Festival underway!"

"And now, the secret storeroom?" Danilo asked.

As they headed out of the barn and closed the doors, Olivia realized the wind was howling. This couldn't be a more atmospheric evening. The elements were conspiring to make it a memorable time.

They scrambled over the pile of boulders, dodged around the rosemary bushes, and bypassed the spindly cedar saplings which seemed to have taken root from nowhere.

And then they were outside the storeroom.

"Do you want to do the honors?" Olivia handed the key to Danilo.

He shook his head.

"We must both do this. You unlock, and I will open."

Olivia inserted the key, wiggling it slightly to make sure it was in the right place.

Turning it carefully, she felt glad that the lock opened a little easier than last time. Her stomach twisted with nerves and excitement, in sync with the key.

"All right. It's unlocked. Your turn!"

Holding her breath, Olivia watched Danilo grasp the rusty steel handle. Just like last time, its hinges screeched eerily. This time, the noise was louder and longer, as he firmly eased the old door open.

Musty, stale air rushed out, snatched away by the wind.

"It's dark in there!" Olivia said.

Danilo snapped on his phone's flashlight.

It shone over raw brick, distressed flooring, with weeds erupting from it, a tangle of ancient spider webs overhead—both Olivia and Danilo flinched at those—and a dusty row of wooden shelves at the back.

That was all? There was nothing more in this secret room?

Olivia sighed. She'd had such hopes. She'd dreamed for months about the mysteries and treasures it might contain! But as she knew, reality was usually more disappointing than wild, imaginative dreams.

"Empty." She let out a sad laugh. "Oh, well. I guess whatever caused the occupants to abandon this farm so long ago also made them clear out the storeroom. Perhaps they hid whatever was in it so well we'll never find it. Maybe they even buried it?"

"Wait!" Danilo handed her the phone and stepped into the shadowy room. As he paced across the floor, he recoiled violently.

"Aaargh!" he shouted in terror.

Olivia squeaked in alarm, almost dropping the phone. The beam veered wildly up to the dark, pitted ceiling beams.

Breathing hard, Danilo removed a thick rope of web from his hair.

"I thought it was an actual spider!" he said, shaking his hands violently to dislodge the trailing strands.

Then he reached over to the middle shelf and picked something up. The object was so thickly coated in dust that Olivia hadn't even noticed it there.

But, as Danilo brushed the dirt aside, Olivia saw that it was a piece of paper.

In fact, not just a piece of paper. Turning to her, he held it out to the light, looking excited as he carefully teased open the ancient document.

"Danilo!" Olivia exclaimed as she realized what it was. "We might find where the contents are hidden after all. This is a hand-drawn map!"

NOW AVAILABLE!

AGED FOR ACRIMONY
(A Tuscan Vineyard Cozy Mystery—Book 6)

"Very entertaining. I highly recommend this book to the permanent library of any reader that appreciates a very well written mystery, with some twists and an intelligent plot. You will not be disappointed. Excellent way to spend a cold weekend!" --Books and Movie Reviews, Roberto Mattos (regarding *Murder in the Manor*)

AGED FOR ACRIMONY (A TUSCAN VINEYARD COZY MYSTERY) is book #6 in a charming new cozy mystery series by #1 bestselling author Fiona Grace, author of Murder in the Manor (Book #1), a #1 Bestseller with over 100 five-star reviews—and a free download!

Olivia Glass, 34, turns her back on her life as a high-powered executive in Chicago and relocates to Tuscany, determined to start a new, simpler life—and to grow her own vineyard.

Spring is in the air, and Olivia is beyond excited to finally debut her home-grown wine at a major wine festival. The festival draws people from all over Tuscany, and Olivia wonders if this will be her big break—until a customer, fighting over the last bottle of her wine, ends up killed.

Can Olivia, stuck in the middle of it all, clear her name?

Hilarious, packed with travel, food, wine, twists and turns, romance and her newfound animal friend—and centering around a baffling small-town murder that Olivia must solve—the TUSCAN VINEYARD is an un-putdownable mystery series that will keep you laughing late into the night.

Book #7 in the series is also available!

Fiona Grace

Fiona Grace is author of the LACEY DOYLE COZY MYSTERY series, comprising nine books (and counting); of the TUSCAN VINEYARD COZY MYSTERY series, comprising six books (and counting); of the DUBIOUS WITCH COZY MYSTERY series, comprising three books (and counting); of the BEACHFRONT BAKERY COZY MYSTERY series, comprising six books (and counting); and of the CATS AND DOGS COZY MYSTERY series, comprising three books (and counting).

Fiona would love to hear from you, so please visit www.fionagraceauthor.com to receive free ebooks, hear the latest news, and stay in touch.

BOOKS BY FIONA GRACE

LACEY DOYLE COZY MYSTERY
MURDER IN THE MANOR (Book#1)
DEATH AND A DOG (Book #2)
CRIME IN THE CAFE (Book #3)
VEXED ON A VISIT (Book #4)
KILLED WITH A KISS (Book #5)
PERISHED BY A PAINTING (Book #6)
SILENCED BY A SPELL (Book #7)
FRAMED BY A FORGERY (Book #8)
CATASTROPHE IN A CLOISTER (Book #9)

TUSCAN VINEYARD COZY MYSTERY
AGED FOR MURDER (Book #1)
AGED FOR DEATH (Book #2)
AGED FOR MAYHEM (Book #3)
AGED FOR SEDUCTION (Book #4)
AGED FOR VENGEANCE (Book #5)
AGED FOR ACRIMONY (Book #6)

DUBIOUS WITCH COZY MYSTERY
SKEPTIC IN SALEM: AN EPISODE OF MURDER (Book #1)
SKEPTIC IN SALEM: AN EPISODE OF CRIME (Book #2)
SKEPTIC IN SALEM: AN EPISODE OF DEATH (Book #3)

BEACHFRONT BAKERY COZY MYSTERY
BEACHFRONT BAKERY: A KILLER CUPCAKE (Book #1)
BEACHFRONT BAKERY: A MURDEROUS MACARON (Book #2)
BEACHFRONT BAKERY: A PERILOUS CAKE POP (Book #3)
BEACHFRONT BAKERY: A DEADLY DANISH (Book #4)
BEACHFRONT BAKERY: A TREACHEROUS TART (Book #5)
BEACHFRONT BAKERY: A CALAMITOUS COOKIE (Book #6)

CATS AND DOGS COZY MYSTERY
A VILLA IN SICILY: OLIVE OIL AND MURDER (Book #1)
A VILLA IN SICILY: FIGS AND A CADAVER (Book #2)
A VILLA IN SICILY: VINO AND DEATH (Book #3)

Made in the USA
Las Vegas, NV
28 September 2022

56177485R00114